LOREN D. ESTLEMAN

Detroit IS OUR Beat

Tales of the Four Horsemen

TYRUS BOOKS

Published by
TYRUS BOOKS
an imprint of F+W Media, Inc.
10151 Carver Road, Suite 200
Blue Ash, OH 45242. U.S.A.
www.tyrusbooks.com

Hardcover ISBN 10: 1-4405-8845-7
Hardcover ISBN 13: 978-1-4405-8845-7
Paperback ISBN 10: 1-4405-8844-9
Paperback ISBN 13: 978-1-4405-8844-0
eISBN 10: 1-4405-8846-5
eISBN 13: 978-1-4405-8846-4

Printed in the United States of America.

10 9 8 7 6 5 4 3 2 1

Library of Congress Cataloging-in-Publication Data

Estleman, Loren D.
[Short stories. Selections.]
Detroit is our beat / Loren D. Estleman.
pages cm
ISBN 978-1-4405-8845-7 (hc) -- ISBN 1-4405-8845-7 (hc) -- ISBN 978-1-4405-8844-0 (pb) -- ISBN 1-4405-8844-9 (pb) -- ISBN 978-1-4405-8846-4 (ebook) -- ISBN 1-4405-8846-5 (ebook)
1. Police--Michigan--Detroit--Fiction. 2. World War, 1939–1945--Michigan--Detroit--Fiction. I. Title.
PS3555.S84A6 2015
813'.54--dc23

2014043510

Cover design by Frank Rivera and Erin Dawson.
Cover images © iStockphoto.com/miljko/lightkey; Gennadiy Kondratyev/123RF.

This book is available at quantity discounts for bulk purchases.
For information, please call 1-800-289-0963.

TO THE GREATEST GENERATION, WITH THANKS

AND

TO ELMORE "DUTCH" LEONARD (1925–2013), WHO MADE DETROIT ONE OF THE GREAT CITIES OF LITERATURE

I wish to commemorate the passing at age 94—all but ignored by our modern media—of Patty Andrews, the last of the singing Andrews Sisters, January 30, 2013. Theirs was the voice of the Home Front.

“There is more law at the end of a nightstick
than in any court in the land.”

—OLD DETROIT COPS’ SAYING

“God, You’ve got a job on Your hands in Detroit.”

—THE REVEREND BILLY SUNDAY

Contents

Preface:
Blackjacks and B-24s

I introduced the Four Horsemen in 1998, in a novel called *Jitterbug*. In that story, the Detroit Racket Squad, part of a skeleton police force struggling to keep the lid on the Motor City during World War II, helped form a mosaic that included black defense workers, the "Arsenal of Democracy," the 1943 race riot that forced President Franklin D. Roosevelt to declare martial law in the city, the black market, and a serial killer known only as "Kilroy," who'd convinced himself he was helping out the war effort by murdering hoarders of ration stamps.

Much of this was authentic history. Kilroy and the Horsemen were not; but the challenges my Racket Squad faced reflected the law-enforcement situation as it existed when most of the male population was either overseas or preparing to ship out.

Although Lieutenant Max Zagreb, Sergeant Starvo Canal, Officer Burke—"Burksie"—and Detective Third-Grade Daniel "Baldy" McReary—my creations, all—were successful in bringing Kilroy to justice, they fell far short of the mark when they failed to recognize the ferment going on in the defense plants. There, white Jim Crow southerners worked cheek-by-jowl with blacks and drew the same wages, circumstances unheard-of below the Mason-Dixon Line.

Historically, the place was a powder keg.

On July 20, 1943, the racial tensions burst forth in a brawl on Belle Isle, then spread throughout the city, with atrocities committed on both sides—although the mostly white police department concentrated mainly on the misdeeds of blacks. The carnage ended thirty-six hours later—by force of five thousand federal troops—with thirty-four slain, twenty-five of them black. After three weeks, a committee appointed by Governor Harry F. Kelly to investigate the affair concluded that the black community was to blame. It would take another generation, and another devastating riot, to expose the inequities behind the violence.

My little plainclothes militia isn't entirely a product of fantasy. It had authentic precedents in L.A.'s Gangster Squad of the late '40s and early '50s, Eliot Ness's storied (and over-romanticized) Untouchables of Al Capone's Chicago, and, in the grim 1970s, Detroit's own STRESS (Stop the Robberies, Enjoy Safe Streets) gang of badge-toting cowboys, whose running firefights and pitched gun battles (sometimes against other law enforcers, and in one delirious case, in a courtroom while a trial was in progress) eventually led to its disbandment by popular demand. At one time or another, many of our major cities have felt the need to ramp up police protection, with or without respect to the statutes the police are sworn to uphold; vigilantism, like chivalry, is not dead. As late as 2013, the Detroit Gang Squad was mustered out for reasons similar to the STRESS situation, its members reassigned to the Major Crimes unit.

As if that would make them go away.

In reimagining the Four Horsemen for the short story form, I cleaned them up a bit in the interests of reader identification, replacing virulent racism with ignorant bigotry (redundancy that that is), but let stand such primitive approaches to police work as a cheerful disregard for due process. (It would be irresponsible to rewrite history *in toto* and whitewash the record.) The result is a tribute to the great crime films of the 1940s, complete with fedoras, exposed electric bulbs, cathedral-shaped radios, sleek roadsters, blackjacks, Tommies, cigarettes, booze, chic women, slick gangsters, and luscious period slang, as well as a tacit condemnation of pre–civil rights thinking. Idealized, like the statues of Egyptian kings and queens, those features were nevertheless a part of the real landscape of the time.

Juxtapose all that with severe police personnel shortages, criminals eager to exploit a perceived breakdown in law and order, and the monstrously lucrative wartime black market, and the writer scarcely lacks for juicy pitfalls to fling his flawed heroes into.

Homework to establish dates, certain details, and the order of events aside, most of what I know about the period came from my parents, who whenever they mentioned "the war" left no question as to which war they were talking about. In their Detroit, the situation was unique and, I'm convinced, never to be repeated. The entire American automobile industry stopped making cars to build tanks, airplanes, ships, weapons, and ammunition. Two thousand miles away, Hollywood celebrities abandoned their glamorous lifestyles to fight or to perform for the USO. Imagine Apple and Microsoft shelving their electronic toys to make communications devices for the military. Picture Brad Pitt and Julia Roberts donning uniforms and braving enemy fire for soldiers' pay. I can't, and the example of a string of conflicts in the current century hasn't supported the image. But to condemn our contemporaries for their decisions would be shortsighted. Pitt and Roberts, among others, have contributed to the greater good in other ways. No two wars are the same.

In World War II, you knew who the bad guys were. They launched sneak attacks and wore black uniforms with skulls and crossbones on the collars. Stateside, they sported silk suits and gorged themselves on black market profits. I didn't invent Frankie Orr, whom you will meet in the pages that follow; I just gave him a snappy name. The gross mistake of Prohibition provided all the machinery necessary to smuggle a semi-normal lifestyle into a time of deprival. Substitute Firestone tires and fresh eggs for Old Log Cabin whiskey, Bugsy, and you're good to go. Hell, you've still got the boats and trucks from the last time.

But for the law-abiding, it wasn't all austerity and sacrifice. Styles in fashion, music, movies, automobiles, and architecture reached their zenith just before Pearl Harbor, and held it for four delirious years before entering a slow decline toward faded jeans, unintelligible lyrics, "experimental" films, cookie-cutter cars, and buildings that look like ice cube trays stood on end. I for one would hang on to such advances as civil rights and modern medical marvels and let the rest go. (Would anyone seriously miss Twitter? Walter Winchell's gossip column served the purpose without amateur help.)

Emphatically, the 1940s were the end of an era. In the next decade, television, the interstate highway system, and the passing of the pioneering patriarchs of the late Industrial Age would change the face of America: The "global village" created by the cathode-ray tube put an end to the small town as we knew it, national chains replaced roadside diners and mom-and-pop stores, and the fate of millions of workers was decided daily in corporate boardrooms. As a result, the second half of the twentieth century bore little resemblance to the first.

It would be irresponsible to pretend that these changes were all bad. The heightened visibility connected with the all-seeing eye of the TV camera led to more intense public scrutiny, so that the brutal interrogation practices seen in these stories sparked outrage, then action. Although these methods are still with us, they occur infrequently enough to attract national attention, official investigation, and punishment. During the heyday of the Detroit Racket Squad, they were routine, and even applauded by citizens fed up with the lawlessness of Prohibition and the Depression. And so I add this improvement to the list of things to keep.

But, damn, I miss those snazzy neckties.

Police Commissioner John H. Witherspoon—whom you also will get to know—is a historical figure, although you're not likely to find a statue erected in his memory. On the evidence of his performance in the summer of '43, he was a fumbling bureaucrat who consistently took all the wrong steps to contain the emergency. His kind of public servant is still very much alive throughout the corridors of power.

I hope I'm wrong, but I doubt Detroit will come back. Myriad attempts to swing that miracle have failed because of political infighting, jaw-dropping graft, and an electorate that votes from spite alone. The city's idea of progress is to tear down the crack houses built by a dim former governor with good intentions and little foresight; it's the nation's leading manufacturer of vacant lots. Malfeasance, incompetence, and jealousy stalk its government. Pressured for payoffs, business executives pony up without protest, and when the public figures involved are caught red-handed, these very victims provide funds for their defense. The local media, knowing at least part of the truth, continued to conduct fawning interviews with Kwame Kilpatrick, the most corrupt mayor in modern history. Even now, those same reporters circle the wagons whenever outside criticism is launched against the city; but then, it's not *their* city. At the end of the day they go home to gated communities in the suburbs and bury their heads in the sodded lawns.

It's a tragedy, because the place has balls. It smokes where it wants, drinks as much as it wants regardless of state law and city ordinance, and no mayor in his right mind would try to wean it off its Coney Islands, paczkis, and pulled-pork sandwiches. Many of its ministers pack iron along with their Bibles, in the grand old tradition of the Wild West; pat down any judge and you're likely to find a magnum under his or her robes. It's a town with blood in its veins, like Chicago and Odessa, nothing like soulless Vegas, however some benighted types would make it so, with their casinos packed with grim seniors in sweatsuits and cocktail bars stocked with forty brands of vodka; as if there were any difference between Five O'Clock and Stoli. Those who drink it don't do so for pleasure, only to get drunk and barricade themselves in their homes with firearms when the neighbors complain about the noise.

Detroit has attitude; maybe not the most pleasant, but an attitude just the same, and the absence on its streets of pedestrians carrying bottled water and containers of antibiotic hand cream is bracing, if you miss men who don't wear cologne and women who don't bikini-wax. It ain't pretty, but you can be sure that what you see is what you get.

I find it comforting, in an ostrich sort of way, to scan old numbers of the *News*, *Free Press*, and Hearst's *Times* on microfilm in the Detroit Public Library, screen archival documentaries at the Detroit Institute of Arts, and revisit the place during its most vibrant period. Then, the fate of the world depended upon its industry, consumers wearing business suits and white cotton gloves streamed through its five major department stores, the Roxy and the Broadway-Capitol changed their features every three days (with live stage shows between programs), and the city itself showed every promise of emerging from the hostilities as the fourth largest in the United States.

Granted, the 1940s of the Four Horsemen is perhaps a little too on the money: a place with the sharp, unnatural contrasts of a *noir* film or a William Hopper painting, the same haunting tune playing over and over on the jukebox, the nickels fed by some hollow-eyed existentialist with a cigarette smoldering between his lips and no real ear for music. Taxi drivers are invariably Irish, and philosophical as to what's wrong with civilization. The rampant racism is muted for contemporary ears. The smoke rises just a little too slowly toward the black pall above the tin shade, and the dialogue is far too glib. The characters go about their business in a twilit limbo; vampires in pinstripes and fur stoles, doomed to burst into flame in the first shaft of sunlight.

Well, what's wrong with that? It's fiction's responsibility to be better than life.

With one exception, "Kill Fee," which was written especially for this collection, all these stories originally appeared in *Alfred Hitchcock's Mystery Magazine*, a superb anthology edited by Linda Landrigan. It's been a happy association from the beginning, when she replaced the late great Cathleen Jordan, as has been my experience with Janet Hutchings, editor in chief of *AHMM*'s equally fine sister publication, *Ellery Queen's Mystery Magazine*. I'm deeply grateful to them both, and not just for myself: Along with the master anthologist Marty Greenberg—sadly, also no longer with us—they've kept the short story alive when the market favors fat tomes populated with bloodsucking teenagers, stumbling zombies, and unhappy couples trapped in a constant state of stale suburbia.

Now, let's return to an era when a dame was a tomato, a Joe was a gee, a butt was a smoke, and everybody came with his own theme, swing or gutbucket or foxtrot; when making love meant kissing (okay, necking), you took Coke from the bottle, got your news from the paper, your home entertainment from radio and the pulps, "going out" referred to a movie and an ice-cream soda, a machine was an airplane or an automobile or a political system, gay meant happy, and when you said you were sore you were pissed off; when the jilted fiancé always looked like Ralph Bellamy or Sonny Tufts, the tough broad like Rosalind Russell or Bette Davis or Joan Blondell, Clark Gable was a barnstorming pilot or an oilfield roughneck or a gambler or the captain of a tramp steamer (sometimes all four in one movie); when the President lit up Luckies in newsreels, the First Lady swathed herself in dead weasels, and all the cars had wind wings and running boards but no seat belts or airbags; when you could catch a floor show in a nightclub without being part of it; when telephones were hard and heavy enough to double as bludgeons, and often did; and when it came to building construction the sky was the limit, with a clarinet playing "Street Scene" in the background. A shadow in a hat and trench coat takes one last drag on his Camel, snaps it into the gutter, and strolls off with his hands in his pockets, whistling "I'll Never Smile Again." It will be the last refrain someone hears in this life; perhaps the shadow himself.

Spoiler alert: Resist reading "Kill Fee" until you've read "Death Without Parole."

It's the 1940s, gate. Don't be a moldy fig. Get hep, jump to the jive, ring up your favorite Jane on the Ameche, and don't spare the horses ("Scrow, scram, scraw!" says Barbara Stanwyck in *Ball of Fire*. "The complete conjugation!" exclaims Gary Cooper); but before you shove in your clutch and step on the gas, remember to ask yourself one question: "Is this trip necessary?"

The LATIN Beat

"Break out the candy, Mac."

The Latin Beat

"Egg-zayvier Coo-got," said Lieutenant Zagreb.

"Egg-zayvier Coo-got," repeated Sergeant Canal.

Zagreb nodded. "'Cause if you pronounce it 'Haviay Cuga,' the way they do down in South America, no one will know who you're talking about."

Canal shook his kettle-size head. "I'll never understand this country, and I was born here."

"I thought you were Polish."

"Ukrainian. Don't make that mistake around another Ukrainian; they're not all as reasonable as me. I never spoke a word of English till I was five, and I spent the next five learning it good. Now you say I got to speak Spanish like some Corktown mick to make myself clear."

"Congratulations. You're a citizen."

"Go to hell, you Balkan bastard."

Xavier Cugat and his Orchestra were performing One Night Only at the Graystone Ballroom, a wartime benefit. It was an opportunity for the Detroit Racket Squad to round up illegal aliens waiting to get in, turn them over to Immigration, and reduce the potential for riots in the beer gardens downtown when soldiers on leave got a snootful and started demanding to see the draft card of anyone with a low hairline and an accent—specifically, anyone who pronounced "Xavier Cugat" correctly. The press took a dim view of jailing America's fighting men, and regarded any sort of foreigner as a saboteur in the making.

"Pre-emptive strike," Zagreb said. "Like the League of Nations should've done to Hitler at Munich. Crack open a zooter's head tonight and save two of ours next Saturday."

Canal said, "We sure don't have any to spare. O'Connor got called up today. That's three this week."

"MacArthur's getting desperate. O'Connor's feet are flatter than skillets. This keeps up we'll be letting out space downstairs."

"What'd the commissioner say about this idea of yours?"

"There's some things he likes not to know about till they make the *Free Press* front page."

"So if one goes sour he can bust us down to Stationary Traffic."

"We can always enlist."

"Not me. I might be shooting at a relative. And they don't make a helmet big enough for your head."

Zagreb raised and resettled his hat, as if such comments upset him. He was fifty pounds lighter than Canal, but from his eyebrows up and from temple to temple his head was as large as the sergeant's. His fine hair scarcely covered it, and he had as much hair as he'd started with. Some subordinates, when they thought he was out of earshot, called him "Donovan," after an episode of the radio program *Suspense* called "Donovan's Brain."

Officers McReary and Burke came in and straddled a couple of straight-back chairs. McReary pushed back his hat to show the freckles that spattered his bald, twenty-three-year-old scalp. Burke, older than any of them but with no ambition to make sergeant, was dark and simian, with hairy paws pushing out of his cuffs. All wore black suits and gray snap-brims, the uniform of the unit. It helped to distinguish friend from foe when the blackjacks came out.

Zagreb looked at his Wittnauer. "Guess you boys forgot about Daylight Savings Time. We were beginning to think you joined the navy."

"Streetcar broke down on Washington," said McReary. "Everything's starting to go to hell and you can't get parts."

The squad room at 1300 Beaubien, police headquarters, was deserted but for them; desks and chairs stood empty and rows of typewriters slumbered under rubberized covers, awaiting the return of their masters from England and the Philippines. These four men made up the Racket Squad, or what was left of it until the Second World War was won. Five months after Pearl Harbor, with the Allies stalled on both fronts, they weren't expecting reinforcements anytime soon.

Each of them was of an age and in good enough condition to pass a military physical, but they all had draft deferments on the grounds of essential service. The Detroit *News*, *Times*, and *Free Press* called them the Four Horsemen; the *Free Press* with irony. The *Herald*, an opposition sheet, called them a disgrace.

-

The department had been promising them a new car since before the war, but with the automobile industry now devoted exclusively to military equipment they were stuck indefinitely with a 1940 Chrysler Royal four-door sedan, black, with its headlamps painted black except for narrow slits to conform during air-raid drills. Swivel spotlights mounted on both sides were designed to turn night into day. The car was tortoise shaped and resembled the tanks Chrysler was building in Warren. Burke, who did most of the driving, was determined to force a replacement and stripped the gears whenever possible.

"What've you got against this heap?" Zagreb asked, bracing himself against the dash. "It's got more horsepower than the state fair and you couldn't dent it with a baseball bat."

"It's uglier'n my wife's rear end. I'm hoping for a Zephyr."

"If you mess this one up we'll be lucky to get an Edison electric."

Burke double-parked next to a five-year-old DeSoto with tiger-striped upholstery ("Mexican pimpmobile," he snarled) and he and Zagreb shared from a pack of Chesterfields while Canal lit one of his four-for-a-quarter cigars. Three windows rolled down in unison. They were waiting for the crowd in front of the Graystone to increase. Inside, Cugat's orchestra or its warm-up band was rehearsing, the brass and marimbas audible for a block.

"Donkey music," Burke said. "I like Wayne King. Nobody ever brawled to a waltz."

"You always were a moldy fig." Canal struck the beat with his big hands on the back of Zagreb's seat.

McReary said. "Irish tenors for me. What about you, Zag?"

"I got a tin ear."

"Right now I'd trade you that Zephyr for it." Burke ground his teeth.

The lieutenant was having trouble getting his Ronson to light; he'd misplaced his good Zippo. McReary passed him a book of matches from the Cozy Corner Grill. He didn't smoke, but he'd started carrying a supply to offer Zagreb. Unlike Burke, he didn't want to retire a lowly officer and knew promotion had little to do with merit.

Canal stopped thumping the seat to crack his window and dump ash. "You ought to get hep, Burksie. There's a lot of white faces out there amongst the coffee-and-cream."

In fact, the Hispanic youths in their zoot suits—baggy slacks, knee-length coats, two-foot keychains, and sailbrim hats with feathers in the bands—were outnumbered, along with their dates in bright Spanish colors, by Caucasian couples, dressed more conservatively in last year's fashions, making do to save material for uniforms, parachutes, and bandages. It was a chilly night in early May and they seemed content to huddle in the press of bodies, chattering and laughing in anticipation of the entertainment that awaited them inside.

With so many native-born bandleaders absent, in uniform or performing with the USO, Latin music had swept the country. Cugat was king, conducting with baton in one hand and his pet

Chihuahua in the other, but Carmen Miranda, Noro Morales, and that smoldering young Cuban conga drummer Desi Arnaz were topping the bill in places where a dozen years earlier they might have been busing tables.

The craze had its detractors, of course, mainly in places like Los Angeles, too close for comfort to the Mexican border for many, and Detroit, where the mix of Negro and white southern defense workers was already volatile before Hispanics had begun joining them in swarms. The same sort of person who'd held that ragtime and jazz undermined society warned that hot blood and spicy music led to anarchy. It was the Home Front, threatened from within as well as from without.

The crowd spilled out from under the canopy, across the sidewalk, and into Woodward Avenue. A big traffic cop, still in his double-breasted winter wool, walked along the gutter pointing at stragglers with his billy to clear the automobile lanes. Passing the big Chrysler, he glanced briefly at Zagreb through the windshield. The lieutenant nodded and poked his cigarette butt out through the window. "Break out the candy, Mac."

As McReary hoisted a black metal toolbox from the back floorboards onto his lap, Burke unhooked the microphone from the dash and radioed for backup. Just before sirens growled and the lubberly paddy wagon came waddling around the corner, the youngest of the Four Horsemen opened the box and passed around the blackjacks.

-

Asa Organdy had been assistant city editor at the *Detroit Herald* until someone in Accounting turned over a canceled check written on expenses and recognized the name of the proprietor of a Vernor Street brothel on the endorsement. After a brief investigation Organdy was demoted to general assignment reporter and placed on probation. In his quest for redemption, he'd taken to dogging the Racket Squad with a photographer he called Speed, after the Speed Graphic camera the reporter was convinced he slept with. Organdy knew the cop who'd given Lieutenant Zagreb the high sign, and had passed him a pint of Four Roses through the window of his chalky gray Plymouth coupe for the privilege of parking beside a hydrant twenty yards behind the black Chrysler. When the excitement started, the reporter and the photographer piled out.

Speed's favorite shot didn't make the paper until the second day. It showed the monolithic Sergeant Canal sapping a young Hispanic, caving in his hat and twisting his face in shock and pain. Instead the photo editor decorated the front page with the four plainclothesmen wading into the crowd in hot pursuit of everyone perceived to be in guilty flight. But that shot went to the morgue when Organdy obtained the names of those who'd been arrested and found one with a military record—the same man Canal had bludgeoned in Speed's photo of choice. After that it ran every day for a week and went out on the AP wire.

Eduardo Natalo was on medical leave from the United States Marine Corps. He'd been aboard a troop transport ship headed for active duty in the Philippines when a Japanese Zero swept down and strafed the deck, killing a dozen men and wounding seven, including Private Natalo. With a bullet in his leg, he'd helped carry men more seriously injured to safety while the plane made a second pass, chopping up deck all around him. A citation written and signed by his commanding officer credited him with uncommon valor and recommended him for the bronze star; the Purple Heart was a foregone conclusion.

-

"He had a cane." Zagreb looked up from the newspaper he was reading in the echoing squad room. "Didn't you see it?"

Canal, standing in the center of the floor with feet spread and his fists at his sides, shook his head. "He turned, I guess to keep from falling down and getting trampled. He must've tripped over it. I thought he was ducking so I couldn't see him. I didn't hit him as hard as it looks in the picture. He was falling already, away from the blackjack."

"You look like you're swinging for deep left field."

"How bad's it going to get?"

Zagreb folded the paper to an inside page and showed him a four-column cartoon of a bull-necked dick slugging a man in uniform with a fist in a chain-mail glove. The soldier's chest was plastered with medals and the dick wore a Hitler moustache.

"Jesus, Mary, and Joseph." Canal crossed himself.

"It don't even make sense," Burke said. "The guy was fighting nips, not krauts."

"Yeah, like *Popeye* stands the test of truth." The lieutenant tossed the paper onto one of the many vacant desks. "The commissioner's on his way. It's been good working with you fellows. Maybe we'll meet up Over There."

Canal said, "It's no good you boys getting canned over me. I'll quit first. I can always pick up security work at the Rouge plant."

Burke cracked his hairy knuckles. "Witherspoon can't can any of us. Who's he got to put in our place?"

"Who says I have to put in anyone?"

At the new voice McReary, who wasn't long out of a blue uniform, got up quickly, almost tipping over his chair. Zagreb and Burke remained seated. Police Commissioner John H. Witherspoon stood in the open door to the hallway with his hands folded behind him. No one had ever seen him actually enter that room. He seemed smaller than he was, too small for the three-piece suit that had been tailored to his measure, too small for the building, too small for the responsibilities of his office. He parted his hair in the center and wore round-lensed Harold Lloyd spectacles.

"This squad was created originally to break up the Purple Gang," Witherspoon went on, his Adam's apple bobbing at each full stop. "The repeal of Prohibition achieved that. It's occurred to me that a prescription for a disease that no longer exists can be worse than the disease."

Zagreb said, "Sir, you're forgetting a little thing called the black market."

"An understandable omission, as I've seen no report of a single tire-smuggling operation smashed apart by your hand." The commissioner took a thick fold of newsprint from the side pocket of his coat. It fell open to the length of a child's letter to Santa. "This is a galley proof of an editorial that will appear in tomorrow's *Herald.* Corporal Natalo—his promotion just came through—was visiting friends in Detroit. He's an El Paso native. His friends call him Eddie. His family has lived in this country for three generations. How far back does yours go, Sergeant?"

"My father came through Ellis Island in ought-three."

"The editorial asks what right you have to conclude on the basis of a man's appearance that he is an illegal."

Zagreb struck twice at his lighter, failed to get a spark, and let his cigarette dangle. "I guess the same one you had to ask Louis Armstrong for a menu when he sat in at the Tuxedo Grill last year."

Color spotted Witherspoon's gray cheeks. "Sergeant Canal, you're suspended without pay pending a hearing to discuss your dismissal from this department. The rest of you are on report." He folded and pocketed the sheet and turned to leave.

The lieutenant unsnapped his holster from his belt, tucked the flap of the folder containing his shield inside, leaned over in his chair, and slid revolver, holster, and shield across the floor. They stopped two feet short of Witherspoon's shoe.

"Pick it up!" he said. "It's city property."

"So's this." Burke leaned and slid sidearm, holster, and shield behind Zagreb's. They fell an additional four inches short.

"Not enough body English," Zagreb said.

Canal stooped, put his badge and weapon on the floor, and kicked them with a toe. They passed Burke's but not the lieutenant's.

McReary's wound up closer to the commissioner's foot than all the rest. "Next time let's play for money," he said.

A tight smile curdled Witherspoon's face. "A picturesque gesture, but bootless. You men provide an essential service. You can't resign without the permission of the War Reserve Board."

Zagreb stood, took out his wallet, and went over to hand him a letter printed on rag paper with the War Department seal on the top. "Picked it up this morning," he said. "I used to go out with the local director's secretary."

"This is extortion. You know the department can't spare four experienced men during wartime."

"We can't spare one. *Three* Horsemen? Forget it."

Witherspoon slapped the letter into Zagreb's palm. "Sergeant, you will apologize publicly to Corporal Natalo at the press conference this afternoon. Your rank depends on it."

"Sure."

"The rest of you will back him up."

"Sure," Zagreb said.

A crease appeared above the nosepiece of the spectacles. "It will be sincere."

"Natch. Anything for the boys in uniform."

-

The press conference took place on the front steps of headquarters, to accommodate the radio equipment and newsreel cameras. Witherspoon was present, with Mayor Jeffries and members of the legal firm that represented the city. Zagreb spoke last.

Asa Organdy pressed forward, with Speed popping his flashgun in the lieutenant's face. "What's crow taste like?"

"Kind of like chicken. How was the hooker?"

He knew the exchange would never reach the public.

A reporter from WXYZ radio asked him why Eddie Natalo was being detained.

"For his own safety," interjected the commissioner. "There are some benighted individuals who wish him harm."

"Worse than what Canal did to him?" Organdy asked.

Canal lurched toward the man from the *Herald*. He was stopped by the blinding flash from Speed's camera and the rest of the Racket Squad, who gripped his arms.

The mayor cleared his baritone throat. "We are all Americans since Pearl Harbor. Some of our citizens could do with enlightenment on that score."

Organdy said, "My paper would like to know if this administration thinks it can sweep an outrage like this under the rug just by having the man responsible mutter a few words in public."

A murmur rumbled through the reporters. Canal stirred; Zagreb and the others tightened their grip on his arms. He shook them off just by flexing.

"Hell," he said. "I'll tell the kid I'm sorry to his face."

-

Eddie Natalo was under guard in a luxury suite at the Book-Cadillac Hotel, all expenses paid by the city of Detroit. It was supposed to be a secure location, but a number of men in rough clothes stood at the entrance. The placards some were holding ran to the "America for Americans" sentiment. The Chrysler was still rocking on its springs when Zagreb got out and placed a hand on the shoulder of a man whose forearms were furred with prison tattoos.

"When'd you get out, Ricky?"

"Last month. I served my stretch. I got a right to be here." He balled his fists at his sides.

"Not with this bunch. I drove two of 'em in the paddy when we busted up the Black Legion. What's your parole officer got to say about your hanging out with the Klan?"

By now the Four Horsemen stood shoulder to shoulder facing the group. It dispersed.

"No kidding, you were in on that?" Canal asked.

"I was pounding a beat on Belle Isle. But it stands to reason they'd send a delegation."

The officers guarding the entrance told Zagreb they were under instructions to let only Canal inside.

"There goes the manager's vote. Good luck, Sergeant."

"No sweat. If he wants to spit in my eye, I got it coming." Canal handed him his revolver.

The lieutenant stuck it under his belt and produced a pint of Old Grand-Dad from his hip pocket. "Never send a man into a dangerous situation unarmed. Remember that when you head up your own squad."

Canal grinned, slid the flat bottle into a side pocket, and pushed through the revolving door. The men in uniform closed ranks to keep out the reporters who'd followed from headquarters. One of the officers shoved Speed aside when he raised his camera.

Twenty minutes later a shot was heard upstairs.

-

At his own insistence—pride, probably—Corporal Natalo had only one guard at the door of his suite, a fellow marine in dress blues with a sidearm in a white flap holster. He admitted he'd let Canal inside without searching him after the sergeant spread his coat to show the empty holster on his belt, although he'd challenged him on the bulge in his coat pocket and the sergeant had shown him the pint of whiskey. When he heard the shot, a sharp crack, the guard drew his pistol, kicked open the door, and threw down on Canal, who was standing over the dead man. Natalo lay on his back on the floor with a bullet in his forehead, fired at close range from a semiautomatic .25-caliber pistol found on the floor near the body; ballistics confirmed it. The marine held Canal until police arrived to take him into custody.

During interrogation at police headquarters, the sergeant said he'd apologized sincerely to Natalo, and when at length the man accepted, took out the pint of Old Grand-Dad, and "got spifflicated with the boy." They'd hit it right off, he said, one fighting man to another. According to Canal, when Canal excused himself to use the john, Natalo had asked him to go for him as well; they were the last words the pair exchanged. When the sergeant finished and washed his hands, he came out to find the war hero dead and the pistol on the floor. It was tiny; he'd have thought it was one of those novelty cigarette lighters if it weren't for the corpse and the stink of spent powder. That was when the guard broke in.

Zagreb asked him why he didn't hear the shot.

"It must've been when I flushed the toilet. Them hotel jobs are loud."

"Pretty thin."

"I didn't do it, Zag."

The Homicide man, Powers, tagged in. He was one of Commissioner Witherspoon's boys, cleanly handsome with a hair trigger. "The pistol was wiped clean. It's untraceable; someone gouged out the serial number. Just filing it off isn't enough to keep the boys in the lab from bringing it out."

"I know that."

"Sure you do, that's why you gouged it out. Everyone knows your kind of cop always carries throwaway in his sock. Comes in handy when you shoot an unarmed man and you want to make it look like self-defense."

"I never did."

"Bull. The marine outside said he heard a lot of yelling. He drank your liquor, but you weren't friends. You blew your top and then you blew his."

"We got loud, yeah. We were drinking, swapping stories. If he says it was anything else he's a liar."

"You and the marines just don't get along, do you?"

"Go to hell."

-

Zagreb left them alone; he wanted to defend Canal, and that was bad police work. The commissioner ambushed him in the hall.

"He'll crack when we get the results from the carbon test. He can't claim he was on the firing range. The logs show he hasn't been in since yesterday. We've taken his shirt, on the off chance he had time to wash his hands after firing the round and before the guard got through the door. It will show powder residue if his skin doesn't."

"What do we know about the guard?"

Witherspoon shook his head. "You're barking up the wrong tree there. His father served with distinction in World War One. His older brother flew in China with Chennault; he was shot down by the Japanese. His younger brother died fighting in the Spanish Civil War. His own record's clean, before and after his enlistment. He ships out for the South Pacific next week."

"Test *him*?"

"We did. Negative." The commissioner pursed his lips; he seemed to consider the expression sympathetic. "Any good cop wants to stand by his partner. Lord knows Canal's not the first member of this department to go bad."

"Go to hell."

"*What?!*"

"I'm quoting Canal. That's what he told Powers. You're going to have to convict him without a confession."

Witherspoon glared, but let the explanation stand. "We may not get the chance. I just heard from Washington. The War Department intends to claim jurisdiction. The penalty for murdering a soldier in time of war is execution."

"No one's been put to death in this state since eighteen thirty."

"I'm sure that's the line Governor Kelly will take. But federal law supersedes Michigan's."

A uniform approached carrying a sheet of paper. He wore bifocals and a hearing aid; the city was scouring the retirement rolls for personnel to fill the empty desks. Witherspoon took the sheet, read it, and handed it to Zagreb. Carbon tests on Canal's shirt had discovered traces of spent gunpowder on the right cuff. He'd discharged a firearm while wearing it.

-

In the interrogation room, Canal read the report and smacked it down on the scarred table. He wore an old sweater Burke had given him to replace his shirt. Burke was the closest to him in size, but the sleeves were three inches too short and his shoulders strained the seams. "It's a mistake. I ain't fired a piece since yesterday at the range."

Zagreb asked him when he'd changed his shirt last.

After a poleaxed moment, a grin spread across the sergeant's broad face.

"Day before yesterday. I get three days out of 'em now before they go to the laundry. Our boys need the soap."

"You just now thought of it." Powers, the Homicide man, showed his teeth.

"Ask Mrs. Chin. She says the war's putting her out of business."

"It won't prove anything. The tests don't show how long the powder's been there."

Zagreb picked up the report. "This is a lot of powder for that size gun. More like a police thirty-eight."

"They don't show caliber either."

"Get the murder weapon up here from ballistics."

Powers straightened to his full movie-star height. "You giving orders now? We're both lieutenants."

"When'd you make rank?"

"October twelfth, nineteen forty."

"December twenty-second, thirty-nine. Get your butt down there, *Lieutenant*, and don't use the stairs."

After Powers left, pulling the door shut hard behind him, Canal said, "It was November of forty. I was at your party."

"He's Witherspoon's man. He doesn't have the brains to check my file."

Powers returned and slammed the pistol on the table. It was less than four inches long from action to muzzle, nickel plated, and looked like a toy.

"Pick it up," Zagreb told Canal.

"Don't get any hot ideas about shooting your way out," Powers said. "It isn't loaded."

Canal picked it up with his big paw. "You check it?"

The Homicide man blanched a shade.

Zagreb said, "Point it at Powers."

He did so. The Homicide man, pale still, rested his hand on his empty holster from reflex. Sidearms were banned from the interrogation rooms.

"Pull the trigger," Zagreb said.

"I can't."

"That's an order, Sergeant."

"I mean I *can't*. Look." He opened his hand. The two lieutenants leaned closer. Canal's finger was too thick to fit inside the trigger guard.

-

The marine guard's name was Norden, like the bombsight. He had a clean jawline, transparent blue eyes, and the standard short jarhead haircut. There wasn't so much as a loose thread on his beautiful blue uniform. His hands were well kept, the nails rounded and buffed lightly. He sat straight as a fence rail behind the window in the interrogation room Canal had just left.

Witherspoon turned from the window and glared at Canal. All the Horsemen and Powers were present. "You checked *both* this man's hands?"

Powers nodded. "He didn't do it, sir. It isn't even his gun. Why carry a weapon you can't use?"

Zagreb tilted his head toward the window. "If Norden could hear voices inside the hotel room, he could hear when Canal went to the bathroom. That's when he made his move."

"But why?"

Burke said, "Let me have a crack at him, Commissioner."

"I'm afraid you mean that literally. Detective McReary?"

As the young man entered Interrogation, Burke nudged Zagreb. "Thinks he's a pussycat."

"It's all those freckles."

They listened over the intercom. Norden shot to his feet.

"Sit down, soldier." McReary's tone was iron.

"I'm a marine, not a soldier."

McReary shoved him with both hands. Norden lost his balance and fell into a chair. When he started to get up, the detective bent and grabbed both his arms above the biceps, paralyzing them. He leaned in close. "How'd you get along with Eddie Natalo?"

The suspect gave up struggling. "Pretty okay." He had a parade-ground tenor. "We didn't talk much. I only met him today."

"How about Sergeant Canal?"

"We didn't talk at all. By the look of him, we could use him to dig foxholes."

"Why didn't you search him for weapons?"

"That was a snafu. I assumed he'd been disarmed. His holster was empty."

McReary straightened. He slid a hand over his prematurely bald head and rested it on top. He seemed unsure of his next move.

"Powers, take his place," Witherspoon said. "He's too green."

"With all respect, Commissioner, there isn't a green man on the squad."

McReary asked Norden where he was from.

"Litchfield, Minnesota. Population thirty-one hundred."

"Don't get many Hispanics up there, I'm guessing."

"Corporal Natalo was the first I ever met."

"Too bad you didn't get to know him. Man like that, a hero, could've given you some tips about how to behave in combat."

"I got plenty of those in training."

"This early in the fighting, those drill sergeants can't have his experience. The military probably would have wasted him on a war bond drive."

"I guess he'd've made a good salesman. He didn't have an accent or anything."

"Accent?"

"You know. Like those Mexican bandits in westerns."

McReary leaned back against a wall and folded his arms. "You're a middle son, right? Your older brother was killed in China and your kid brother got it in Spain. Your dad was wounded at the Marne. I imagine his boys made him proud."

"Jack did. He took out two Zeroes before they shot him down. Pop was just plain mad over Andy. His first day out, a Fascist sniper put one in his head from a tree two hundred yards away. He never had a chance."

"Fascist? One of Mussolini's thugs?"

"One of Franco's. Some lily-livered spick that couldn't even look him in the eye when he murdered him. Just like one of those banditos." Norden's face was dark.

"Well, there are spicks and Hispanics, just like there are micks and Irish. Eddie Natalo was a credit to his ancestors. If Jack and Andy had come back, they'd be proud to have their picture taken with him at a bond rally. Your pop too."

"He'd've spit in his face! Just like Andy would've done if that yellow guinea came down out of his tree and faced him like a man. They're all the same. One of our boys got himself killed helping those men on the ship and Natalo took the credit."

"Who told you that?"

"No one had to. Look what one of them did to my little brother!"

McReary pushed himself away from the wall and unfolded his arms. "You're out of uniform, fella."

Startled, Norden glanced down at his tunic.

"Where are your gloves?" McReary asked.

-

"Tell me about the gloves," said Witherspoon.

McReary said, "Yes, sir. A marine's not in full dress uniform without white cotton gloves. I took a squint at the manual of arms when this thing started, to bone up. They had it at the recruitment center. I barely made it back out in civvies."

The Four Horsemen and the commissioner were in the squad room. Witherspoon was two feet inside the door, a personal best, and Zagreb and Burke straddled chairs. McReary had risen when Witherspoon came in. Canal, wearing a fresh shirt under his blue suit, sat on one haunch on a windowsill looking down on Beaubien. Lieutenant Powers was absent, supervising Norden's confession.

Zagreb held out a report rolled into a funnel for the commissioner to take. "Scrub team found the gloves in a bin behind the hotel. I make it he took them off while everybody was crowding into the murder scene and stuffed them in the waste receptacle of a maid's cart. They tested positive for spent powder. I told him his prints were on them."

Witherspoon stared at the sheet. "I don't see anything here from the fingerprint team."

"They weren't needed. You can't lift a decent print from fabric."

"Ah."

"It was premeditated," Zagreb said. "When Norden drew the guard detail, he bought the piece, or had it, intending to use it in place of his service automatic, which would've nailed him to the crime. Canal coming to apologize was an answer to a killer's prayers."

"How can a man hate a stranger enough to kill him?" asked the commissioner.

"That's one for the military. They trained him. We're going to have to beef up Homicide once this war's over."

When Witherspoon left, Zagreb asked Canal why the long face. "You should be celebrating. Open that window and fire up one of those torpedoes you smoke."

The sergeant didn't move. "I liked Natalo. You drink with a man, it's the same as fighting with him; you find out what he's made of. I don't think I'll go out on the Latin beat next time, Zag. You can suspend me for insubordination if you want."

"Me, too," Burke said. "I don't like the music anyway."

Zagreb stuck a Chesterfield between his lips. "What about you, Mac?"

"I'll go if you order me, Lieutenant."

"Uh-huh." He snapped open the Ronson. "Let's find out where Ricky and the Klan went after we rousted 'em from the Book-Cadillac and bust heads." He spun the wheel and got a flame for the first time.

SOB Sister

"Keep the change."

Sob Sister

Arabella Lindauer was the highest-paid sob sister on the staff of the *Detroit Times*. Her boss, William Randolph Hearst, had said that if you assigned Arabella to a fire with nothing worse than a singed dog for human interest five minutes before deadline, she'd pound out a story that would draw tears from a stone. Her five-part series on the Lindbergh kidnapping had failed to win a Pulitzer, but Walter Winchell had choked up while quoting from it on the air (which she said was better).

A self-described spinster (although she had no shortage of suitors), she never left home or the office in anything other than her uniform: pillbox hat, print dress, chunky-heeled shoes, and of course white cotton gloves. She bought these by the box and seldom wore a pair more than once; red lipstick gravitated to them no matter how careful the wearer and didn't wash out. She carried clutch purses with just enough room for her pencil and pad, a roll of nickels for the telephone, her compact and rouge, and the keys to her Hudson on a ring attached to a set of brass knuckles.

For a time, she'd been seen about town in the company of Lieutenant Max Zagreb of the Detroit Racket Squad, but when they'd exhausted all the ballrooms and picture shows and sat down to talk, they discovered that they lived at cross-purposes. It was his job to jail predators with a gun and hers to free them with an adjective. They parted on grounds of self-preservation, but not with finality. When the two-burner range, the radio, and the post-nasal drip of the faucet in the apartment kitchen surrendered their charm, one would call the other and they would go out for Clark Gable and a Coney Island. A palpable lack of a social life was the one thing they had in common.

This was a matter of career alienation, not unattractiveness. She was a handsome woman of thirty, with a trim waist and an abundance of auburn hair, he slightly older, whipsaw lean, large in the forehead—the sign of a thinker—and had a lazy smile like Dan Duryea's. One knew them only briefly before realizing that his eyes didn't always smile when his mouth did, and that she spoke the way she wrote, with the main subject on top and all the other details following in descending order of importance, in the shape of an inverted pyramid. Satellites from outside their solar system didn't stay long in their orbit.

On the day the marines landed on Guadalcanal, Arabella and Zagreb went to see *Mrs. Miniver* at the Broadway-Capitol, with a Betty Boop cartoon and newsreel footage of the Japanese in New Guinea, and lingered over coffee in the J.L. Hudson cafeteria while waiting for their hamburgers to digest. Zagreb was first to break the comfortable post-prandial silence.

"I ought to call in. Some draft dodgers might celebrate this Guadalcanal business by busting up a tavern."

"Isn't that the uniform division's baby?" She slid a Lucky between her lips.

He snapped his Zippo under it. "Most of them are in Pearl and the North Atlantic. We all have to make do, isn't that the line?"

"The only line I know is the fake seam girls draw up the back of their legs till the Air Corps stops using nylons for parachutes."

"That never makes sense to me. How do you show you're helping the war effort by pretending you're not?"

"Nothing about this war makes sense. We've got Hitlers right here."

"You better watch who you say that to." He kept his voice light, but his gaze swept the nearly deserted room for junior J. Edgar Hoovers, gray men in pinstripes with notebooks.

"I'm talking about that snake Frankie Orr."

"What'd he do, sell you a bum set of tires?"

"He can make a million off the black market for all I care. I interviewed a GI on leave from the Aleutians who said he helped set fire to a thousand gallons of gasoline just to de-ice a runway. Rationing's a joke."

"When's the piece come out? I'll read it."

"You already did, if you saw yesterday's paper, but you didn't see that bit. The old man blue-pencils anything that might remind people he was an isolationist before December seventh. The rest was columns of sludge about the GI's tearful reunion with his teenage bride. They'd been separated a whole six weeks when he got sent home with a nasty case of frostbite."

"What are you beefing about? That's your specialty." He lit a Chesterfield.

"I can do it in my sleep. I've gotten all I can out of kittens and Christmas Eve car crashes and one-legged prom queens. I want to quit making people reach for the Kleenex and make them look for a stamp instead, to write their congressman. Frankie's hired guns have made more widows locally than Tojo."

"The war's young. Give Tojo a chance."

"I want to write about him."

"Who, Tojo?"

"Don't play dumb, Zag. You know who I mean."

"So write about him. Who's stopping you?"

"He is. I can't even get in to see him at that restaurant where he hangs out, a public place. But you can."

"You want I should ask him for an interview?" He'd forgotten how much she amused him when she wasn't being exasperating.

"You're planning a raid. Take me along."

He'd forgotten, too, how thin the line was between amusement and exasperation. "Who told you that?"

"My hairdresser. She's dating a member of your squad."

"Which one?"

When she shook her head he said, "There are only four of us, Belle. I'm not dating a hairdresser, Canal's saving himself for a girl from the Old Country, and Burke talks nookie like Cesar Romero speaks Spanish: no hairdressers recently. That leaves McReary. By the time that little mick takes off his hat and shows his bald head, it's too late. He's already charmed you half into the sack. It's Mac, isn't it?"

"I'm not saying, but don't blame him. He didn't spill the beans. Women are smart and dumb, same as men. This one isn't dumb. She's spent enough time with him to know when he's strapping himself down for a rough ride."

"Busting Four-F shirkers' heads on Woodward isn't a pleasure cruise."

"You don't spend days planning those raids."

He shook his head. "If it's true, I couldn't take the chance. If you got hurt, the commissioner would have my head. He's wanted it ever since he took the job."

"I can look after myself."

"Then again, you might get one of *us* hurt. I'm short a dozen men as it is."

"For old times' sake?"

"No soap. It's this job or storming some beach. Damn sand gets in everything."

She said something uncomplimentary, dropped her cigarette butt into her cup, and left. He pushed the cup out of his line of sight while he finished his Chesterfield and his coffee. That brown floating debris could put him off nicotine and caffeine at the same time.

-

McReary was in his twenties, fair and freckled, and self-conscious about his bald head, a souvenir of scarlet fever, or one of those other diseases that stalked children between wars. The rest of the squad called him Baldy only when they were sore at him. Zagreb, on the rare occasions when the young man had his hat off, thought he looked sleek and predatory, like a hood ornament.

He found Mac at his desk, tapping out a report with two fingers on a Royal typewriter of Spanish-American-War vintage, his snap-brim tipped forward to shield his eyes from the glare of the gooseneck lamp. He struck a wrong key when the lieutenant spun a chair and straddled it backward to face him. The detective third-grade was a capable cop, but all his confidence in his abilities evaporated in the presence of the commander of the Four Horsemen.

"Anything?" Zagreb jerked a thumb at the loudspeaker mounted on the wall. It was connected directly with Dispatch.

"Not a peep, L.T. For us, anyway."

Officer Burke, seated nearby, said, "Some criminal genius busted a window in the A-and-P after closing and made off with a dozen cans of peas. Went right past a display of Maxwell House coffee to get to 'em. Canned peas ain't rationed yet."

"That's because it's unpatriotic to poison the troops." Sergeant Canal, perched on one massive ham on a windowsill, exhausted cigar smoke out over Beaubien. The rest of the squad had petitioned him never to fire up one of his bargain-basement specials without ventilation handy. Zagreb's second-in-command was a big man, as light on his feet as Sonja Henie on the ice, and all muscle under a layer of fat, like a grizzly. "Me, I'd make a beeline for the freezer."

"Not everybody can carry a side of beef under one arm." Burke, who was determined never to be second-in-command of anything, was big also, but not by Canal's standards. He'd compensated by cultivating a mossy growth of black hair that stuck out of his cuffs and grew above his collar, where it blended with his around-the-clock shadow.

"I could manage six, seven capons," McReary said. "I'm wiry." He grinned nervously. Zagreb was studying him.

The lieutenant addressed the others without looking away. "Why don't you two boys get some air?"

The others exited without comment. Every man on the detail knew Zagreb seldom disciplined a member in front of the others. This decision was both diplomatic and practical: All three were armed.

"How's your sex life, Mac?"

McReary's face flushed deep copper.

"Okay, I guess. No complaints, anyway."

"I went out with a lady barber a couple of times. She talked the thing to death in the end. They sure can gab up a storm."

The color drained from the young man's face.

"What's Agnes been up to?" he asked.

"Agnes? Seems to me a blade like you can do better than an Agnes."

"She didn't even know I was a cop till she saw the gun. I had to tell her."

"She'd know that anyway. We're good copy, we make the front page whenever there's nothing doing overseas. How much you tell her about Express?"

Sound travels across empty space. With most of the desks in the squad room vacant and a skeleton police force riddled with paid informants, the Horsemen had followed the lead of the U.S. military by assigning code names to their activities. On the street, Frankie Orr was known as "the Conductor," for an old murder aboard a streetcar. Operation Express was in place to break up his black market organization.

"I never told her a goddamn thing, L.T. I don't have so many miles, but I'm no rookie."

"Rationing's a war priority. You know they shoot you for treason."

"Where are you getting this?"

Zagreb watched him closely another moment. Then he sat back and tipped his hat past his crown.

"Some women can read a man," he said. "It takes time to learn how to keep your nerves under your vest. In the meantime, try to stay away from gossipy dames. The *Times* has it."

"Holy smoke!"

"It's all right, the reporter's a friend of mine. But just till this one's in the can, go to the pictures by yourself. Betty Grable's more fun to look at when you're stag."

"Okay, L.T." McReary took his hat off, mopped his forehead with a handkerchief, and resettled it. "L.T.? Would you really have me shot?"

"Hell, no. Uncle Sam needs the bullets. I'd do it myself."

-

When he came to Detroit, at the height of the booze wars, Francis Xavier Oro had been touted as one of the new breed, applying modern business methods to the rackets. That meant quieter murders and a fairer system of graft. He'd expunged the Sicilian from his name, replaced his loud suits and silk shirts with bankers' colors and white button-downs, and expanded his activities to embrace gambling, drugs, labor unions, and other difficult-to-obtain goods and services after liquor resumed flowing legally. When America entered the war and the OPA restricted traffic in meat, eggs, butter, gasoline, and automobile tires, Frankie Orr had annexed the black market to his territory without a single assassination.

It was better than hooch; better even than girls and heroin. In Grosse Pointe, where defense-plant profits were put up in barrels to mellow, a porterhouse steak on the table and a new set of whitewalls on the Packard translated into instant prestige.

"I seen—saw—it coming when Schicklgruber muscled in on Munich," he said. "Man of vision, that's me."

"That's I," corrected his English tutor.

"Forget it. You was one of them, you wouldn't be teaching school."

Orr procured his inventory exactly as he had in earlier days, through hijacking, bribery, and midnight deliveries from Canada by way of the Windsor Tunnel, the Ambassador Bridge, and boat landings in the City of Monroe and Detroit Beach, a flea-speck just north of there, where the grease spread farther.

Although not all the way to the Detroit Racket Squad.

On a crickety, mosquito-thick evening in August 1942, Officer Burke shoved the foot-feed to the firewall of the two-year-old Chrysler Royal, muttering curses like Popeye as he twisted the wheel this way and that to keep the tires from snatching in the sand drifted across the highway from the beach. He'd disliked the heavy sedan from the day it was issued, but was the only one of the Horsemen who could get the best out of it.

"Take it easy, Burksie." Sergeant Canal gripped the ceiling strap in the back seat and took the cigar out of his mouth to stare at the spot where he'd bitten through the wrapping. "They don't make new brakes for cars no more, just tanks and airplanes."

"What's your beef? I ain't touched the brakes since Dearborn."

"Once in twenty miles won't hurt," said Zagreb, seated beside him in front.

Burke took the hint and slowed down.

He passed the turning, switched off the lights, and coasted to a stop on the gravel apron in front of a bait-and-tackle shop that had been boarded up since the Bank Holiday. The four got out and gathered at the trunk, where the lieutenant handed out flak jackets and heavy artillery: a sawed-off shotgun for McReary, a Thompson for Canal, and a flare pistol for himself. Squat-barreled Police .38s rode on their belts.

McReary watched the sergeant fitting a fifty-round drum to the machine gun. "Just once I'd like the Tommy."

Canal grinned in the trunk light. "Not till you pack on the pork, junior. When this starts to spit it'll jerk you around like a turd in a twister."

"Who you calling a turd, you big piece of—"

Zagreb whistled sharply between his teeth. "Save something for the enemy."

They walked down to the beach, Burke cursing at the sand he shipped in over the tops of his wingtips. Between them and the spot where boats landed loomed a canvas-shrouded bandshell, once host to the Casa Loma and Les Brown orchestras but now a place for winos to shelter and teen couples to grope. Farther out, an ancient dock, landlocked by a receding waterline, decrepitated under a shoe-heel moon. McReary pumped a round into the shotgun and joined Burke under its cover while Zagreb and Canal ducked under the canvas of the bandshell. The sergeant used his jackknife on the rotted fabric to create observation posts. This made a V-shaped firing perimeter with the landing in the middle and the two men under the dock closest to the action.

Canal sat with his back against a timber, cradling the Thompson in his lap. "What if they check out this place?"

"It's a bandstand. Play 'em a concert on that fiddle." Zagreb remained standing.

"It ain't like the Conductor to take a chance with the feds and the Mounties both at once. This ain't the dry time, when it was only against the law on this side."

"He's not shipping from Canada. He's following the shore up from Toledo. He knows there are guardsmen at the state line."

"His snitches are better than ours. I hope yours wasn't pulling your leg."

"He better not have. He's looking at three to five on a granny warrant if Frankie comes by land instead of sea."

"Frankie coming along, you think?"

"Nah. He's probably polishing off a mess of spaghetti at Roma's."

"What's the cargo, meat or tires?"

"One or the other. He only deals gasoline when he's strapped for cash. One stray round during a hijack and he's out some men he can't spare. General MacArthur's got all the best."

"Right now I'd settle for two or three more of our own, second best or no."

"Can't risk it. You might have noticed that what we got left to draw on isn't USDA Choice. Department's calling back cops it dismissed for grafting."

"They're the ones should be drafted. If this foreign business drags on, I wouldn't give a Confederate nickel for what we end up with." The sergeant chewed on his cold cigar.

"Maybe you should enlist and finish it quick."

Canal smacked the deck of the bandshell. "What, and give up showbiz?"

The night wore on. The wind freshened off Lake Erie, blowing away the mosquitoes and carrying a snatch of studio laughter from a radio program. It could have come all the way from the Canadian side.

In a little while the ground trembled beneath a heavy piece of machinery shifting gears down the highway. The big man gathered his legs under him, tightening his grip on the submachine gun.

"Keep your pants on. Could be a bread truck." But the lieutenant forgot his craving for a Chesterfield.

The diesel rumble increased. When the vehicle downshifted to make the turn, they felt it in their testicles. Canal said, "If that's bakery products, they're making 'em out of cement."

"Now."

The sergeant rose and they crept to the hole in the canvas, taking turns peering through it.

A rounded radiator grille appeared in the moonlight filtering down onto the highway. Two slits of electric light winked on briefly from blackout lamps, locating the twin tracks in the sand leading to the shoreline. The cab's divided windshield was dark; not so much as a dashboard bulb illuminated the occupant or occupants. Behind it, sliding into line as it followed, the trailer cut a square blank out of the scatter of lighted windows belonging to what remained of the beach community on the other side of the pavement. The truck was painted dull black from stem to stern.

"Listen," said Zagreb.

A wheezing sound rose above the engine when it slowed to a purr.

"Refrigerator truck," said the lieutenant. "It's not tires."

Canal said, "Hot damn. I'm throwing a barbecue Saturday."

The truck stopped. Gears changed. It backed around until the end of the trailer was pointed toward the lake. Air brakes whooshed and two men climbed down from the cab.

The one from the passenger's side started toward the bandshell.

Zagreb whispered. "Don't move a muscle."

A flashlight snapped on. The man trained the beam on the ground, an obstacle course of driftwood, broken beer bottles, and trash from Canada. A square pistol showed in the reflected glow.

"Get ready." Zagreb thumbed back the hammer on his revolver.

Canal stepped back from the opening and raised the Thompson to his hip.

The man holding the flash and semiautomatic came within ten feet of the shell.

"Gus!"

He stopped walking, hesitated, then turned and trotted back toward the truck.

The two men inside the canvas relaxed.

A new chugging sound reached them, laboring against the offshore current. The word from the underworld was Frankie Orr had bought a decommissioned World War I minesweeper and refurbished it for cargo. When the frosty moonlight limned the sharp, Dick Tracy nose of the prow, Zagreb put away his .38 and tugged out the flare pistol.

The chugging slowed. A thousand-candlepower spot slammed on aboard ship and swept its blinding shaft across the beach. Zagreb and Canal withdrew farther into shadow.

The shaft made two more passes, combing sand and structure, then stopped.

Abruptly the light went out. For a moment, green-and-purple blossoms swam before them, spoiling their night vision. They resumed recycling oxygen. They hadn't been spotted.

For an instant, the light had illuminated a second pier, this one jutting twenty feet beyond dry land—new construction, added since their last visit. As the craft approached, the pitch of the engines changed; the props were reversed. After a moment they stopped. Silence then, except for water lapping the hull as the ship continued under its own momentum. It ghosted alongside the pier, and now the men watching saw human silhouettes above the railing, guiding the man at the wheel with gestures.

Water splashed; an anchor released. The ship yawed against the pull of the cable, steel plates scratching submerged sand. It stopped just short of beaching itself.

A pair of silhouettes clambered over the railing and leaped to the pier, landing with a double thump. More maritime business while they caught a pair of lines cast over the side by a third silhouette, pulled them taut, and maneuvered the pliable craft closer to the pier. They tied them to rings attached to posts.

A hatch lowered, creating a gangplank. The man on deck vanished, to reappear (Canal and Zagreb guessed) among two others walking down the ramp carrying stout cartons on their shoulders.

"Shoot," murmured Canal. "I was counting on sides of beef and pork."

"Smaller cuts. Chops and tenderloins." But the lieutenant was troubled. Something was missing. What?

The sergeant stepped toward the opening. Zagreb put a hand on his arm.

"Let 'em finish loading. It's a sin to let fresh meat spoil while our boys are eating Spam."

"I'm worried about Burke. He's the impatient type."

"Mac'll keep him tame. That's half the reason I put him on this detail. Learned it from an old horse trainer. For some reason, putting a goat in with a stallion keeps it from kicking down the stall."

"Mac's a goat?"

"Don't tell him. He's too good with that scattergun."

But Zagreb was only half listening to himself. That crack about meat spoiling had told him what was missing.

"No vapor," he said. "That boat ought to be smoking from dry ice."

Canal peered at the minesweeper. There was nothing issuing from the open hold. "Maybe it's refrigerated, like the truck."

"Yeah." Only he doubted it. "Well, we came all this way. Take the safety off that chopper." He stepped into the open and fired a rocket into the night sky.

-

"I'm still blind in my right ear." Canal twirled a thick finger inside it.

McReary said, "Try cutting loose with a twelve-gauge under a dock."

"Shut up, both of you."

The lieutenant was testy. The flare he'd shot off still lit the beach, a miniature sun in a white sky. The men they'd arrested sat on the beach leaning forward, each with a wrist shackled to an ankle, a Four Horsemen specialty that discouraged flight.

There were eight men in cuffs, with the truck driver, the driver's partner, the men who'd helped with the unloading, and the two armed guards, who'd dropped their guns and surrendered when Canal and McReary fired warnings close enough to kick sand over their shoes. Burke had pistol-whipped the man with the semiautomatic when he'd drawn down on the squad. He sat listless, one hand raised to keep his brains from leaking out of his cracked skull.

The ship's captain and what remained of his crew had slipped through the snare. Props still reversed, they backed away from shore, unmindful of bullets thudding against the hull. Once outside range, they'd turned and gone all-ahead full, out to sea.

A half-dozen stout cardboard cartons lay split open on the beach where the detectives had dumped them, their contents scattered: paperbound copies of *The Autobiography of Benjamin Franklin*, Caesar's *Conquests*, *Treasure Island*, and the works of William Shakespeare; servicemen's editions of literary properties long in public domain.

"Not one stinking Edgar Wallace," complained Burke. "No wonder we're losing."

There wasn't so much as a pork chop in the whole cargo, or anything else remotely resembling contraband.

Zagreb, as angry as the squad had ever seen him, kicked one of the shackled men in the ribs. The man grunted and fell sideways, rolling himself into a tight ball. "That's for the goddamn reefers aboard the truck," he said. "You just had to be sure we took the bait."

Canal fired a short automatic burst into the trailer. Hissing, the refrigeration units poured ammonia and liquid oxygen into the air.

"Ammo's rationed like everything else," said the lieutenant. "That's coming out of your salary."

The sergeant took aim at the piles of books and emptied the drum. Confetti littered the surface of the lake. "Keep the change."

-

Commissioner John Witherspoon was a sour apple of a man who parted his hair in the middle and smeared it to both sides with a butter knife. He stood behind his slab of desk at 1300

Beaubien, Detroit Police Headquarters, with his hands clasped behind him Napoleon fashion and glared through Coke-bottle spectacles at the Four Horsemen standing before him. "What've we got to hold them on?"

"Sullivan rap," Zagreb said. "Two of 'em, anyway, the trucker's partner and one of the loaders. The goons standing guard had permits for their weapons. Frankie got them private detective licenses under Bowles. Renews 'em every year like clockwork."

"Wide-Open Bowles." The man behind the desk measured out a bitter expression appropriate to a mayor removed from office for corruption. "Orr had a contract with the War Department to supply reading material to servicemen. He set up a printing press in Sandusky and offered them for pennies above cost. A front, of course, but legitimate. Who told you he was shipping anything else?"

"C.I., sir. He's been reliable in the past. We sweated him. I'm convinced he didn't set us up." If he was wrong, the snitch would be passing blood for a week for nothing.

"Who else knew a raid was planned?"

"Nobody outside the squad." Zagreb stared at the commissioner, who looked away. He was a career politician and a coward who feared and despised the street cops under his command.

"Well, someone made a serious mistake. It may be years before we have another opportunity to put Orr out of business. Meanwhile I'm reassigning your squad to riot control."

"That's a uniform detail!" shot Burke.

Witherspoon looked at Zagreb. "You'd better get your men into line. In this office, I'm addressed directly only by lieutenants and better.

"The uniforms can use assistance," he went on. "The defense plants pay the same wages to Negroes and white southerners, which doesn't always sit well with the sons of the Confederacy. Security's tight on the assembly line, but tensions boil over in the saloons between shifts. Perhaps managing a roomful of drunken bigots is not beyond your abilities."

-

Back in the squad room, Burke spat on the linoleum. "We need to invite that walking ulcer along on beer garden detail some election year; see do his capabilities stand up to a bunch of rednecks pumped up on Rebel Yell."

"Shut up. For once he's right. We got hornswoggled like a bunch of rookies." Zagreb dropped into the nearest chair, wrung-out as a bar rag.

McReary came forward, holding out his gold shield and .38.

"Thanks for not throwing me to the dogs, L.T. Maybe I can make myself useful in the Pacific, as long as nobody trusts me with the invasion plans for Tokyo."

"That only works with the commish. Put 'em away before I take you up on it."

He didn't. "I'm the one put us on dipso duty."

The lieutenant looked up at him. "You think you're the only cop in the world got sucker-punched by a dame? Brother, you're not even the only one in this conversation."

-

Max Zagreb didn't see Arabella Lindauer again until after the new series had run its course.

The Confessions of Frankie Orr: Notorious Racketeer Spills All had appeared in the *Times* throughout the summer and into early fall, by which time the Four Horsemen weren't the only ones battling their way back from the starting line: The Allies were encountering heavy resistance in North Africa, the Philippines, and Stalingrad.

"Makes you wonder who Eisenhower and MacArthur been going out with," Canal said.

The lieutenant was drinking a beer between sets at the Cozy

Corner swing joint when Arabella came in on the arm of a vapid-faced corporal in Class A uniform and found a table far enough from the dance floor for talk and a quiet drink. When the band picked up its instruments, they got up to dance to a Tommy Dorsey tune, but when it finished and the next one was a jitterbug, she shook her head and led her disappointed escort back to their table. Zagreb checked his Wittnauer several times, and when the soldier left to make curfew, he carried a fresh beer over and took the vacant seat.

"Lindy Hop a little much?" he asked.

Arabella, tapping a Lucky on the back of a pigskin case, gave him a cool look. "The war's destroyed the proprieties, I see. Gentlemen used to wait for a lady's invitation to sit down."

"All's fair, I'm told." He lit her up, then himself. "'Racketeer tells all,' my fanny. Frankie didn't give you the dope on anything the statute of limitations didn't run out on under Herbert Hoover. He's personally responsible for four murders I know of. We're still toting up the score on the ones he catered out."

"He's a louse, but he's not stupid." She moved a bare shoulder. "Modern-day crimes bore readers: hoarding ration stamps, big bellies in brown shirts at Bund rallies. They like touring-car chases and choppers and bathtub gin: nostalgia stuff. Circulation's up. The old man wants to put me on police beat. First female reporter in the city to ride in a prowl car. Without handcuffs, that is."

"Congratulations. No more one-legged prom queens."

"I turned him down."

"Offer come with a ticket to Atlantic City? I didn't know you were so picky who you creased the sheets with."

"Get your mind out of the gutter. I'm holding out for a government assignment."

He lifted his glass in a toast, then drank. "Read any good books lately? Servicemen's editions?"

"I was wondering when you'd get around to that. I didn't give him anything but an educated guess. You wouldn't provide details or even confirm there was going to be a raid. The rumor was enough to get me into that private room of his at Roma's. The rest was horse-trading over the marinara."

"Mac's hairdresser friend was just a gossip. She was too dumb to know better. You're nobody's idea of dumb."

"No one got hurt. You didn't even get demoted."

"I've been there. I didn't mind it so much. Frankie suckered us with that refrigerator truck, just to set the hook deep. I minded that." He smoked. "How many you think he's hurt since you gave him his get-out-of-jail-free card?"

"Now you sound like one of those Home Front do-gooders. Why don't you donate a coffeepot to the aluminum drive? Give up your morning brew to help build a B-25?"

He put out his cigarette. "Last time we discussed Frankie, you called him a snake. Whacking him with a stick was part of the reason you wanted to write about him, you said. Now he's just a louse. Next time around, he's a fuzzy puppy. I always knew you had a price; I just didn't know you came so cheap."

"This isn't about Frankie," she said. "It's about the big-time crimebuster trusting a woman and getting burned."

"Or not trusting her. If I'd agreed to let you ride along on that raid, you'd have sat on it till it hatched, or risk losing the scoop. Don't tell me you didn't think I got what was coming to me when it went bust."

"Listen to you: Robert Taylor in his own movies. The world doesn't spin around you."

He put money on the table and rose.

"Buy yourself a bottle of bubbly. Enjoy it while you can. Just because Frankie makes good on his debts doesn't mean he likes it. Right now the feds are too busy chasing Fifth Column saboteurs to worry about an old-time bootlegger, but as soon as this war turns our way, all those headlines will hang on him like a bucket of rocks. A grand jury will want to talk to you."

"I don't know anything that isn't already public record."

"The jury won't know that. By that time, Frankie may not be able to remember everything that passed between you. You've got a reputation now for wheedling information during weak moments. He's famous for not taking chances. He didn't with the National Guard at the Ohio state border and he won't with a sob sister."

She stubbed out her lipstick-stained Lucky and smiled up at him. She wore her pillbox hat at a fashionable angle, as always.

"I'll buy that champagne and save it to share with you when we kick Hitler's butt."

-

She didn't make it to V-E Day; she barely made it through the Battle of the Bulge. After a trial period covering the capitol in Lansing, Arabella Lindauer drew a national assignment, to cover President Roosevelt's fourth inauguration in January 1945. Her private plane went down in a wooded area in Maryland fifty miles north of the District of Columbia, killing her, a *Times* photographer, and the pilot; leaky fuel line, investigators decided. She'd been subpoenaed to testify before a grand jury looking into the wartime black market as soon as she got back.

Soft Lights — AND — Sabotage

"Senators are a lousy team."

Soft Lights and Sabotage

McReary said, "We got Nazis."

"The whole world's got Nazis," Zagreb said, "even Africa. You see the last Tarzan, Johnny Weissmuller chopping down storm troopers with a machine gun?"

"You know, Weissmuller trained for the Olympics in the big pool at the Detroit Athletic Club," Canal said. He was working the crossword puzzle in the *Free Press* and only half listening.

Burke, looking over Canal's shoulder, asked what kind of name Weissmuller was, anyway.

Zagreb said, "German."

"Huh. I'm surprised Schicklgruber ain't had him shot for treason."

"Hitler's got his hands full just now." Canal tapped the pencil eraser on a paragraph about Stalingrad, continued from a story on page one.

Officer McReary, the youngest member of the Detroit Racket Squad—known popularly and unpopularly as the Four Horsemen—waited with exaggerated patience for the banter to subside. He kept his prematurely bald scalp covered indoors and out. "I mean we got Nazis right here in town. Scuttlebutt downstairs says the FBI's appointing a new Special Agent in Charge to investigate Fifth Column activity in the defense plants."

"His name rhyme with *mover*?" Officer Burke straightened and rolled his meaty shoulders. People considered him a big man until they laid eyes on Sergeant Canal. "The way you know it's not a false alarm is when the fat little twerp comes in by army plane with a couple hundred Washington reporters."

"It's legit," Lieutenant Zagreb said. The squad leader wore a perennially tired expression, as if his face had grown weary of supporting his large cranium. He had his hats made to order at J.L. Hudson's to accommodate it. "The commissioner sent a memo to every division this morning. We're supposed to put all our manpower at this guy's disposal."

Canal lowered his newspaper, paying attention now. "Most of our manpower's on active military duty. Should we send a cable to Patton asking to please loan some of it back?"

It was quiet at 1300 Beaubien, police headquarters. In order to make things easier on the janitor, whose son was serving in the Philippines, the detail was using four desks in the middle of the big room and sharing a single wastebasket. All the other desks were unmanned for the duration of the war.

"Let's just cooperate, okay?" Zagreb said. "The more help we give him, the sooner he'll be out of our hair."

"Speak for yourself." McReary tugged down his hat brim.

The telephone rang on the lieutenant's desk. Canal happened to be sitting at it—the detectives weren't territorial about office furniture, and kept no personal items in the drawers, to streamline the clearing-out process in case the commissioner made good on his threats to dismantle the squad—but he was still scrambling to get his size sixteens off the blotter when Burke scooped up the receiver. He listened, said, "Thanks," and cradled it. "Grady downstairs. Washington's on its way up."

"Hide the silverware," Canal said.

The man's name was Holinshead. He was suspended in age somewhere between thirty-two and forty-six, with a marine crewcut and eyes as flat as pewter cuff links. His navy suit, black rayon tie, and white shirt might have come in one piece and zipped up the back. He snapped his credentials-case open and shut. "Which one's Zagreb?"

Zagreb unfolded himself to his feet and offered his hand. He felt brief pressure and then cold air on his empty palm.

"I'm detaining a man at the Packard plant this afternoon," said Holinshead. "I want to borrow one of your detectives for backup and I need a place to question the suspect outside of the federal building."

"Two interrogation rooms on this floor," the lieutenant said, "no waiting."

"No, no place official. I want to keep him disoriented, uncertain whether he's been taken by the law or the Gestapo working behind enemy lines or the Nazi-American Bund or a bunch of vigilantes from the American Legion. He'll have a different set of lies for each one, so he's bound to stumble."

Burke said, "What'd he do, take a shot at Wendell Willkie?"

The FBI man ran his dull metallic eyes over the officer, lingering on his tie hanging at half-mast and sleeves turned back to expose the thick hair carpeting his wrists. "It's not what he's done. It's what he might do."

"We arresting 'em for that now?"

The eyes slid to the big man who'd asked the question, still seated with the *Free Press* spread on his lap. "Name and rank?"

"Starvo Canal, Supreme Knight, Knights of Columbus."

"Sergeant," supplied Zagreb, looking wearily at Canal.

"Stand up, please, Sergeant. Put out the cigar."

Canal looked at the lieutenant, who rolled his eyes and nodded. He set aside the newspaper, took a long last pull on the smoldering black stump, pressed it out in an old burn crater on the desk, and rose. Before the war had suspended such amusements he'd rejected offers from several other divisions to join them and play for their side in the annual intradepartmental football tournament. He was a defensive line all by himself.

The Special Agent in Charge shook his head. "Too intimidating. If he sees you coming he may bolt and fall under a drill press." As the sergeant resumed his seat and picked up the dead cigar, Holinshead turned to McReary. "You. At least you look like you've been near an ironing board recently."

The young man snapped to attention. "Sir, Daniel McReary, sir. Detective third-grade."

"At ease, son. I'm not MacArthur. Take off your hat."

McReary uncovered his pink scalp.

"Keep it on when we enter the plant. You'll look less like a CPA. Does any of you own a suit that isn't black?"

"I don't own *this* one," Burke said. "I borrowed it from my uncle before they buried him."

"We don't get a uniform allowance." Zagreb took a key off a ring from his pocket and gave it to the agent. "Room eleven-oh-two, the California. It's in the Negro section."

"Satisfactory. These fascists fear the colored man."

"What's this kraut's name?" Zagreb asked.

"Fred Taylor."

"Fred Taylor?" Canal struck a match. "I partnered with a Taylor in a prowl car. He was as German as a fox hunt."

"It was Alfred Schneider before he changed it. These Fifth Columnists are clever at assimilating. You won't trip them up by asking them who won the World Series."

Burke said, "Do *you* know who won the Series?"

"The Yankees."

"Wrong, *mein fuhrer*! It was the Cardinals."

Holinshead looked at Zagreb. "Lieutenant, if you can't control your men, I'll ask the commissioner to do it for you."

"Phone's free."

After a pleasing season of silence, Zagreb spoke to Burke. "Sit down and shut up."

The officer shrugged and obeyed.

"Taylor's burrowed in deep," the FBI man said. "Before Pearl Harbor he hung doors on Packards while contributing to the North American Aryan Alliance, a group that funneled money directly to the Reich. Now he puts bushings on Rolls-Royce aircraft engines. All he has to do is drop a wrench on the right spot to send a bunch of our boys crashing to the ground."

Zagreb said, "It's that easy?"

"I was simplifying, to make my point. Surely you see the danger."

"Danger's right. Those line workers are rough as hard times. Two of you enough?"

"We're stopping at the federal building to pick up Junkers and Dial, experienced men in the field. We'll handle it. Let's go, Detective."

"He's right, by the way."

The agent stopped in mid-turn. "I beg your pardon?"

"What Burke said about the Series," Zagreb said. "Four games to one, St. Louis. DiMaggio did bupkus."

Nothing appeared to be happening between the pewter studs in Holinshead's face. "I'm a Senators rooter myself."

After the FBI man left with McReary, Burke yawned. "You don't get fruitcake from him come Christmas."

"None of us will be here come Christmas if you don't learn to keep your mouth shut."

"Sorry, Zag."

"You, too, Canal. You don't even belong to the Knights of Columbus."

"They kicked me out when they found out I was Greek Orthodox." The big sergeant was puffing up gales of thoughtful smoke. "I worked a kidnapping with Junkers and Dial when I was with Missing Persons. They was always talking about the old days in Chicago. Once, they tied up a barber they thought was harboring John Dillinger, took off his shoes and socks and put a hot iron to the soles of his feet."

"He talk?" Zagreb waited. Canal's stories didn't always go anywhere.

"Dillinger stuck up a bank in Ohio while they was toasting his tootsies. They let the poor schnook go in an ambulance. The barbershop smelled like a wienie roast, they said. What reminded them, we was eating hot dogs in the Coney Island. Hard guys."

"Senators are a lousy team," Burke said.

-

Two hours passed, of which twenty minutes were diverting. Burke straddled a chair backward and practiced tossing his hat onto the clothes tree. Canal, his cigar gone cold again between his teeth, gave up on his puzzle and tuned the Philco to H.V. Kaltenborn for news from the front. Zagreb chain-smoked Chesterfields, correcting the grammar in arrest reports with a green fountain pen and checking the Wittnauer on his wrist from time to time. At three o'clock a call came in from the police in Warren and they put on their hats and drove to a beer garden across from the Chrysler tank plant to assist the locals in breaking up a brawl, employing blackjacks and a pool cue cut down to a handy length.

"Be easier with Mac along," said Burke during a lull in the action. "I miss his backhand."

On the way back they stopped at a call box. Canal hung up and got into the sedan beside Burke at the wheel, rubbing with his thumb at a spot of blood on his cuff. "Mac ain't checked in yet."

Zagreb said, "Let's swing over to the California."

"Suits me. Nazis and rednecks are like peanuts. Once you start beating on 'em, you can't stop."

The residential hotel stood on Hastings, a squat building of tar-stained yellow brick where the 31st Michigan Infantry had stopped before boarding a train to Mexico to fight Pancho Villa in 1916. When the black Chrysler boated into the curb and the three plainclothesmen got out, a young black man in a lavender pinstripe suit tightened his grip on his female companion's arm and they trotted down the block.

The lobby smelled of stale cigarettes and spearmint gum. The trio nodded at the horse-faced clerk reading *Sixgun Stories* behind the desk and boarded an elevator operated by an ancient Negro in a bellhop's uniform.

"Where's Hank?" Zagreb asked him.

"VFW meeting, boss."

"Which war'd that be, eighteen-twelve?" asked Burke.

The scent of DDT greeted them when the doors trundled open on the eleventh floor.

McReary answered Zagreb's knock. The young detective was in shirtsleeves with his hat pushed back from his glistening forehead. "I was just about to hunt up a phone." He stood aside. The squad entered.

Holinshead stood next to the only window, whose sash was propped open with a block of wood that belonged to the room. It did nothing to relieve the fug, but the FBI man looked fresh with his jacket buttoned and his tie knotted snugly. There were three other men present: one standing, one seated sideways in a straight wooden chair with his legs crossed and an arm resting on the back, the third stretched out on the bed.

Both the man standing and the man sitting were jacketless, in suspenders with their ties hanging loose. The man in the chair was stocky and wore lizard skin boots, old but polished. The other was gaunt, with an Adam's apple the size of a cue ball and a cigarette smoldering at a sixty-degree angle from the corner of his lips.

Zagreb knew at once these weren't the Arrow Collar men J. Edgar Hoover liked to parade before cameras, but two of the cowboys the Bureau employed to toughen its center—former Texas Rangers, peace officers from Arizona and Montana, and posse men who'd dispensed justice with a rope and a Winchester in the days of John Wesley Hardin, pickled since in brine and rye whiskey and as ageless as the single-action Colts on their belts. Their eyes were dead in faces burned deep brown.

"Glad you could make it, Lieutenant. I don't know if you've met Special Agents Neil Junkers and George Dial." Holinshead swept a hand from the standing beanpole to the lunk in the chair.

Canal said, "I have. Somebody else must be using the iron from the lobby."

Zagreb studied the man on the bed. He lay spread-eagled with wrists and ankles bound to the posts with twine, wearing nothing but a pair of BVDs soaked through with sweat or urine or both. The rest of what the lieutenant guessed were his clothes lay in a sodden heap on the floor. He looked to be in his early thirties, fair, with ribs that stuck out. One eye was swollen shut and his lower lip was split and bleeding and twice normal size. He was conscious, breathing heavily, but his open eye was opaque. The point of passing out was close.

"Oh, and Alfred Schneider, the enemy." The Special Agent in Charge sounded bored.

"My name is Fred Taylor."

This information came in a mumble, with all the inflection pressed from it as if through constant repetition. The German accent was slight.

"That's the name you write on the back of your paycheck, just before you turn some of it over to the North American Aryan Alliance," Holinshead said. "It always clears, but that's between you and the bookkeepers at Packard."

"I told you I have never heard of the North—the North Aryan Alliance. You have—"

Junkers, the gaunt one, took a step and backhanded him hard across the cheek. One of his big knobby knuckles split it open. Taylor made a choking noise and his body lost all tension.

Dial, the stocky one, got up, scooped a pitcher off the grubby nightstand, and dashed water into the unconscious man's face. Taylor groaned and his head rolled over, but both eyes remained closed.

"Damn it, Neil, now we got to start all over again."

"So what, you got a date with Betty Grable?"

"Here, kid, make yourself useful and fill this up." Dial thrust the pitcher at McReary, who reached for it.

Burke put a hand on McReary's arm, stopping him. "Fetch it yourself," he told Dial. "He ain't your errand boy."

The stocky man looked Burke up and down. The city detective had three inches and twenty pounds on him, but for someone who had a little too much padding around the chest the agent seemed confident of whatever outcome this discussion might have. "Whoa there, hoss. I didn't just bring any carrots with me."

Burke bunched his muscles. Zagreb inserted a shoulder between him and the G-man.

"It won't hurt to give the kraut a breather. He's no good to you in a coma."

"Let him rest, Dial."

Dial nodded at his superior's quiet command and sat back down, dangling an arm over the back of the chair.

Holinshead regarded Zagreb mildly. "Don't tell me you never bruised a knuckle on a stubborn suspect, Lieutenant."

"We usually leave enough to stand up at the arraignment. What've you got on Taylor?"

"That's classified."

"Huh. Snitch." Canal lit a cigar and tossed the match on the floor.

The FBI man nodded. "I can confirm that, without going into detail. Our informant identified Taylor as a contributor to the Alliance."

"Finger him in person?" Zagreb asked.

"Too risky. He's in deep."

"He just gave you the name Alfred Schneider, alias Fred Taylor? My grandmother spoke four languages; she taught me a little German. Schneider in English is tailor. He can't be the only one who took that name when he came here."

"So far he's the only one who's turned up in a position to threaten our national interests."

Burke said, “He’s a grease monkey in an aircraft plant. There’s thousands of ’em.”

“But only one Fred Taylor.”

The lieutenant pierced his face with a Chesterfield and touched his Zippo to the end. The acrid stench of fear and bodily fluids from the man on the bed was oppressive.

“A little random sabotage don’t call for a Special Agent in Charge; or are you trying to make an impression your first day?”

“Even the smallest fish knows who leads the school. We offered him a pretty good deal if he’d give up some of his associates, but he turned us down. Isn’t that right, Detective?”

“They said they’d hold him for the duration, then deport him to Germany,” McReary said. “It was either that or life in Leavenworth. It wasn’t *Beat the Band*.”

Canal asked, “Can’t you get those names from your rat in the Alliance?”

“I didn’t say our informant was a member. In any case, our methods aren’t open to analysis outside the Bureau.”

Junkers chuckled, his Adam’s apple doing the Lindy Hop in time with the cigarette that never left his lips. He kept his head cocked to one side to keep the smoke out of his eyes, but it appeared to have cured his weathered brown face like leather. So far he’d spoken only once, to ask Dial if he had a date with Betty Grable.

Canal shifted his attention to him.

“Hope you got the right man this time. I heard that barber you gave a hotfoot to had to close up shop. Can’t cut hair sitting down.”

“We got Dillinger in the end, didn’t we?” The man’s southwestern accent was sharp enough to cut barbed wire.

“Well, sure. You couldn’t miss him once you ran out of barbers.”

Taylor groaned again and muttered something in German. He was coming around.

Holinshead glanced from him to Zagreb. "You can file any grievances with the Director in Washington. Meanwhile our boys are dying while we're losing the war at home."

"Put it on a poster." Zagreb looked at his men and jerked his head toward the door. The squad left.

-

That night, responding to an anonymous tip, the Four Horsemen staked out a machine-tool warehouse on Orleans near the river, where an exchange of black market tires for cash was expected. Before leaving 1300, Zagreb called the personnel department at the Packard plant, where a female clerk agreed to look up Fred Taylor's employee file and report back.

The tip turned out to be a dud. When the squad returned to clock out two hours later, the sergeant at the desk handed Zagreb a message.

"What do you mean it's missing?" demanded the lieutenant over the wire the next day. No one had answered the night before.

"That's not exactly true." This voice was male, and wearily patient. "The person you spoke to last night couldn't find it because it wasn't there. I gave it to the FBI yesterday, a man named Holinshead."

"He show you a court order?"

"I didn't think he needed one. There's a war on, you know."

Zagreb's knuckles whitened on the receiver, but he kept his tone even.

"Who's foreman on Taylor's shift?"

There was a pause. Metal scraped against metal, paper rustled. The man's voice came back on. "Orville Sack, but he's busy on the line. He's on the eleven A.M. rotation for lunch."

The Packard plant sprawled on East Grand at Mt. Elliott, as palatial and orderly as it had appeared on Albert Kahn's drawing board forty years before. Directed by an employee, Zagreb clanked a tin lunch pail onto the cafeteria table opposite where Orville Sack sat munching an egg-salad sandwich. "Swap you a Baby Ruth for your apple."

The foreman looked up with his mouth full, first at the stranger, then at the gold shield in his palm. He had thin, ginger-colored hair and an expression that seemed resigned to any sort of tragedy. Zagreb wondered if his acquaintances called him Sad Sack.

Sack chewed and swallowed. "Nobody offers a trade like that."

Zagreb opened the pail and set the candy bar in its bright wrapper in front of the foreman. Then he sat down facing him.

"Where'd you get the points for an egg sandwich?"

"I didn't. It's powdered. I got a nephew in the navy."

"Good for you. Fred Taylor."

"Uh-uh." Sack pushed away the Baby Ruth. "Bad enough you took one of my hardest workers off the line. I won't put him in worse Dutch over no dessert."

"I'm not federal. I'm trying to find out why they're interested in him."

"Beats me. He's a good Joe for a kraut. He usually sits right where you're sitting, telling me how much he loves this country and how he wouldn't go back to Germany if they made him *Reichsfuhrer*, whatever the hell that is."

"He wouldn't be a very good spy if he didn't say that."

"If he's a spy, I'm Mata Hari. He hates Hitler more than Churchill does. His girl's Jewish, for God's sake."

"What's her name?"

"Molly something-or-other. She's a secretary in the Fisher Building, he said. She was a campaign volunteer for FDR in nineteen forty. I guess that makes her a regular Axis Sally. You sure about the Baby Ruth?"

"Go ahead. Sugar hurts my teeth." Zagreb accepted Sack's apple, a McIntosh with a brown spot. "Where's Molly work in the Fisher?" He bit into it.

Sack shrugged, peeling down the candy bar wrapper like a banana skin. "I need Fred on the line. The dames are okay, but they don't come here Rosie the Riveter; that takes training. These krauts got machine oil in their veins. They held a monkey wrench before they could pick up a spoon. Henry Ford ought to hire Krupp away from Berlin if he wants to win this war."

"I'll see what I can do. About Taylor, not Krupp. Henry don't return my calls."

"If Fred's a spy, I'm Sergeant York."

"You've got your wars mixed up. We're fighting Nazis, not the Kaiser."

"I got no beef with either of 'em. My nephew's in New Zealand. All I want to do is make quota. I can't do that if I got to train somebody from scratch every day 'cause somebody on the line don't talk American as good as me."

Zagreb asked a few more questions, but got nothing more he could use. He threw his apple core into a trash bin, went back to headquarters, and put the lunch pail on the desk Burke was using.

"Hey, I been looking for that." The officer undid the catches.

"Eat while you work. I need you and Mac to call every office in the Fisher Building and ask if they've got a woman named Molly working there. She's Taylor's girl."

"We investigating Taylor now?" McReary had a game of double solitaire going on a pair of desks left vacant by a sergeant training at Fort Bragg and a detective first-grade missing in action in the Pacific.

"We're investigating Holinshead."

McReary looked up from his cards and Burke looked up from his lunch pail. Canal, smoking a cigar near the open window assigned to him on such occasions, grinned around the stump.

"That don't leave this room," said the lieutenant. "The commissioner thinks J. Edgar Hoover shit the moon."

"The commissioner thinks we should be storming a beach

somewhere." Burke scratched his chin, making a sound like a snow shovel scraping concrete. "I thought we was supposed to be all in this together: Us versus Them."

"That's what they say to sell war bonds. Holinshead's working on some gripe of his own. Even a flag-waving nut takes a coffee break now and then."

"Maybe he's got a bet down on the enemy," Canal said.

McReary shuffled the pasteboards back into the deck. "I always knew I'd wind up in dog tags. Who's got the Yellow Pages?" He began opening and closing drawers.

"Here." Burke tore the directory in two and handed him half.

Canal asked Zagreb what he wanted him to do.

"Hop over to the hotel and find out if Taylor's still breathing. Pick up a sack of burgers on the way, just in case he is. I doubt those bastards have been feeding him."

"What if they don't like it?"

"That's why I'm sending you."

The sergeant grinned wider, tossed his cigar out the window, and buttoned his jacket around his barrel torso. Whistling, he rolled on out.

"I bet they stick me in a submarine." McReary planted a finger on the page in front of him and picked up a receiver. "I get claustrophobic just putting on a vest."

"I heard they feed you good in them tin cans," Burke said.

"That's just for ballast when the depth charges start dropping."

"You're dreaming, both of you," Zagreb said. "It's the infantry for us all if we blow this."

Burke stared into his pail. "Where the hell's my Baby Ruth?"

-

They found Molly Wenk in the mailroom of an insurance underwriter on the Fisher's fourteenth floor, putting letters and reports in tin canisters and poking them into rows of pneumatic tubes connected to the various offices. Her best asset was her auburn hair, which she wore in a shoulder bob, Andrews Sisters style. She had sharp, rodentlike features and spoke in a harsh New York accent that Zagreb had heard previously only in Patsy Kelly movies.

She found someone to spell her and accompanied the lieutenant and McReary to a coffee shop on the ground floor. Zagreb had left Burke behind to answer the phones on the theory that a single woman in her late twenties might find the younger officers' presence less daunting. He determined quickly that Miss Wenk wouldn't be daunted by anything this side of a German .88.

"I ain't heard from Fred in a couple of days." She tapped a Camel on the back of a pigskin cigarette case and set fire to it from a book of matches in an ashtray before Zagreb could get out his Zippo. "I thought maybe the five o'clock whistle didn't blow; you know, like in the song."

"I wouldn't," Zagreb said. "I got a tin ear. Known him long?"

"He was the first person I met when I came here on the bus. I was schlepping this huge suitcase, looking for a cab, when suddenly somebody jerks it out of my hand. Well, I'm a Brooklyn girl. I kicked him in the nuts."

McReary said, "Jesus. This guy was born under a bum star."

Zagreb glared him into silence.

"Turns out he was just trying to give me a hand," Molly said. "He carried the suitcase to a streetcar stop and told me how I could get to my friend's address where I was staying without having to transfer. Next day he showed up at the door with a bunch of flowers. I'd've thought he was a real smooth operator, except his English was all mixed up. He was cute. We go out to dinner and a movie sometimes. I wouldn't call him my boyfriend, exactly. All he ever done was kiss me on the cheek. What kind of a girl do you think I am?"

"How's he feel about the war?"

"Oh, he's all for it, buys bonds and contributes to the scrap drives. He's registered for the draft, but his number's high on account of he works in a defense plant where he's needed. Which is just as well, I say."

"Why?"

"On account of him being a kraut and all. It stands to reason he don't want to kill somebody that might be a friend or family."

"He could join the marines and fight nips," said McReary.

She studied him under lowered lids. "So could you. Can I see them badges again? I didn't get a good look upstairs. You could be Cracker Jack cops for all I know."

They showed her their shields and IDs. She sat back, blowing smoke at the ceiling. "What kind of jam's he in? He's no rackets boy, I'd swear that on a stack of Bibles."

Zag rolled the dice. "He's in custody on suspicion of spying and sabotage."

"Banana oil. He came here to get away from the Nazis. I'm Jewish on my father's side. Hanging around with me wouldn't win him points back home."

"On the other hand, it's good cover."

She stabbed out her cigarette.

"You boys are full of hooey. If you had Fred in jail, if you spent any time with him at all, you'd know he's a better American than the two of you put together. He couldn't tell a lie if lies was water and he was on fire."

"I didn't say we had him in jail. I said he was in custody. The FBI's got him."

She'd plucked another Camel out of her case. She stopped in mid-tap and stared at Zagreb.

"Tell me something about the man in charge. He have a crewcut?"

"Plenty of them do."

"Maybe thirties, maybe forties, eyes like a dead mackerel?

Slings around words like 'satisfactory' and never sweats or takes off his coat?"

The two plainclothesmen exchanged a look.

Zagreb rested his forearms on the table. "Didn't you tell us you came here from Brooklyn?"

"I left when I was eighteen. I was a file clerk in Bureau headquarters in Washington for seven years, the last three of which I threw away on that snake in the grass. He's the reason I bought a bus ticket, just like Fred leaving Germany to duck Hitler." She lit the cigarette and shook out the match viciously. "I dropped fifteen pounds, changed jobs twice, went through four stylists, got a complete new wardrobe. It's just like that creep Holinshead not even to change the way he cuts his hair."

-

Time seemed to have stood still at the California since yesterday, and for that matter since Repeal; even the flies in the bowl fixtures lay frozen in the same death throes. The same bored clerk was reading the same pulp magazine behind the desk. Only the elevator man was different, and that was just Hank, who wasn't likely to take another day off before old age caught up with him.

This time Canal opened the door to 1102, minus his jacket and cigar. The air in the room was fetid as ever and he wore two dark circles under his armpits. A thread of dried blood bifurcated his lower lip. Zagreb asked if he'd run into something.

"Washington red tape." The big man grinned, wincing when a fresh trickle broke through the scab.

Inside, Holinshead was at his station near the open window, looking as crisp as usual. The color scheme was the same, but he must have gone home to rest and change, because the two cowboys had the unpressed look of men who'd taken turns sleeping in the hard wooden chair. Both men needed a shave. Junkers, the scarecrow, had a purple welt under one eye the size of Canal's ham fist. Dial, his stocky partner, leaned back against a grimy papered wall with his arms folded and a swelling on one side of his jaw.

Zagreb grinned. Holinshead bridled.

"It took my service piece to back that mad bull of yours off my agents. I'm considering filing federal charges."

Canal grunted. "I told 'em they ought to take better care of their pets. Some guys just don't take advice."

Fred Taylor, alias Alfred Schneider, was sitting up now on the edge of the bed, dressed in wrinkled Packard Motor Car Co. coveralls and oil-stained black work boots. His hands dangled between his spread knees and his chin rested on his chest. The lieutenant approached and lifted Taylor's chin gently. His face was swollen and his breath whistled through a broken septum.

Zagreb lowered the prisoner's head. A greasy paper sack leaned at a drunken angle on the nightstand. "He eat anything?"

"Couple bites of burger," said Canal. "That's all he could chew. I gave him some water, he took more of that. I wouldn't go away and trust these boys to water my plants."

"Let's all file charges, starting with false arrest and unlawful detention." The lieutenant looked at Holinshead. "This isn't the Fred Taylor your snitch gave you; but you knew that."

The Special Agent in Charge smiled, lips pressed tight.

"You're a day short and a dollar late, I'm afraid. This man has confessed. Your sergeant's a witness."

"That's right, Zag. I think he said he started the Chicago fire, too. There was something about a quake in Frisco, too, but I didn't catch it. He mumbles."

Zagreb said, "We get a lot of confessions in this room; something about the atmosphere. After a half a dozen or so you pick up a sense for when they're on the level and when they're talking just because when they're talking they're not getting slugged. Taylor!" he barked. "Who burned down the Reichstag?"

"I did." The man on the bed spoke into his chest.

"That was pointless," said Holinshead. "He's not so far gone he wouldn't recognize a way out when you gave him one. I told you these spies are clever."

"Tell your men scram."

"This is a federal operation, Lieutenant. You don't give orders. The commissioner—"

"Molly Wenk."

The FBI man's mouth closed with a snap.

"Chief?" Dial looked at his superior. Junkers' eyes were on him too.

"Step outside. If I need you I'll call."

Canal opened the door. "Scat."

Junkers took a step the big man's way. Canal let go of the knob and squared off in front of him. Dial's hand wandered to the butt of the revolver in a holster snapped to his belt. McReary drew his own in one smooth motion and flicked the barrel across the stocky man's temple. Dial stumbled, caught himself on a bedpost, and clapped a hand to the side of his head. Blood oozed between his fingers.

Burke said, "Told you he wasn't your errand boy."

The cowboys left, Dial still holding his head and muttering. Burke kicked the door shut behind him.

"I thought they'd never leave," Canal said.

Holinshead spoke calmly. "Molly Wenk was next on our list. If you've spoken with her, you've compromised our case. Your behavior is treasonous."

"Molly?" Taylor raised his head, blinking his one visible eye.

"She's okay, Fred. Worried about you." Zagreb didn't look away from the FBI man. "Investigating her for what, running out on you? That's outside your jurisdiction."

"Is that what she told you? I'm surprised a professional like you would fall for such an obvious attempt to divert suspicion. We've had her under surveillance for years as a premature anti-fascist."

McReary laughed. "A premature *what*?"

"You heard me. She came out against Hitler well before the war, when he posed no threat to America. We have files to cover that. Taking such a stand so early put her under suspicion as a possible Communist sympathizer."

Canal shoved his hat to the back of his head, exposing his unruly black curls. "Jeez, you miss Winchell one day, you fall behind. Last I heard, the Communists in Russia was our allies."

"You're confused. That's understandable. In Washington, we're engaged in fighting more than one war: the next one as well as this. The Bolsheviks represent just as great a challenge to our national interest as Hitler, Mussolini, and Tojo combined. If we don't identify and isolate the enemy now, we'll be at a serious disadvantage after the cessation of the current hostilities."

Burke scratched his chin. "Hell, we might as well take out the Dutch while we're at it. Get 'em before they sneak up on us in them wooden shoes."

"You could burn Molly as a witch," Zagreb said. "It wouldn't be any less trumped up. You lived with her for three years in Washington, and when she got fed up and dumped you, you tailed her to Detroit, wangled yourself an assignment here, and arrested the first man she took up with, to use as leverage to get her back. You're lucky he didn't croak on you. Next time try hiring less enthusiastic help."

Taylor seemed to be paying attention now. His chin was off his chest.

Holinshead stood immobile. "You'd take the word of a subversive over that of an agent of the United States government?"

"No."

"Well, then."

"I'm a pro, like you said. We ran up a whale of a phone bill getting corroboration. Her old landlord and her former neighbors backed up her Washington story. The landlord still has the lease with both your signatures on it. Not enough? We can ask Molly about scars and moles. I don't guess you can claim she saw you out swimming in the Potomac."

Holinshead paled. "Taylor's file—"

"You'll have a drawer full of files on Fred Taylors and Alfred Schneiders. If one of 'em didn't show up in ledgers at the North American Aryan Alliance, it's easy enough to plant it through your snitch." Zagreb shook his head. "I gave you too much credit. I had you down as a flag-waving fanatic. Turns out you're just a jealous ex-boyfriend."

"All right, we were involved. I can still link her to a conspiracy to overthrow the government."

"How'd that look, one of Hoover's own twiddling toes with a Red? You're washed up, Holinshead. They probably won't shoot you. Maybe you'll get a work detail: carrying a shovel after Patton's horse in the Victory Day parade."

"That dirty little tramp!" He went for his revolver. The Four Horsemen beat him to the draw; but Fred Taylor obstructed their field of fire.

With an animal roar, the defense worker sprang from the bed and tackled the Special Agent in Charge, who fell against the window behind him, shattering it. He got his gun free, just as his attacker collapsed at his feet; he was too weak to follow through. Burke and Canal barreled into Holinshead as he pointed the muzzle at the man on the floor. He went down under their weight, gun arm flung to the side. Zagreb took two steps and brought his heel down hard on that wrist. It cracked like a stick of kindling.

Junkers and Dial burst through the door, guns first. McReary and Zagreb drew down on them, pinning them in the crossfire. The cowboys dropped their weapons and threw up their hands.

"Hi-yo, Silver," McReary said.

"The Lone Ranger." Canal got up off Holinshead, who writhed

on the floor, clutching his splintered wrist. "Another Detroit invention. Just like Johnny Weissmuller."

-

"Fred and Molly." The big sergeant folded the *Free Press* to the society section and handed it to Zagreb. "Sounds like somebody you'd have over for bridge."

As always happened in those photos, the bride looked radiant, the groom as grim as a pallbearer. Taylor's face had healed, but he looked wan. It had only been five weeks. U.S. warships were pounding Guadalcanal. Rommel was in trouble in North Africa. "Poor sap thought he had it tough with the feds." Zagreb gave back the paper and bent over his arrest reports.

"How you getting on with the new Special Agent in Charge?" Canal asked him.

"Swell. Been here a month and I haven't met him yet."

"Maybe he's scared."

The lieutenant consulted his Wittnauer. "Mac and Burke should've checked in by now."

"They're still softening up that guy gave us the bum tip on the warehouse on Orleans. He'll spill his guts okay, if Burksie's fists hold up. He's got delicate knuckles."

"It means more stakeouts when he does."

"Our work's never done." Canal returned to his crossword. "Here's one I been saving. What's another word for 'government agent'?"

"Convict Number 6672, Alcatraz."

GET Sinatra

"What, no whitewalls?"

Get Sinatra

Belle Isle Beach was white in late sunlight; Westinghouse white, Max Zagreb thought. Slanting rays put a Gillette edge on the waves where the river broadened into Lake St. Clair. Little boys searched the water with toy telescopes for U-boats, pretty girls cocoa-tanned their legs so they could pretend they were wearing nylons when they danced at the Club Congo, the Green Hornet was busy stinging the bejesus out of Japanese spies on someone's portable radio. It was a peaceful summer Saturday in the middle of a war, and here he was with a stubby .38 stuck inside his swimming trunks.

"Lieutenant? I mean Zag?"

Zagreb looked up, scowling at the slip-up, then felt his face crack into a grin as McReary came trotting up from the water, trunks wet and sagging, holding down a winter-weight gray fedora with one hand against the wind from Canada. He was freckling badly and resembled nothing so much as a polka-dot scarecrow.

"You might as well give me the rank, Mac. That hat screams cop. Where's your shoulder holster?"

The young detective flushed. McReary was a good-looking kid, but he'd lost his hair early and was sensitive about it. "Sorry. I had a Panama, but I think I threw it out during the last snowstorm." He sat on the edge of Zagreb's beach towel, drew his service piece from under it, and put it in his lap. "I don't think they're coming. It's almost sundown, and torches mean gasoline. Even phony Nazis aren't crazy enough to burn up all their ration stamps just to celebrate the anniversary of the fall of France."

"We got another hour. Eastern War Time, did you forget?"

"Half this town's got kin serving overseas. They had that kind of guts, why not enlist in the *Wehrmacht*?"

"Keep your shirt on. Put it on, I mean. Vice picked up the *Bundesfuhrer* an hour ago, trying to lure a fourteen-year-old girl into his Studebaker with a lollipop."

"Where'd you hear that?"

Zagreb pointed at the radio, still playing *The Green Hornet* under someone's colorful umbrella.

Suddenly they were both in shade. Sergeant Canal stood over them with his square feet spread, listening to the Hornet's chauffeur reporting to his boss. In a striped robe, green cheaters, and a glob of white zinc on his nose, he was as quiet and petite as the Big Top. "Didn't Kato used to be a nip?"

"That was before Pearl," Zagreb said. "Now he's a Filipino."

McReary said, "You hear? We nabbed Heinrich on a jailbait rap."

"Maybe he was recruiting for the Hitler Youth." Canal bit down on his cold cigar and spat out sand.

They were joined by Officer Burke. He wasn't as big as the sergeant, but made up for the difference in body hair. Tight white trunks made him look like a Kodiak bear that had been shaved for gallbladder surgery. Briefed by the others, he said, "I bet the girl was Shorty O'Hanlon. When he puts on a girdle he looks just like Linda Darnell."

Lieutenant Zagreb broke the pungent little silence that followed this remark. "Mac, I'm putting you on that black market case at the Detroit Athletic Club. Burksie's been staking out the locker room a little too long."

Burke's face darkened while the others laughed.

"Why didn't you call us an hour ago?" McReary was the youngest member of the Racket Squad and the most earnest.

"When's the last time any of us got the chance to top off his tan?"

"This detail's the bunk anyway," said Canal. "We can't even make an arrest, just get a look at the faces under the storm trooper caps and match 'em to the mug books downtown."

Zagreb said, "So far there's no law against playing dress-up and singing love songs to Schicklgruber. If they've got a record we can haul 'em in and sweat 'em later, put the fear of FDR in 'em."

Burke scratched his chest hair. "Busywork's what it is. The commissioner can't break up the squad because we get headlines, so he's going to bore us into quitting and joining the army."

Canal said, "The navy for me. Them sailor boys get laid more."

McReary said he thought Canal was saving himself for a nice girl from the Old Country.

"There won't be any left if we keep dropping bombs on 'em. Man's not made of stone."

Zagreb got up and folded his towel. "Let's get dressed. I'll talk to the commissioner."

Burke leered at Canal. "I hope you know all the words to 'Anchors Aweigh.'"

-

"These rats in the Bund are a serious threat to the Home Front," Commissioner Witherspoon told the lieutenant. "You'll stay on the detail until further notice."

Witherspoon, a sour parsnip in a stiff collar, considered the Racket Squad the chief impediment to his ambition to run for mayor. He resented the tag the press had hung on Zagreb and his men—the Four Horsemen—and reprimanded any department employee who used it.

"Setting up their leader on a morals charge has scared the sauerkraut clean out of them. They're tearing up their brown shirts to donate to the armed services."

The commissioner put on his pinch glasses and shuffled the papers on his desk, gesturing dismissal. "You're insubordinate, Lieutenant. This department doesn't railroad innocent men."

"Heinrich and I bowled in the same league before the war. He's a blowhard and he's got a screw loose when it comes to Jews, but he's never so much as looked at a woman except his wife. Putting Sergeant O'Hanlon in a pinafore wouldn't change that."

"It wasn't O'Hanlon. I'd like to know how these rumors get started. We used a female volunteer from the steno pool."

"So it *was* a frame."

Witherspoon sat back and unpinched his spectacles. "What is it you want, Zagreb? Half my men are overseas and I can't keep a secretary; they all want to build tanks for Chrysler. I don't have time to listen to you gripe."

"You just made my case. You're wasting four experienced men on a piss-ant detail that Uncle Sam's Whiskers should've been doing in the first place."

"The last time I let in Hoover's boys, it took a can of Flit to get them out." He twirled his glasses by their ribbon, lips pursed. Then he put them back on and reshuffled his papers. "Here. A job for experienced men."

Zagreb hesitated before taking the sheet, a letter typed single-spaced on heavy bond. He didn't like the commissioner's constipated little smile.

-

For fifteen seconds after the lieutenant stopped speaking, the only sound in the squad room was Canal mashing his cigar between his teeth. They had their hats on—matching pearl-gray fedoras, to avoid bopping one another with blackjacks when they waded into brawls—because the nights were beginning to get cool. They were alone except for an officer flipping through files in a drawer. He was ten pounds too heavy for his uniform and five years past retirement. Witherspoon was desperate for manpower but too cheap to restore the man's sergeant's rank. The room was filled with empty desks and typewriters covered like canary cages.

"Bodyguard duty," spat Burke. "That's actually a step down from watching fake Nazis."

Canal said, "I can't stand Sinatra. He sings like olive oil coming to a boil."

"He's okay," McReary said. "Next girl I have, 'I'll Never Smile Again' will be our song."

Canal snorted. "If you ever *had* a girl, you'd know you don't get to pick your song. It's the one that's playing the first time you plant one on her."

"Your luck, it'll be 'Thwee Iddie Fishies.'" Zagreb held up the letter. "It's from Frankie's manager, asking for police protection when he plays the Fisher next month. He's been getting anonymous calls promising to lay a lead pipe across his throat if he doesn't agree to pony up five grand."

"Worth a shot, if it improves his singing." Canal blew an improbably long jet of smoke out the open window next to him.

Burke said, "Hell, anybody can drop a nickel. Some soda jerk's sore because his broad's in love with that twig."

"The manager thinks it's the McCoy. Remember that lug tried to throw acid in Mae West's face?"

"Serves him right for aiming at her *face*," Canal said. "It's a publicity stunt."

McReary was still fuming over that crack about his love life. "I've had more girls than you've had cheap cigars. You fall in love with Hedy Lamarr every time you go to the can."

"I told you, her picture came with the wallet."

Zagreb said, "You're both Errol Flynn, okay? Let's get back to business. Frankie's the job, that's it. I don't know about the rest of you, but I've had it up to here with beating up on ham radio operators with Lawrence Welk accents. What's so wrong with show business? Maybe we'll get to meet Ann Sheridan."

"We've got a couple of weeks," said Burke. "I'm thinking we might wrap this one up before we have to dive into a mob of obsessed fans. Don't this sound like just the kind of lay that another Frankie dear to our hearts would love to sink his teeth into?"

Deep contemplation followed. The Greektown bar where they hung their hats off-duty had a picture of Francis Xavier Oro on the dartboard. Frankie Orr had his paws on every automobile tire and pound of butter that passed through the local black market. If he'd attended high school in Palermo, his classmates would have voted him Most Likely to Succeed in Organized Crime.

"I'd like five minutes with that greaseball in the basement," Canal said thoughtfully. "I'd swap it for my pension."

Burke chuckled. "Big talk. Someday you'll punch a hole in Witherspoon's face and your pension'll be dead as Valentino."

Zagreb lit a Chesterfield with his Zippo. "There isn't a man in this room won't be on the dole the minute the boys come back from Berlin and Tokyo; the commish will see to that. Meanwhile, let's have some fun with *our* Frankie."

-

Orr's office of record stood high in the Buhl Building, an Art Deco hell designed by a firm of chorus boys from Grosse Pointe, with a checkerboard of ebony and pickled-birch panels on the walls and a chrome ballerina hoisting a lighted globe on his glass desk. He sent someone there to pick up his mail and read it in his private dining room in the Roma Café, a Sicilian restaurant in which he owned part interest; that was speculation. His name didn't appear on the ownership papers.

A freestanding sign in front of the dining room read PRIVATE PARTY. As Canal lifted it out of their path, a man nearly his size took its place. His suit coat sagged heavily on one side.

"'S'matter, junior, you only read the funnies?" Canal said.

Zagreb smiled at the man. "Hey, pal, you like Vernor's?"

"Never heard of it."

"Out-of-town," Zagreb told the sergeant. "Frankie rotates 'em like tires so they don't get lazy. It's not his fault he don't know we're famous." He flashed his shield. "Boss in?"

"No."

"Then what the hell you doing here?" Canal swung the sign at his head.

The bodyguard tried to roll with the blow and reached under the sagging side of his coat. McReary, stationed on that side, slid the blackjack out of his sleeve and flicked it at the back of the man's hand as it emerged. The big semiautomatic pistol thumped to the carpet. Burke kicked it away.

"Just like Busby Berkeley," Zagreb said. "Show some manners. Knock on the door."

The bodyguard, bleeding from the temple, ungripped his injured hand and complied. When a muffled voice issued an invitation, he grasped the knob. "What's Vernor's, anyway?"

"Just the best ginger ale on the planet," Canal said.

"I like Canada Dry."

Canal swung the sign again. Zagreb caught it and took it away.

Frankie Orr, seated in a corner booth, closed and locked a strongbox on the table and looked at the bodyguard without expression. "Call New York. You're still on the payroll till your replacement gets here. I don't want to see you after that."

The man left, closing the door. Orr turned his gaze to Zagreb. The gangster was handsome, if you liked the gigolo type. He trained his glossy black hair with plenty of oil, practiced his crooked Clark Gable smile in front of a mirror, and the man who cut his silk suits at Crawford's swore he hadn't added an inch to his waistline in ten years. "I wish you'd put a leash on that St. Bernard of yours," he said. "There's a war on. Good help's scarce."

"He's still a pup. I don't want to break his spirit." The lieutenant spun a chair away from a vacant table—they all were, except Orr's—and straddled it backward, folding his arms on the back.

"Sinatra's coming, did you hear?"

"I bought a block of tickets. I didn't know you followed swing music."

"Der Bingle for me. Crosby was here when he came and he'll be here when he's gone. That might be sooner than we think. That goon on the Manhattan subway, before you came here; didn't you beat him to death with a lead pipe?"

"I never killed nobody, not with a lead pipe or a gun or a custard pie. If that's why you're here, you need a warrant. Small talk, Sinatra and Ish Kabibble, won't do it."

"They don't call you the Conductor because you shook a stick in front of the Philharmonic, but that's New York's headache. One less of you heels back East doesn't annoy me one little bit. Some joker's making noise about doing plumbing on the Voice's throat, maybe right here in town; that does. Since you both like the same weapon I thought we'd start here."

"You're barking down the wrong hole, Lieutenant. I don't piss in the wind, especially when it's blowing from Jersey. You know how Sinatra went solo?"

Burke said, "We ain't deef. Willie Moretti got Tommy Dorsey to release Frankie-boy from his contract by twisting a .45 in his ear. Every little girl in Hoboken sings about it skipping rope."

"I heard it was a .38," Orr said. "Anyway, the organization has plenty tied up in Sinatra. Anything else you heard is bushwah."

"His manager don't think so." Zagreb got out a cigarette and walked it back and forth across his knuckles. "I believe you, Frank. It's easy enough to find out if you bought all those tickets, and everybody knows you're cheap. Any loose cannons in your outfit? Some driver thinks he didn't get his end smuggling a truckload of Juicy Fruit past the OPA?"

"You got to do better than that if you want me to say I got anything to do with the black market. Say, where'd you learn that trick?" Orr stared, fascinated by the lieutenant's sleight of hand.

"I used to deal blackjack before I got religion. Okay, so when it comes to waving Old Glory, you're Kate Smith. But say you weren't, and one of your boys wanted to cross you. Who'd it be?"

"I clean up my own messes. Listen, there's a showgirl at the Forest Club'd think that thing with the cigarette's swell. I can get you a deal on a set of whitewalls if you teach me how to do it. Prewar, never used, so there won't be any trouble over stamps."

Canal drew his shadow over the booth. "Frankie, I think you're trying to corrupt us."

"*Signora* Oro didn't raise any dumbbells, Sergeant. It's a friendly trade is all."

Zagreb stood and put the Chesterfield back in the pack. "Keep your nose clean, Frankie. We don't want to have to come back and blow it for you."

Out in the public area, the lieutenant stopped.

"You boys wait in the car. I forgot my hat."

They left him. None of them looked at the hat on his head.

He found Orr putting the strongbox in a wall safe. The gangster shut the door, twisted the knob, and covered it with a print of St. Mark's Cathedral in Venice. He jumped when he turned and saw Zagreb. "Jeez, you fellas are light on your heels. I thought you all had Four-F flat feet."

"Relax, Little Caesar. If we wanted to shake you down, we'd just bust holes in the walls with sledges. It occurred to me you don't trust my boys not to go running to Jersey if you gave me the time and temperature in front of them."

"I know you since the old days," Orr said. "You hauled me downtown with ten cases of Old Log Cabin in the back seat. I offered you half a C-note, but it was no go. I got my cargo back, you got foot patrol for a month. You're a sucker cop, but a right gee. You could take a certain bellyacher off my neck, but what'll you tell the others when you come back with a name?"

"I'll say I taught you the cigarette trick."

"Jersey'd laugh 'em clear back to Detroit if they went to them with a story like that." Orr gave him the Gable grin. "So how do you do it without bending the butt?"

Zagreb shook his head. "Can't risk it, Frankie. You couldn't resist showing it off if Jersey asked, and there goes your cover. I can't have your blood on my hands."

The grin shut down. "Serves me right for trusting a cop."

"Now give me the name before I bring the boys back in with the toys from the trunk."

The others were sitting in the unmarked black Chrysler with the windows down to let out the reek from Canal's cigar. The lieutenant got in beside Burke at the wheel and said, "Lyle Ugar. Drops a grand a month to his bookie on a dock foreman's pay."

"What, no whitewalls?" McReary said.

-

They discussed using the California Hotel, the flea hatchery where the squad conducted unofficial interrogations, but since a street thug wasn't likely to squawk to the commission they took him to the basement at 1300—Detroit Police Headquarters—still wearing his coveralls, artfully smeared with grease in case his parole officer came to call. Ugar had gin blossoms on his nose and brass knuckles in his pocket. "My good luck charm," he said.

Canal tried them out on the prisoner's abdomen.

Ugar spit up on the sergeant's shirt. Canal, mildly irritated, straightened him back out with his other fist.

"Slow down." Zagreb yawned. "You got a train to catch?"

"I'm stuck with this shirt for the duration. My Chinaman charges double to scrub out puke." But the big man took pity on Ugar and shoved him gently into a kitchen chair soaked deep with sweat and worse. The impact tilted the front legs off the floor. They hung for a second, then came back down with a bang.

McReary was sitting on a stack of bulletproof vests left over from the Dillinger days, holding a wrinkled sheet of onionskin. Generations of mice had chewed holes in the vests and pulled out steel wool to snuggle their young. "Says here in your personnel record you were a pipe fitter on your last job. Take any pipes with you when you left?"

"That's what this is about, pilfering from the job?" Ugar hugged his stomach. A violet knot marred the line of his underslung jaw. "Christ, I'll donate 'em to the scrap drive."

Canal placed one of his gunboats against the foreman's chest and pushed. A building less solid would have shaken when chair and man struck the floor.

Zagreb lit a cigarette, watched the smoke spiral toward racks of sports equipment untouched since December 1941. "What kind of music you listen to, Lyle?"

"Wh-what?" Ugar's lungs were still trying to reinflate.

"I like Bing Crosby. 'Wunderbar,' but I don't guess we'll be hearing that one for a while. How about you fellas?"

"Polka," said Canal. "Oom-pah-pah."

Burke said, "Pass. I'd rather hear the fights."

"Kay Kyser," McReary said.

The other three groaned.

Zagreb said, "See, we're making conversation. What do you think about this skinny kid has the little girls' bobby sox rolling up and down? Sinatra."

"Never heard of him." Ugar remained sitting in the chair with his back on the floor and the soles of his Red Wings showing. "I hocked my radio when the U-boats was taking down all our ships. My kid brother was on one."

McReary showed Zagreb the personnel sheet.

"No next of kin, says here," Zagreb said. "It's dated July nineteen thirty-nine."

Canal bent over Ugar, grabbed the back of the chair in both hands, and stood it back up, man and all.

Burke touched the sergeant's arm. "Take five."

When Canal stepped aside, Burke snatched Ugar by the front of his coveralls and lifted him out of the chair. From the shrieking it seemed he had a fistful of chest hair.

Zagreb said, "Burke's favorite cousin went down aboard the *Arizona*. Maybe you were mistaken about that brother. I had an imaginary friend once. Bet it was yours you were thinking of."

The prisoner, his face close enough to the officer's to scratch himself on stubble, made a sound that was not quite human.

The lieutenant nodded. "What I thought. You probably took one on the noggin when you roughed up Reuther and Frankensteen at the overpass and haven't been right since. Go easy on him, Detective. He's a veteran of the labor wars."

Burke released his grip, letting Ugar drop back onto the chair. He wiped his palms on his shirt. "Strikebreakers all got cooties."

"I don't think there's scientific proof," Zagreb said. "This isn't the USO, Lyle. We wouldn't lay off you if you *had* a brother and he flew a plane up Hitler's ass. When you're not goldbricking on the loading dock or busting heads for Harry Bennett, you're pouring antifreeze on the horse feed at the fairgrounds, fudging the race results for Frankie Orr. He passed you over for a juke route you thought you had in the bag, so you decided to shake Sinatra down for case dough and incidentally tick off the Conductor and the people he answers to back East.

"Look at me when I'm talking to you, Lyle," he said.

Canal and Burke moved toward Ugar.

"I don't get you, honest!" He held up both palms. "I wouldn't know Frankie Orr if he sat down next to me on the streetcar."

Zagreb said, "If you know his history with streetcars, you know you're better off with us. We can let him handle it, if you like. If you don't know each other, we're just wasting our time."

Ugar's face paled beneath the broken blood vessels. Then he breathed in and out deeply.

"It ain't my lay. I'm strictly heavy lifting: Somebody says go here and screw up a guy, I go there and screw up a guy. I don't ask how come. The one time I went out and did something on my own, plotted out a juke route in neutral territory, they took it away and gave it to somebody else. I was sore, sure, and I guess I wasn't quiet about it, but that's as far as it went. I never took one on the noggin so hard I'd commit suicide."

The lieutenant blew smoke at him and crushed out the butt on a floor strewn with them like fall leaves.

"This one needs more tenderizing, Sergeant. He's still too tough to chew."

"And us fresh out of red points." Canal, in shirtsleeves with the cuffs rolled back, dark half-moons under his armpits, squeezed his sausage fingers into the brass knuckles and flexed them. "Face or body?"

Zagreb told him to surprise him.

-

They dumped Ugar in third-floor Holding and convened in the toilet, all booming marble with white pedestal sinks and urinals a man could stand in upright. Canal soaked his swollen knuckles in cold water and splashed it on his face. "I'm getting rheumatism. If this was the military they'd put me in for a Purple Heart."

"Ugar made me mad when he sucker-punched you with his nose," Burke said. "I almost took a hand, but it was your ball."

McReary adjusted his hat in the mirror. "He's not our guy. He's too dumb to dial a phone."

"The dumb ones and the smart ones are the hardest to crack," Zagreb said. "He's a thousand miles from smart, but he ain't dumb enough to clam up and swallow medicine he don't have coming. He's been on the other end of plenty of beatings. He knows how many things can go wrong."

"With him, maybe. I'm an artist." Canal smoothed back his

hair, thick as the Black Forest. He caught McReary looking at it and grinned; winked at him. The balding detective third-grade looked away. "He'll wake up soon. Maybe he'll be smarter for the experience."

"Spring him." Zagreb pushed away from the wall. "Mac, stop primping and run down to the stand and pick us up some copies of *Good Housekeeping*."

"We taking up cooking?"

"Babysitting."

-

"He's here," McReary said, first thing inside the squad room door. "In the lobby."

"*Who's* here, Omar Bradley?" Zagreb scratched his OK on an arrest sheet and spindled it atop a tall pile. They'd had a busy two weeks separating Polacks from hillbillies in beer gardens; security in the defense plants was tight, so their basic differences boiled over after the whistle. It was beneath the Racket Squad's dignity, but it was either that or go back to spying on the Bund, and the weather was getting too nippy for beach detail.

"Sinatra. And he brought armored support."

Minutes later, the elevator outside gushed to a pneumatic stop and the squad room door opened at the end of a long arm in a heavy-duty coat sleeve. The coat was as big as they came off the rack, but a king-size safety pin had been added to close it in front. The man was as big as Canal, with so much scar tissue on his face it looked like a bunch of balloons. No hat; a barber's enamel basin wouldn't have covered that head. He darted a pair of tiny, close-set eyes about the room and grunted.

The man who came in past him was a third as wide and a head shorter, but taller than he looked in newsreels. His suit was sharply cut, with extra-wide lapels, and he wore a narrow-brimmed hat cocked just above his right eyebrow. A floppy polka-dot bow tie accentuated his slender neck. He stopped and looked around.

"Holy moly, it looks like *The Frame-Up*. I thought you boys would've redecorated after the St. Valentine's Day Massacre."

Canal said, "That's Chicago. The Purple Gang ran Capone out of Detroit on his fat ass."

"Just kidding, Dumbo. Who runs this zoo?"

"That'd be me," Zagreb said, "and I caution you not to poke the elephant. We call him Canal. You'll call him Sergeant. He's in charge of the reptile house when I'm out. The gorilla is Officer Burke. I don't know what kind of animal Detective McReary is, but he bites."

The big man in the tight coat gathered the balloons on his face into a smirk. "When's the last time you shoveled out his cage?"

McReary said, "We lost the shovel. Your face free?"

They were squaring off when the thin man in the sharp suit spun and stamped his heel on the bodyguard's instep. When he howled and bent to cradle his foot, the thin man seized his lapels and brought his face to within an inch of the big man's. "You're a guest here. Tell them you're sorry."

A sagging lower lip twitched twice before anything came out past it. "I beg your pardon."

The thin man let go, shoving him away in the same motion. He produced a fold of bills, removed a gold clip initialed F.S., and stuffed them into the bodyguard's handkerchief pocket. "You're fired, Clyde. The first string just clocked in."

The big man went out, limping slightly. The thin man tugged down his coat and shot his cuffs. "Sorry for the scene, gents. A joke's only a joke when you're breaking the ice."

McReary coughed, interrupting a short awkward silence. Zagreb looked toward the door. In another moment he was alone with the thin man. He held out a pack of cigarettes. The other shook his head, indicating his throat. "Not before a concert."

The lieutenant took one and used his lighter. "Why Clyde? His name's Laverne."

"I call everyone Clyde I don't like." The thin face smiled warily. "On the square, Laverne? No wonder he got so big."

"Is 'Frankie' okay? We don't exactly dress for dinner here."

"I prefer Frank."

"Max." They shook hands; Sinatra's bony grip tried a little too hard. "Frank, next time you cast a play out of town, don't hire locals. Laverne's a palooka. He went into the tank so many times he grew gills. He'd've scrubbed the floor with your brains if you didn't cross one of those big mitts with silver."

Sinatra flushed deeply. "Do the others know?"

"Canal dropped two weeks' pay on him in the Carnera fight."

"I wanted to make an impression."

"We don't need impressing, Frank. You're our assignment."

"Max, you ever been to Hoboken?"

"I never even heard of the place till you came along."

"When you get in a jam on the street, the only way to duck a beating is to pick the biggest, ugliest cretin in the crowd and hit him hard as you can; the rest will leave you alone. Well, I was the runt of the litter. Paying him to take a fall was cheaper than dental work."

"They didn't always pull their punches. That's quite a scar."

Sinatra traced it with a finger, a long vertical crease down his left cheek. "Doctor's forceps. He didn't stand on ceremony when he delivered me. I was born dead, you know."

Zagreb searched the narrow face for humor, found none. "I didn't, but I'd like to."

"I'll make you a deal. You square me with the rest of the squad, and I'll tell you the whole story."

-

Zagreb let Sinatra tell them about the streets of Hoboken. Burke sneered, but Canal appreciated the idea.

"Stomping a tame pug so you don't get stomped yourself makes plenty of sense to me. It beats starting a fight in a saloon so we don't have to bust up a riot later, which is what we do all the time. Next Saturday, let's draw from petty cash and pay some Four-F slacker to take the fall."

Zagreb said, "Have another snort, Sergeant. You haven't spilled all our trade secrets yet."

Sinatra said, "Not on my account. I just *look* wet behind the ears. Things aren't any different where I'm from."

They'd left 1300, with ears built in every wall, for the relative privacy of the Lafayette Bar, whose noisy program of Greek music and dancing didn't start until after dark. Zagreb had a beer, Burke and Canal bourbon; McReary, a teetotaler, sipped Coke through a straw. When Sinatra asked for Four Roses, Canal said, "It's on us, Caruso. You don't have to drink piss just 'cause it's cheap."

"I'm not much for booze. It's all the same to me."

"Well, I can't stand looking at a dog dragging a busted leg or a grown man drinking Four Roses. Jack on the rocks," he called to the bartender.

McReary, who wanted to be sergeant someday, got back to business. "Tell us about these threatening calls."

"I wish my manager never found out about 'em. He wouldn't have if my wife hadn't answered one and got upset. There's a heckler in every audience; usually it's some bum whose girl thinks I sing pretty."

Burke said, "That's what *I* said."

"How many calls there been?" Zagreb asked.

"Two at home. One in Atlantic City, another up in the Catskills, couple in Philly. He must collect phone books."

"Determined-sounding bum," Zagreb said. "Recognize the voice?"

"If I did, we wouldn't be talking. I've got friends in low places. It sounded whispery, but I don't think he was trying to disguise it. Maybe someone hit him in the throat once and that's where he got the idea."

"Any accent?"

Sinatra gave the lieutenant a bitter, tight-lipped smile. "You mean was he a wop?"

"Not all of you have the gift of music."

"Some of us are barbers."

"I'm a hunky, pal. Mac and Burke are micks, and I don't know what Canal is."

"Ukrainian," Canal said.

"Who gives a shit but the Cossacks? The point is there's none of us here won't take the gas pipe if Hitler lands in New York, so get the chip off your shoulder and help us out. You're the one snipping hair if we screw up."

Sinatra looked genuinely contrite. "Sorry, Lieutenant. I swing from top-of-the-world to rock-bottom blue faster than Jessie Owens runs the track. It's a medical condition, according to the shrinks."

Canal said, "Everybody's got something. I got corns the size of bowling balls, but you don't see me taking it out on folks."

McReary changed the subject. "What's this guy say when he calls?"

"'Gimme five G's or I'll take out the Voice with a lead pipe.' 'The Voice,' that's what the publicity flacks call me."

"A poet," Zagreb said. "He say where to send the dough?"

"I hang up first." The singer sipped from his glass. "Say, this stuff's not bad."

Canal grunted. "World's full of good hooch. Life's short."

Zagreb said, "Next time don't hang up. If we nab him at the drop, we won't have to pick him out of a crowd."

"Like we wouldn't spot a guy in a skirt-and-sweater set with a bow on his head," said Burke.

"If it was that easy, I'd nab him myself."

But Burke wasn't through. "No, you wouldn't. He wouldn't

stand still and let you step on his foot."

"Clyde, you're getting on my nerves."

"How come you ain't in uniform, by the bye? Too puny?"

"Punctured eardrum. What's your excuse?"

"Essential service," Zagreb put in, before the officer could rise to the occasion. "Isn't a singer with a bum ear like a dancer with a wooden leg?"

"If I'm twice as good as what I hear, I'll go all the way."

"Jee-sus." Burke sat back. "This guy's got more gas than a Mexican restaurant."

The lieutenant studied Frank Sinatra, a blue-eyed, cocky-looking youngster with his hat on the back of his head and famous tousle of hair falling over his forehead. He thought he might like him more if he liked himself less. "Can you lay hands on five grand?"

"I could have my manager wire it to me, but why should I pay this creep?"

Zagreb asked if he'd ever heard of a guy named Joe E. Lewis.

"Comic. He opened for me in the Catskills. He's got a voice like a cement mixer, but it's not the one I hear on the phone, if that's what you're thinking."

"It isn't. Lewis was a singer on his way up when he got on the wrong side of some thugs in Chicago. They cut his throat just for fun and now he tells jokes for a living. You're not that funny."

-

Sinatra was registered at the Book-Cadillac Hotel. Zagreb went up with him to his suite and stationed Canal in the hallway and Burke in the lobby. McReary got the switchboard. The supervising operator, a gum chewer with rhinestone glasses, liked his looks enough not to give him any trouble about listening in on calls placed to the suite. They had four hours until the curtain went up at the Fisher.

The call came in with thirty minutes to spare. McReary threw in his hand of canasta, motioned for the earphones, and held one up to the side of his head. He didn't want to take off his hat and disappoint the girl.

"Hello?"

"Frankie! How's the Voice?" It was a harsh whisper. The detective had to press the receiver hard to his ear to make out the words. "We can deal or you can pound rivets at Lockheed."

"I don't think I'd be good at it." Sinatra sounded tense.

"Got the cash?"

"I got it. Where you want to meet?"

"Knew you'd come around. See you after the show."

"You're in *Detroit*?"

There was a click and a dial tone. McReary held on. Zagreb came on the line. "Make him?"

"Nah, he doesn't sound like any of our squeezeboxes."

"Well, it was a long shot. Meet us at the car."

-

The singer wedged himself between Canal and McReary in the back of the Chrysler. He had a light topcoat on over a white dinner jacket and another of his floppy bow ties. "I still don't see why you had me get the money. It doesn't inspire confidence."

"Money can speed things up," Zagreb said. "It can also slow 'em down. Maybe long enough to put one of us between you and a hunk of plumbing."

McReary said, "That's me. I don't draw as much water as the rest of these guys."

The girls were lined up all the way down Grand Boulevard to the corner, dressed nearly identically in letter sweaters, A-line skirts, saddle shoes, and bobby sox; the mounted patrol was out to keep them from storming the theater. Sinatra slid down in the seat and tipped his hat over his eyes to avoid being swamped.

"I heard your people pay them to scream and faint," Burke

said.

"Maybe they did in the beginning, but nobody's got pockets *this* deep."

"Six-to-one says Boris Karloff's got the record."

Canal said, "No sign of Orr."

Zagreb said, "He'll be inside already, with the guys he pays to carry his guns. I'd be tempted to take a potshot at him myself if he stood out on the street."

Sinatra asked who Orr was.

"He's in the way of being you," said the lieutenant. "If Tommy guns was trumpets and the fans didn't get back up after they fell."

"Oh. Those guys. I been around 'em my whole life."

They turned the corner and found out that the line did as well. Now there were men in army and marine uniforms, and a bus unloading naval cadets from the University of Michigan, some holding passes. Part of the proceeds had been pledged to the armed services. Sinatra sat up and straightened his hat.

"See, there are more ways to win a war than just with a rifle."

McReary, the least conspicuous of the Four Horsemen, accompanied Sinatra through the stage door. Burke parked in a loading zone and the three went inside and fanned out. Minutes after the doors opened to the public, every seat in the theater was filled, but it didn't stay that way long.

When the orchestra played and Sinatra bounded onstage, the girls leapt to their feet and the men in the audience were forced to do the same, to see over their heads. Jitterbugs made their complicated maneuvers in the aisles until they got too crowded to do more than jump up and down and squeal. Only the group of men in silk suits and their female escorts in the front row kept their seats. Frankie Orr's sleek head showed in Zagreb's binoculars in the middle, next to a stack of blonde hair that was not his wife's.

Sinatra didn't hold back. He opened with "All or Nothing at All," slid seamlessly into "I'll Never Smile Again"—McReary's favorite—and a lively, finger-snapping rendition of "That's Sabotage," a novelty hit with a wartime theme, while the girls screamed "Frankie!" over and over, each hoping to catch his eye and pretending it was her waist he was holding and not the microphone on its stand. He grasped it in both hands and tilted it, made love to it.

Zagreb was impressed—not enough to throw over Bing Crosby, but it was clear the singer took that chip off his shoulder and left it backstage when he performed. Long before he got to "I'll Be Seeing You" (wasn't that where he said he was going?"), he proved he was born for the spotlight.

The lieutenant noted all this on the edge of awareness. It was the man he was concentrating on, not the entertainer. Just in case the would-be attacker had changed his choice of weapons, Zagreb scanned the manic figures on the floor for suspicious bulges and arm movements; matters of instinct, easier to see than guns. He knew Burke and Canal were doing the same in their respective quarters, and McReary in his, back there among the chalk marks and dust. They'd divvied up the place the same way FDR, Churchill, and Stalin had each claimed his part of the war.

In that moment, he felt a surge of premature nostalgia. Did the rest of the Horsemen realize these were the best times of their lives? Come hell or high water, nothing that came after could ever measure up to this complete sense of confidence in partnership; the absolute faith that every man would play his role to perfection. Someday, fat, tired, and disappointed by life, they might attend a reunion, and share memories of experiences they'd failed to appreciate in the moment, laughing at circumstances that had scared them shitless, then stagger home to the patient wife and uncomprehending kids: *What did you bring me, Daddy? Just your future, you little bastards.* He supposed it would be the same for the men serving in foxholes and cockpits and the holds of ships, so they weren't alone. But it made a man feel old beyond his years.

At length the concert ended, and with it the reveries. Sinatra, as prearranged, tugged loose his bow tie and cast it out into the audience, where a hundred pairs of hands snatched at it and tore it to pieces for souvenirs.

(Canal: "You do that every place you play? How rich are you, anyway?"

(Sinatra: "It doesn't cost much. My wife makes 'em."

(McReary: "That's the kind of wife I hope to land.")

This time, the tie gag served as a signal, alerting the squad to join the singer backstage and form a flying wedge around him toward the exit.

A sea of hysterical fans filled the narrow corridor leading to the stage door. Pens and autograph pads came at the moving party from all sides, but Burke and Canal deflected them with their forearms and McReary and Zagreb kept a death grip on Sinatra's biceps, propelling him forward.

"C'mon, fellas. Let me sign a couple."

In response, they heaved upward, lifting the singer's patent-leather heels off the floor, carrying him now. He was heavier than he looked.

"Should've allowed for his swoll head," gritted Burke.

A group of sailors in white stood smoking near the door. Grins broke out when they recognized the man being swept their way; they'd been training hard, and he'd put on a swell show. They called him Frankie and asked him when he was coming to Pearl.

"Well, they ain't the cavalry, but let our mug try busting through this bunch." Canal sounded relieved.

Zagreb said, "You know the navy. What's 'dress white' mean?"

"Hell, it's the uniform of the day; everybody knows that."

"Why's this one in blue?"

A sailor who'd been standing apart from the group lunged between Canal and Burke, sliding a hand inside Sinatra's dinner jacket as his other came out of his blue blouse with a shrill tearing sound.

Canal clubbed him with an elbow while Burke clamped down on his wrist. The hand attached to the wrist sprang open and the object in it bounced off Zagreb's knee and struck his toe, sending a bolt of pain to his ankle. It was lead, all right.

Cursing, he snatched the envelope from the sailor's other hand and shoved him off his feet. He stuck the envelope back inside Sinatra's jacket.

McReary and Zagreb let go of the singer to help Canal and Burke hoist the sailor to his feet. Sinatra turned immediately to sign a piece of paper one of the men in white was holding.

"This for you, pal, or you trying to get in good with some dame?"

-

"I'd look spiffy in one of those sailor suits." Sinatra played with his Jack on the rocks. "In a movie, I mean; I've had offers. I tried to join. Sometimes I think I should carry around a sign saying it."

Burke said, "I'm Four-F myself. Colorblind, as if I couldn't tell a nip or a Jerry from just his uniform."

The two touched glasses.

They were all back in the Lafayette Bar. The Greek band was between sets, giving them the chance to talk without shouting. Zagreb was looking at his notebook.

"Morty Tilson, not affiliated with the U.S. Navy or any other branch of the armed services. He was catching in a pickup ballgame when the ball bounced off the plate and hit him in the throat. He'd signed to sing with Benny Goodman; now he can't even get in the military. Hoboken boy. Your story could've been his."

"I don't know him. Hell with him." Sinatra signaled the bartender for another round. "I could forgive him for the pipe; everyone gets jealous. He had to have the cash too."

McReary said, "He needed it for the black market. Driving

from New Jersey to Detroit burns a lot of gas."

The bartender, a brick-colored Mediterranean with a brow like a spacebar across both eyes, set down the drinks and asked Mr. Sinatra if he might indulge his customers in a song. He rolled his head toward a bright young thing seated at the bar, smiling at him over a bare shoulder. Her swarthy escort glowered at him over his padded one.

The singer shook his head. "Put their drinks on my tab."

Burke asked Canal what the hell he was playing with. It was making him edgy.

The sergeant unwound the flexible silver square from a thick index finger and showed it to him. It was torn on one side.

"It's what Tilson used to stick the pipe to his chest. Lab monkeys have the rest. Duct tape, it's called. The flyboys in the navy and air corps use it to patch the hydraulic cylinders on planes. Holds better'n Scotch tape, especially to skin. I guess he got it from the same guy who gave him the uniform."

"He'll tell us about that too. It might mean the difference between one-to-three and five-to-seven in the Jackson pen." Zagreb pointed his beer bottle at Sinatra. "You owe us a story. You don't have to sing it."

The singer lit a Camel off a pigskin lighter and blew twin strands out his nostrils.

"You earned it, with or without accompaniment. Yeah, I was born dead; bluer than Tilson's shirt. I weighed thirteen and a half pounds, can you believe it, a rake like me? The doctor jerked me out any old way to save my mother from bleeding to death. My grandmother scooped me up and dunked me in a sink full of cold water and I started yelling. My first solo."

"No wonder you pay to even the odds," McReary said after a moment. "You started out a strike behind."

Burke said, "I got three nipples."

Quiet settled over the table.

"What I mean," he said, turning red, "everybody's got

something."

Sinatra smiled his brittle smile. "Sure you're not counting your dick?"

Burke colored all the way to his fingertips.

When the laughter faded, the singer lifted his glass to his chin. "So I guess I *am* funny."

"Just sing, Frank," Zagreb said.

Death
—WITHOUT—
Parole

"You guys ever ashamed you're a cop?"

Death Without Parole

Canal said, "Friday," and sat back as if he'd predicted the day Hitler would surrender. A jet of smoke shot diagonally from the corner of his mouth opposite the one where he'd parked his cigar.

"Sucker bet," Lieutenant Zagreb said. "He doesn't get out till tomorrow—that's Thursday—and that's confidential to the squad. You've got to allow time for shock to set in. Action comes later."

"Not if one of us does it." Burke spat on his iron. It sizzled and released a cloud of steam into the general exhaust in the room.

Zagreb shook his head, waggling a finger. "That's cheating. Monday, at the earliest. Who wants to work the weekend?"

"I feel like I came in on the middle of the feature," McReary said. "I got no idea what you fellas are talking about."

"Office pool. That thing's too hot, Burksie," Zagreb told the man with the iron. "You want the cotton setting."

"Shows how much you know for a lieutenant. It's rayon." Burke snatched his shirt off the ironing board and showed him the label. He was the hairiest man on the squad. In his BVD undershirt he looked like a grizzly wearing a white vest.

"Even worse. You'll set it on fire and burn down the joint."

The California Hotel, deep in the heart of Detroit's Negro district, had opened soon after *The Birth of a Nation*, to capitalize on the public's sudden fascination with Hollywood. The potted palm in the lobby had been dead for nine years and the flies in the ceiling fixtures a few months longer. The city Racket Squad used Room 1102 for discussions of sensitive material, unofficial interrogations, and in Detective Burke's case, assignations with women not his wife. He was preparing for one at present, which explained the operation involving the shirt.

"A fin still says Friday. I'm a cockeyed optimist." Canal relit his cigar, which promptly went out again. The brand he smoked was made by Jackson Prison inmates who mixed tobacco with steel shavings from the machine shop.

McReary, the youngest and lowest-ranking member of the squad, nudged his hat to the back of his head, exposing his prematurely bald scalp. "What pool? The Series don't start for a week."

"Screw the Series. Bunch of Four-F shirking bums." Burke pressed the iron to the collar of the rayon shirt, scorching it. Zagreb snickered.

Canal said, "We're betting on what day a cop knocks off Eddie Karpalov."

"Who's Eddie Karpalov?"

"Before your time, rook." Zagreb slid a mug card out of his suit coat hanging on a chair and handed it to him.

McReary looked at Edward Illyich Karpalov in front and profile, swarthy and hollow-cheeked, with no more expression than a bucket of sand. "Says here he killed a cop. What's he doing out?"

"Judge at his second trial said the cop wasn't a cop because he failed to identify himself as a cop," Zagreb said. "So when Eddie charged out of that savings and loan with the alarm clanging and shot the first guy came at him with a gun it was self-defense."

"I may take a crack at him myself." McReary gave back the card.

"Better step on it. He goes back to Russia soon as they process him out of County." Burke shrugged into the shirt and turned up the collar, hiding the burn mark. "Whaddya think?"

Canal said, "You look just like Cary Grant after a bad accident."

"This ain't worth it. I might as well go home to Sadie."

"Not tonight," said the sergeant. "I'm taking her out dancing."

McReary said, "Card says Karpalov ran with the Purple Gang. I didn't know those boys messed with banks."

Zagreb yawned; he hadn't slept eight hours at a stretch since Pearl Harbor. "They didn't, until Prohibition was repealed. The demand for bathtub gin and guns-for-hire dropped off sharp. What was he going to do, go straight?"

Sergeant Canal got off the bed to throw the dead stogie out the window. He and Burke were the biggest men on a force that didn't employ officers much below six feet, or didn't until the draft came along and cut the department in half. But Burke didn't look big when Canal stood up. Zagreb kidded the sergeant that the only reason he made plainclothes was they couldn't find a uniform his size. "State Department's shipping him home as an undesirable. I know a shorter word means the same thing."

"Since when do we deport people in wartime?"

"Since we hooked up with Uncle Joe," said the lieutenant. "Maybe he'll slap a helmet on him and send him to the Eastern Front."

"Where I'll personally pin the Iron Cross on the kraut that nails him." Burke fastened the spoiled collar and put on a necktie with a cannibal painted on it. Canal blew him a kiss. He glowered back.

McReary said, "When they start a pool on the judge, count me in."

"They did, down at the Tenth," Canal said. "I got Sunday."

The young detective stripped the foil off a stick of bubble gum, read the little comic strip that came with it, and chewed. He was the only one of the famous Four Horsemen ("famous" in the *News*, "notorious" in the *Free Press*; the *Times* was on the fence) who didn't smoke. "So much for the feds. What's our end?"

"We get to put him on the train," Zagreb said. "That's how

come we're sitting around the presidential suite, waiting to hear time of release. The marshals will meet us at Michigan Central and see the undesirable putz off on the boat in New York."

"'Putz' wasn't the word I had in mind," said Canal.

"I know, but there's a child present."

"You crumbs." McReary blew a bubble.

The phone rang, an old-fashioned candlestick. The lieutenant picked it up, put the receiver to his ear, and dangled the standard by its hook from the same hand. "Racket Squad, Zagreb. Yeah. Ants in his pants, hey? Okey-doke." He hung up and held the phone in his lap. "Twelve-oh-one ayem. Chief turnkey wants him gone pronto. Sorry about your evening, Burksie."

"I can do what I need by ten." Burke leered.

"Provided you start by nine-fifty-eight." Canal grinned.

Zagreb thrust the telephone at Burke. "Give her a rain check. We may need that nervous energy later."

"Okay, L.T., but you and the boys don't listen in. It tears me up when a dame starts crying." He took the instrument and got the switchboard downstairs.

Canal, who never wore a watch, took hold of McReary's wrist and read his watch. "So what do we do for six hours?"

The lieutenant took a deck of cards out of the drawer in the nightstand and shuffled. "Maybe Burke'll get lucky and win a new shirt."

-

"Looks just like his picture, don't he?" McReary said.

Burke nodded. "Them shutterbugs in Records are the best in the business. I never laid eyes on Rita Hayworth, but I bet she looks less Rita Hayworthy in the flesh than on the wall in Canal's toilet."

"Shows how much you know, smart guy. Toilet's down the hall. I share it with the whole third floor."

The chipped Bakelite radio in Admissions—bound with air corps–issue duct tape and stenciled PROPERTY OF WAYNE COUNTY JAIL—was playing Arthur Godfrey, a repeat broadcast; most of the talent was in the USO with Jolson. They watched Zagreb swap manacles with a sheriff's deputy, officially assuming custody of Edward Illyich Karpalov, a.k.a. Eddie the Carp and a host of other names: former bootlegger, ex–bank robber, and cop-killer for all time.

"What do we call this guy?" McReary asked. "He's got more aliases than—"

"—Clara Bow's got crabs," finished Canal.

"Who's Clara Bow?"

Burke and Canal spoke together. "Before your time, rook."

"Movie star, I bet. Don't you guys ever go to a ballgame?"

Burke scowled. "Bunch of Four-F shirking—"

"So what do we call him?"

"How about DOA?" Canal unholstered his .38, spun the cylinder, and put it back.

McReary was right. The man in the two-hundred-dollar suit—wrinkled from long storage—was as cadaverous and swarthy under his prison pallor as he looked in his picture. It took a photographer of uncommon skill to capture his absolute absence of expression without erasing his features altogether.

If only his vocabulary were as bland as his face.

"What's with the bracelets? I'm an innocent man, judge said." He had a thin voice with a cellblock rasp.

"Wear 'em while you can, Eddie," Zagreb said. "I still owe two payments."

"I hope you birds got me a lower berth. Riding in trains makes me puke."

Zagreb said, "We took up a collection and bought you a first-class compartment. Otherwise the marshals won't know where the puke left off and you started."

"Go ahead, crack wise. I'm gonna get me the best lawyer in Rooshia and sue all you flatfeet for false imprisonment, clear up to J. Edgar. Come back home on the *Queen Mary*."

"Drop us a card before you board. We'll tell the U-boats you're on the way. There must be one commander with a brother walking a beat in Berlin." Zagreb, cuffed to him by the wrists, nearly jerked his arm out of its socket heading for the exit.

When they were all in the Chrysler, Karpalov sandwiched in the back seat between McReary and the lieutenant, Canal riding shotgun—literally, with a twelve-gauge across his lap—Burke stomped on the starter and threw in the clutch, stripping the gears. He was a better driver than that, but he hated the car. "I had a Russian lawyer once," he said. "My first wife got the house and the dog and I got half a carton of cigarettes."

"Chesterfields, I hope." Zagreb lit one one-handed.

"No dice. One of them injun reservation brands, they don't charge tax. But I got no beef. That damn dog ate a good pair of Florsheims."

"How would I know how things are over there?" Karpalov said. "I was in diapers when I left."

"Shoot a cop in Moscow, you'll be in diapers when you get out." Canal blew cigar smoke over the back of the seat, gassing McReary also. He opened a window.

Burke said, "Wrong. They walk you down a hall in Lubyanka, only you don't get to the end of the hall. Say what you like about the commies, they don't have the storage problem we have here."

"Wiseacres. I imagine they got a black market there too. I'll make a killing."

"Poor word choice." Zagreb jerked up his arm, splitting the prisoner's lip with the edge of his own handcuff.

"Cripes!" He threw his free hand to his mouth, smearing blood. "You guys are supposed to deliver me in one piece!"

The lieutenant took out a document printed on heavy stock

and passed it across to McReary. "Read me the part where it says we got to."

McReary handed it back without unfolding it, grazing Karpalov's mouth on the way; he sucked in breath sharply through his teeth. "It don't say."

They had their choice of parking spaces by the great gaunt brick barn of the Michigan Central Depot, another structure predating women's suffrage. "Sure the trains run this late?" Karpalov kept touching his lower lip, which was puffing up like a handful of boiled rice.

Zagreb said, "Only the specials. You're riding with boxcars of bullets from the Chrysler plant."

"Jeez, hope you don't hit a bump." Canal patted back a yawn.

A streamliner locomotive sat on the tracks, looking sleek as a destroyer, with a passenger coach behind it and then a chain of freight cars stretching into an infinity of darkness where the station lights failed. As the four men approached flanking the man in their charge, two men in blue business suits, one tall and thin and sallow, the other shorter and broad and deeply tanned, came toward them across the platform, each holding a leather folder open showing star-shaped badges. They wore their hats at opposite angles, making a *V* for Victory.

"Zagreb? I'm Deputy Marshal Rudnicki. This is Deputy Marshal Cash. We're here for Karpalov." The short broad one spoke in clipped government tones.

"Are you? I thought you were here for the tulip festival."

Burke glanced around. "Where're your horses?"

"That gets funnier every time. Take the cuffs off, please." Rudnicki produced a pair of his own.

"Not till you sign this. I don't want him coming back stamped 'Return to Sender.'" Zagreb held out the document.

Rudnicki hesitated, peering at Karpalov. "He looks a little used."

"Accident. People drive like maniacs since the war. Too many women behind the wheel."

"My sister flies cargo planes for the navy." Cash, the thin one, had a honking New York accent.

"We need more of her on the ground."

Rudnicki juggled the handcuffs and the paper in one hand and took out a fat fountain pen. A gust of wind rattled the sheet just as he got the cap off. Zagreb said, "Use Cash. He looks sturdy."

Cash turned and bent with his hands on his knees while his partner spread the document on his back. He started to write.

"Hold on!"

This was a new voice, belonging to a fat man with 1930s lapels waddling his way from the direction of the station. He was clutching a battered hat to his head with one hand and waving an envelope with the other. When six handguns pointed his way, he braked to a halt, nearly falling on his face from his own momentum.

"Don't shoot! I'm Winston Sweet, with the legal firm of Roylston, Ryker, and Reed. I have a court order enjoining you from remanding Edward Illyich Karpalov into U.S. custody pending investigation of his immigration status."

"Roylston, Ryker, and Reed." Zagreb kept his revolver trained on the newcomer. "Never heard of 'em."

"Must've met in the same homeroom," Canal said.

"It's quite legal. We have evidence Mr. Karpalov was born a U.S. citizen, in Cleveland."

Burke said, "That's no improvement over Moscow."

"Take a look, Mac. You studied law."

McReary put away his weapon, took the envelope, and opened it, turning the paper toward the light. "Three weeks of night school says it's the McCoy. Signed by Judge Springer."

"'Spring 'em' Springer." The lieutenant rammed his .38 back under his arm. "The mook that acquitted him. This your lawyer, Eddie?"

Karpalov grinned, starting his lip bleeding again. "I don't know him from Baby Snooks. But if it means I get to stay, he gets all my business from now on."

"Who's paying the bill?" Zagreb asked Sweet.

"That's privileged."

"Well, he's government property now. Take it up with Cashnicki and Rudd."

"That's Rudnicki and Cash." The short broad marshal smiled. "No soap, Lieutenant. I didn't finish signing the receipt." He gave it back. "Guess we'll take in those tulips after all."

"Joke's on you. They're out of season."

Canal snatched a look at McReary's watch. "Nuts. Day's fifteen minutes old and already it's shot to hell."

-

Judge Vernon Springer had been a prosecutor under Mayor Charles "Wide-Open" Bowles, racking up an impressive number of convictions for public intoxication and none at all involving the bootleggers who'd supplied the fuel. He'd resigned under threat of a grand jury investigation, gone into private practice for a few years, and won the bench after the reform ticket wore out its welcome after one term. He entertained the Four Horsemen in his chambers in the Wayne County Building, a riot of carved scrolls and statuary and decorative holes in the concrete through which a couple of million taxpayer dollars had drained away. He sat with a bright window at his back.

"Lawyer Sweet dug up a Karpalov cousin who signed an affidavit claiming he was born in his parents' house two blocks from Lake Huron," Springer said, pulling a tuft of hair from his long fleshy nose; another replaced it immediately, like paper towels in the men's room. "It looks genuine, but a hearing will determine that. Meanwhile I'm ordering your men to see he makes it there upright and not feet first."

Zagreb squinted against the sun as if it had no business in the same room with his hangover. "I kind of wish you'd told us that seven hours ago. With that start, Eddie could make Denver."

"It was a stay of deportation, not a release. Can't you read?"

"If I knew there was a literacy test I'd've joined the merchant marines."

"Don't give up the dream," Springer said.

"My fault, Judge." McReary was bright-eyed, no poisons in his blood. On sober days like this the others drew straws to see who got to give him a hotfoot. "I looked at the paper, Zag didn't."

"And who is Zag?"

"Lieutenant Zagreb."

"Well, tell *Zag* that if Karpalov doesn't show up in court Monday—*breathing*, it seems I must add—your lieutenant had better brush up on his sea chanteys."

"Tell him yourself. He's right in front of you." Burke was still partly drunk, and even less fun than usual.

Springer fixed him with his peashooter eyes. "Which one are you?"

Burke stared back. "Sergeant Starvo Canal."

"That'll cost you twenty-five dollars for contempt, Sergeant."

Canal glared at Burke. He'd drunk his hair of the dog for breakfast, and peppermint schnapps didn't sit well on an empty stomach.

"I know your commissioner," Springer said. "He'd love to have a reason to throw you all off the force into the draft."

"Speaking of reasons, why give Karpalov life without parole, then cut him loose just because the cop was too busy doing his job to show his buzzer?"

"That was part of his job, Lieutenant. Had I presided at the first trial, I'd have directed the jury to acquit and saved this community the expense of a second."

"Thrifty, that's you," Burke said.

"That will be another twenty-five dollars."

Canal swore under his breath. Springer swung his head his way. "What's the matter, Detective? He owe you money?"

"He does now."

The judge's telephone rang. "Pay the clerk, Sergeant. Don't make me jug you. Your detail hardly qualifies as a squad as it is."

In the marble hallway, Canal stopped Burke with a big hand on his shoulder. "Fork it over, Jack Benny. Fifty smackers."

"Take it out of the sixty you owe me for the Louis fight."

"You characters cut the comedy." Zagreb stuck a cigarette in his mouth and patted his pockets. McReary, who always carried matches to confirm his value to the squad, lit it for him. "Where'd Eddie hang his hat when he had a hat to hang?"

"Tip-Top Club on Twelfth," Canal said. "The OPA pushed it in last year on a rationing beef."

"The beef being they was charging eighteen points a girl, same as canned peaches." Burke grinned.

"Not a help. Someplace where they aren't rolling bandages for the Red Cross."

"Oh, detectives!" Springer practically sang the words.

They turned in a body to see the judge's head sticking out the open door of his chambers. "Get your sea legs ready," he said. "That call was from Homicide. They scraped your responsibility out of a phone booth on West Lafayette half an hour ago. Two slugs in the chest, one in the head, right through the glass."

-

On West Lafayette, a busy street in a busy town, sawhorses cordoned off a Rexall Drugs roughly halfway between the *News* and *Free Press* buildings. Most of the local reporters stopped there for hamburgers and Cokes sweetened from hip flasks. They stood outside looking hungry and disgruntled, frozen out of a scoop right on their doorstep.

Burke kicked the shrouded body on the linoleum. "Deader'n ragtime. Hey, Ox, every time I see one of these it's already got a sheet over it. You run around with 'em in your pocket or what?"

"Give me the rank, Officer. Or go on report." Lieutenant Osprey, Homicide, swigged from the pint of Ten High he carried to balance out his handcuffs and sidearm. "'Lo, Zag. Remind me not to ask you and your boys to look after my dog when I'm in Florida. He might get shot by a cat."

"Long time no see, Oswald. I thought it was good-bye for real after the McHenry investigation."

"Didn't you hear? I got washed in the blood of the lamb after the last draft lottery. A little grifting don't look so bad with all of them desks standing empty downtown." He swung his head. "Lay off that, you big ape! You'll spoil it for ballistics."

Canal drew a thick forefinger from one of the jagged holes in the booth. The floor was a litter of shattered glass and wood splinters. "I don't need calipers. These're too small for my .45-caliber fingers."

"Not to mention feet like torpedoes. And they call *me* Ox."

"It's not your size they're talking about," Zagreb said. "What about the mouthpiece, see anything?"

"He says not. He's over by the soda fountain, drying out his drawers."

The medical examiner arrived, a fat white-haired retiree returned to active duty, who uncovered the bloody corpse and opened his case, whistling "Popeye, the Sailor Man." McReary put the comic book he'd been reading back in the rack. "What makes you stiff-jockeys so happy all the time?"

"Patients never gripe about the bill."

Passing the counter, Zagreb glanced at the soda jerk, wearing a white coat and a paper hat and fingering a lump of acne under his chin. Osprey said, "In the stockroom when the ball started, he says. The shyster was sitting at the counter getting his coffee juuuust right, like Goldilocks. You can see the razor display blocks the view of the entrance." He pointed to a cardboard cutout of a smiling Robert Taylor holding up a Gillette.

"Calling a lawyer a shyster is actionable." Winston Sweet sat at an ice-cream-parlor table in the corner, looking deflated inside his out-of-date suit. His voice sounded like an air raid siren grinding down.

"Sue my bookie," Osprey said. "That's where I keep my dough. These guys missed the first reel, so let's take it from the opening titles. What was Karpalov doing here?"

"He said he wanted to call a woman."

"What woman?" Zagreb barked.

"'Some dame,' that's how he put it. He said any dame would do after a deuce in the joint. Understand, I'm using his own language. The King's English is colorful enough for me."

"You here for a dame too?"

"Certainly not. I'm a happily married man. I came along to see he didn't wander off. My client insisted I keep an eye on him."

"You did a swell job. Who's your client?"

"That's privileged."

"Nuts," Zagreb said. "Murder's got its own set of rules and clamming up ain't in it."

"I'd argue that in court and win."

"Where'd you and Eddie go after you left the train station?"

"An awful place called the Ruby Lounge. I think the trumpets were hooked up to air horns."

"On Hastings?"

"I have no idea. I'm from Cleveland."

"Admitting that is the first step on the way to health," said Canal.

Burke gripped the edges of the table and leaned in close to Sweet's face. "You can do better than that, Counselor. We padlocked the Ruby six weeks ago for operating after curfew."

Canal said, "It's open again."

"Since when?"

"Since five weeks ago. I guess it took 'em a week to sweep up the pieces."

"You might tell a guy."

"You wouldn't've liked it. Sweet's right about the trumpets."

"After that," Sweet said, "we went to an even worse place in a basement, where the music came from a jukebox and I think they made their own whiskey. I poured most of mine into a fire bucket. Then we went to an apartment where a friend of his lived, only after a few drinks he wasn't very friendly and they got into a fight."

Zagreb asked what friend.

"Frank somebody. Karpalov tried to pull this Frank's woman onto his lap and Frank told him to lay off and Karpalov threw a punch at him, but Frank ducked under his arm and twisted it behind him and threw him out into the hall. I went out right behind him. By then the sun was up and we came here so he could make that call. He wasn't in the booth ten seconds when I heard shooting. A bullet smacked into that wall and I fell off the stool and stayed on the floor until I heard sirens."

Zagreb looked at the hole in the lath. "What was the name of this Frankie's girl?"

"An exotic sort of name." Sweet massaged his temples. A vein throbbed in one. "Nola."

"Nola Van Allen," Canal said. "Blonde in the chorus at the Broadway-Capitol. Dances like a duck with a wooden leg, but it don't matter because of who runs the stagehands' union."

"Frankie Orr." Zagreb found his Zippo and lit up before McReary could act. "Whenever the wife and kid hang on him like a cheap suit, he scrams that crypt in Grosse Pointe and makes a beeline to that apartment. He was twisting arms for Joey Machine at the same time Eddie tailgunned for him along the river. How about it, Sweet, was Frankie sore enough to follow him here?"

“This is a farce.” The lawyer looked at Osprey. “Lieutenant, I want to swear out a complaint against this man and the three thugs who work for him.”

“What’s the squeal, no regard for the King’s English?”

“I believe they murdered my client.”

-

“It’s still Thursday,” Canal said. “Who had it in the pool?”

“Nobody, that’s who.” Burke stroked his wire-brush stubble.

“Let’s roll it over on what day we all draw one-A.”

“Thursday.” Zagreb, Burke, and McReary spoke together.

“No sweat,” Burke added. “They’ll have to bust us out of stir to get us into basic.”

“Eddie bit the linoleum about seven,” Zagreb said. “We all met in Springer’s chambers at seven-thirty. Who was where when?”

“After we finished tying one on at Sportree’s I caught up with my dame and left her place at seven,” Burke said, “but I’d sure hate to see her have to say it for the record.”

“On account of your wife?” McReary said.

“On account of her husband.”

Canal bit the end off a cigar and spat it into a cuspidor next to the oaken bench. They were waiting outside the commissioner’s office. “Hell, Burksie, you don’t need to worry about prison. Somebody’ll shoot you long before then.”

“Canal?” Zagreb looked at him.

“When I can’t sleep I go to the Pussycat Theater on Telegraph. Grindhouse: stag films twenty-four hours a day.”

McReary shook his head. “I’m serious. You and Burke have got to go to the circus once in a while.”

“Ringling don’t give free passes to cops,” Canal said.

Zagreb asked him what was playing.

“Search me. I was out like the Charleston as soon as the lights came down. I told you I go there when I can’t sleep.”

"Mac?"

"I went straight home."

"Anybody see you?"

"My mother."

"An unimpeachable witness, I don't think. Well, I'm no better off. I went back to my place and nodded off counting roaches."

The commissioner's secretary called them in. John H. Witherspoon was a small man in a big job, with bicycle-shaped spectacles and the kind of face that made lemons pucker. He asked the squad the same questions Zagreb had asked, but didn't appear to hear the answers. He had a file open on a desk the size of a Murphy bed.

"In his complaint, Winston Sweet says Karpalov told him you men made statements of a threatening nature."

"Balls," Burke said.

"Eloquent, Officer, but hardly satisfying." He pursed his lips at Zagreb. "Did you tell your prisoner that if he tried to come back on the *Queen Mary* you'd give that information to the Germans?"

"That was a rib. My butcher's the only kraut I know, and he's a Jew."

"Beside the point. I'm not accusing you of high treason." His face registered regret for that omission. "Officer Burke. Did you tell the prisoner he should be marched down a hall and shot in the back?"

"That's what the Russkies do, I said. It was a joke, Commish."

"Commissioner. Sergeant Canal. Did you brandish your revolver and make a remark about DOA within the prisoner's hearing?"

"Jeez. Who knew the little snake had such big ears?"

"I'll take that as an affirmative."

"I was just kidding around."

"You men were on an assignment, not *Amos 'n' Andy*. What about you, Detective Third-Grade?"

McReary sat up straight. "I never said a word to the prisoner."

"Why not? Everyone else had a turn. Were you afraid your words might come back to incriminate you?"

Zagreb scraped back his chair. "Now we're on the hook for what we *didn't* say. If that's all you got, can we get back on the job? Letting killers run loose is sloppy police work, even when it's Eddie the Carp on the slab."

"Keep your seat, Lieutenant. I didn't say that's all I've got." Witherspoon turned the page. "All the slugs fired in the drugstore were .38s. Ballistics tested your guns, all .38s. The results were inconclusive."

"Zero for four's low," Zagreb said. "They better not try moonlighting at Briggs Stadium."

"The bullet they dug out of the wall was misshapen. The three the medical examiner got from the corpse were in fragments. Comparing the striations was impossible."

Canal said, "Dum-dums. Frankie Orr's practically got the patent."

"Lieutenant Osprey's bringing him in for questioning. Three of your weapons have been eliminated; dust had accumulated in the barrels since their last cleaning. The fourth was in bandbox condition. Ordinarily I commend taking care of one's sidearm. In your case, McReary, this morning's session with the rag could mean a life sentence in Jackson."

McReary paled. "I clean and oil it regular."

"That's no baloney. The kid takes care of his piece like it was a dame." Burke was bristling.

The commissioner slapped shut the folder. "All your alibis stink. The squad's suspended until all the facts are in. With pay, it pains me to add. Karpalov belongs to Homicide."

"Sweeter words were never spoken," Zagreb said. "What about our guns?"

"Impounded, and give me your shields. That should keep you

heroes off the streets until the police clean up your mess."

The four rose and flipped the leather wallets containing their gold badges onto the desk. Witherspoon opened the belly drawer, scooped them inside like a poker player gathering in his winnings, and slammed the drawer shut.

Down on the street, Canal stopped chewing his cigar and set fire to it. "Well, we ain't in combat boots."

"Stripes neither," Zagreb said. "Just a bunch of guys on a busman's holiday."

McReary's eyes went round. "You mean we're investigating?"

"Ox can't find his fly, much less a triggerman. Jackson's no place for us. We're the reason the warden made quota."

"I don't know, L.T.," Burke said. "I'm naked without my piece."

"No one wants to see that." Zagreb put his hand in the side pocket of Burke's coat, got his keys, and popped the trunk of the Chrysler parked at the curb. Inside were two pump shotguns, a Thompson submachine gun with three drum magazines, a box of smoke bombs, and assorted blackjacks and brass knuckles. "Careless of Witherspoon to overlook these," he said. "He was a better bean-counter before he came down with a bad case of politics."

Canal grinned around his stogie and bent to scoop up the Thompson. The lieutenant slapped his hand.

"Let's try it *a capella* for now. That 'heroes' crack upstairs got my goat."

"So he got your goat." Canal rubbed his hand. "You want Frankie to get the rest?"

"Let's give him a couple hours with Osprey. Even a cheap hood needs a laugh now and then. It won't take more than a breadstick to bend a twig like Winston Sweet."

-

They didn't have access to the file, but out-of-town lawyers weren't hard to find in Detroit. Sooner or later they got wind of the attorney-friendly staff in the bar of the Book-Cadillac Hotel, where the Recorder's Court crowd flocked to drop their briefs after a hard day of litigating.

At sight of the Four Horsemen entering the cool dim interior shoulder to shoulder, half a dozen bail bondsmen drained their glasses and left by the side door. The counselor from Cleveland shared a leatherette booth with a public defender Burke knew well enough to remove by his collar and propel toward the exit with a boot from behind. Zagreb shoved himself in beside Sweet and the others crammed themselves in opposite.

"What is the meaning of this?" The fat little man righted his glass, tall and misty with a gardenia floating in it.

Burke waggled his fingers at Canal. "He said it. Pay up."

Canal told him to deduct it from the fifty he owed him. "I had him down for 'I beg your pardon.'"

"Naw. That's doctors. With lawyers it's always questions."

The lieutenant stuck two fingers in Sweet's drink and tasted them. "Gimlet." He wiped his fingers on one of the man's wide lapels. "Too late in the season. Who's your client?"

"Bartender! These men are annoying me."

The short, athletic-looking man in the green suede vest gathering empty glasses off tables nodded to Zagreb and glanced at Sweet. "It's what they do, mister. None better."

"Thanks, Sully. Schlitz all around." Zagreb smiled at the lawyer. "Sully goalied for the Red Wings, the only mick on a team full of Canucks and Russkies. He's got more gold in his mouth than the Black Hills."

"I don't follow football."

"That's it. I'm shooting him on general principles." Canal groped at the empty holster hidden under his coat. The little man squeaked.

"Stand down, Sergeant. You might miss and hit the inventory." Zagreb's smile vanished. "You got us suspended, Winston. Me, I can use the sleep. Burke's got his dames, Mac's got his dear old white-haired mom."

"Redhead. She bought a five-year supply of henna the day after Pearl."

"His dear old flame-haired mom. It's Canal I'm worried about. Lonely bachelor walking up and down his crummy cold-water flat, listening to *The Guiding Light*. You know what it's like when a guy his size cracks down the middle?"

Canal crunched his knuckles, creating a sound effect. Sweet jumped again, sloshing more of his drink. The top of the table was getting wet and sticky.

"I don't know either," Zagreb went on, "and I don't want to. Who's your client?"

"What you're asking could get me disbarred."

"You think we're going to broadcast where we got the information? There isn't a cop in the world who don't sit on his own personal snitch."

"I detest that word."

"That's more like it. We're sharing our likes and dislikes. No more small talk."

Conversation flagged while the bartender set out their beers. When he left, the lawyer glanced around the table, then leaned over and whispered in Zagreb's ear.

"That's a reasonable request. You boys take your beers over to the bar."

They obeyed. McReary worried at the label on his bottle with a thumbnail. "You guys ever ashamed you're a cop?"

Before anyone could answer, the lieutenant threw two dollars on the table and joined them.

"A.E. Smallwood, Cleveland Heights."

Canal said, "Never heard of him. What's his racket?"

"I didn't ask."

"*You?*" Burke's mouth hung open.

"Sweet's just a fat little guy in a Salvation Army suit. Probably the first job he ever had where he didn't have to worry about smacking into the back of an ambulance. I got a heart."

Burke said, "What's having a heart got to do with lawyers?"

"That's swell, Zag." McReary sounded like Christmas morning.

"Hell with him. If that Karpalov cousin he dug up is the real deal, I'm Billy Sunday."

"Who's—? Aw, skip it. You guys and your washed-up movie stars."

When they left, Winston Sweet was drinking from the glass Zagreb had filled for him, his highball abandoned.

-

On East Jefferson, Burke coasted the Chrysler to a stop behind a black Packard with nickel wheels and set the brake. There were two men in the front seat. "He's home. Guess his mouthpiece followed him downtown."

McReary said, "Could be he's still downtown. The commish said he was brought in."

"That's Rocco Marconi next to his driver," Zagreb said. "You couldn't pry a city block between Frankie and his nursemaid."

Canal looked up at the rundown building. "What's a big cheese like Orr doing keeping his broad in a dump like this?"

Burke said, "He owns the dump. Wait'll you see the crib."

"Yeah? When were you there ever?"

"I seen it in *Good Housekeeping*."

"Less talk, more do." Zagreb got out, followed by the others.

The man on the passenger's side of the Packard saw them coming and opened the door. Canal kicked it shut, just missing his hand. "Stay put, Rocco. This is a social call."

The window cranked down. "Lots of lip for a cop on relief. I hear you boys got kicked off the force." The bodyguard had cauliflower ears and a nose like a twist of rope. Canal took hold of it and twisted it back the other way. He howled. The big sergeant looked at the driver for more, but he merely folded over his *Racing Form* and resumed reading.

On their way upstairs, Burke said: "You really think he knows this bird Smallwood?"

"If he's a rackets guy," Zagreb said. "They're clubby as hell."

A sharp-faced blonde in green lounging pajamas answered the apartment door. She was barefoot and all her nails matched the pajamas. "Uh-oh. Somebody left a cage open at the zoo."

Canal leered. "That's no way to greet an old friend, Nola. I know you since you checked hats at the Oriole Ballroom."

"Pants, too," Burke said.

She started to slam the door. Zagreb stopped it with his shoulder.

"We want five minutes with Frankie. Here or at the California, only there it'd be more like an hour."

"And seem like a week," McReary said.

Burke raised his brows at the young detective. "Hey, you're coming along."

Nola Van Allen walked away from the door. The living room was done all in black-and-white and chromium. An albino zebra skin lay on the floor. As they entered, Frankie Orr came in from another room drying his jet-black hair with a towel. He wore a silk dressing gown embroidered with silver thread and slippers with heraldic crests on the toes. "Aw, c'mon, fellas," he said. "I just scrubbed off the last of Osprey."

"Ox just looks like he stinks," Zagreb said. "Simmer down, Frankie. You only kill when there's dough involved. Who's A.E. Smallwood?"

Orr got rid of the towel, palmed back his hair, and took a silver-tipped cigarette from a doohickey on a bar with rubber wheels. He lit it with a platinum lighter and blew smoke at the ceiling, showing a tanned throat. "Smallwood. Sounds like a medical condition."

"You're hiring better writers. Coming up in the world." Zagreb waited.

"Seems to me I had a drink once with an Abner Smallwood. I forget just where."

"Try Cleveland Heights. After the city of the same name."

"*You* try it. I lost a good man there once. He went swimming across Lake Huron with a Hupmobile tied to his back."

"This Smallwood paid to get Eddie Karpalov out of hock."

"That so? I got a bone to pick with him then. Eddie insulted Nola."

"You call practically getting raped an insult?" She was sitting on the black leather sofa holding a jade cigarette holder with nothing in it. "Your friends can go piss up a rope."

"He wasn't a friend. He thought he was and tried to put the arm on me for a getaway stake. Then he got fresh with my girl. But I wouldn't sell out an enemy to the cops, dead or alive. The way I hear it, you ain't even cops no more."

"Your boy Rocco heard the same thing. The way news travels in this town, it's a wonder anyone bothers to tune in Walter Winchell. So tell us about Smallwood. We're all civilians here."

"Go swipe an apple."

Zagreb took a step and hit him on the point of his chin. Orr fell back against the bar, which rolled two feet and dumped half its cargo in an explosion of liquor and crystal. He caught his balance, but his hair was in his face and his eyes lacked focus.

"Excuse our bad manners, Frankie." Burke ground out Orr's cigarette on the floor. "The commish took away our guns."

"Yeah? Maybe telling me wasn't so smart."

Zagreb sucked his knuckles. "Put your pants on. Threatening us buys you ninety days in County."

"You said you weren't cops."

"I stretched it a little. Witherspoon just sent us off to summer camp. He thought we looked tired."

Orr spat blood on the zebra skin. He'd bitten his tongue.

Nola leapt to her feet. "You cheap gangster! That won't wash out."

"Shut up and go in the bedroom. Turn on the radio. Loud."

She threw her cigarette holder at him and ran into the next room. The door slammed. In a little while noise came out. It sounded like a pair of wrestlers falling down the service stairs.

"Had to be 'Drum Boogie.'" Canal shook his head. "Couldn't be Fred Waring."

Orr browsed the containers left on the bar, found leaded glasses in the cabinet underneath, poured. "You boys never had stuff like this. You never even been in the same room with it."

"Thanks. For a thief you got a generous heart." Zagreb jerked his down, as did Canal and Burke. McReary sipped, made a face. He was a milkshake man.

Orr winced when his drink touched his tongue. "You can't make that threatening charge stick."

"If you're so sure, why send Nola to her room?"

"I'm a busy man, and I already lost half my day, so here's a crumb. Abner Elias Smallwood. He's out of my league. If I fix things between a mug and the mayor, he fixes 'em between Shell Oil and Washington. Can't get a defense contract? Talk to Smallwood. In a month you're cranking out hatch hinges for the navy."

"What's his end?" Zagreb asked.

"Half a percent."

Canal snorted. "You built him up like he was big-time."

"You got any idea what just one plant cleared last year?"

Zagreb helped himself to another drink. "What's a minnow like Winston Sweet doing swimming with a whale like Smallwood?"

"My guess is this Roylston, Ryker, and Reed outfit sails close to shore. No legit firm would touch the case."

"Why Eddie the Carp?" Zagreb drained his glass again.

"I said Smallwood talks to the big fish for the little fish. That don't mean it can't work the other way. Somebody big wanted him out on the street bad enough to meet Smallwood's price."

Zagreb said, "Out in the open, you mean."

"We're just talking, understand. You can get to a man in the joint, but it leaves a trail. On the street it's anybody's game."

-

Zagreb locked the call box on the corner and got back into the Chrysler next to Burke behind the wheel. "Smallwood's out of town, meeting with Cordell Hull."

Burke said, "The attorney general?"

"I think he's secretary of state."

"Wonder who *he* wants rubbed out?" Canal asked.

The lieutenant swigged from a pint he'd swiped from Orr's bar and passed it over the seat to Canal in back. "What's the name of that cop Eddie smoked way back when?"

"Jim Hooper." Canal took a pull and gave it to McReary. "He went in the front door when we busted up the Oakland Sugar House Gang in thirty-nine. I was a harness bull then same as him."

"Married, wasn't he?"

"Sure. I heard she moved in with her mother in Hamtramck."

Burke got the bottle from McReary, who hadn't partaken, drank, capped it, and slid it into his coat pocket. "Hamtramck it is. I know a market there sells kielbasa under the counter, no stamps." He started the car.

McReary said, "Don't that put money in Frankie's pocket?"

"It's a screwy war," Zagreb said. "We'll get all the bugs worked out in time for the next."

They found Bernice Hooper packing a lunch pail in the kitchen of a small house on Joseph Campau. She was a thick-waisted woman with gray in her hair who said she was working the swing shift at Dodge Main.

"I'm sick of having coppers in my house," she said. "I had 'em in every house I ever lived in. My father and uncle were cops, I married a cop, I got a brother who's a cop. I'm glad now I never had a kid. I'd be pinning his diapers on with a shield."

"Tough break." Canal was sincere.

McReary had his hat off, baring his bald head. "We're sorry for your loss."

"Every copper says that. It must be in the department manual."

Zagreb said, "Eddie Karpalov's dead, if it helps."

"Gee, let me check. Jim!" she called over her shoulder. She waited, shrugged, threw a box of Sun-Maid raisins in the pail. "Nope. Still in the ground."

"Can you tell us where you were at seven this morning?" Zagreb asked.

"Welding tanks, midnight till eight."

"You pulled a double shift?"

"I don't have a husband to come back to, mister. My mother talks about Jesus all the time, so I don't figure I'm missing much in the way of conversation."

Burke said, "We'll check with your foreman."

"Check or not, I don't care. I'm glad he's dead, but my life's the same either way."

Zagreb paused in the midst of lighting a cigarette. "Mind telling us your maiden name?"

-

That night they reconvened in Room 1102 of the California and wolfed down kielbasa sausage and cabbage cooked by Canal on the hotplate, chasing it with beer. The big sergeant was a lifelong bachelor and the only one of the Horsemen who could apply heat to a meal without needing a fire extinguisher or a stomach pump. They were sitting around burping when the candlestick phone rang. Zagreb said "Okay" three times and pegged the receiver.

"Washington P.D. picked up Deputy Marshal Cash an hour ago," he said. "He rolled over on his partner, but he says all he did was drive the getaway car, a rental. He never heard of anybody named Smallwood. Deputy Marshal Rudnicki lives on the Virginia side. They're rounding up the locals to help snag him. We'll know in a little."

"Bernice Rudnicki." McReary shook his head. "How'd you guess, Zag?"

"I didn't. When she said she has a brother who's a cop, I got a hunch, but I didn't figure Rudnicki. The Justice Department checked with his bank. He cashed in all his war bonds last month. That's how he paid Smallwood to arrange to spring Karpalov."

Burke picked his teeth with a thumbnail. "It don't make sense. They could've taken a crack at him on the train all the time he was in their mitts."

"And explain it how?" Zagreb said. "Rudnicki called in some markers to get the assignment. The shooting team would start with that, and when it came out he was Hooper's brother-in-law, he'd be hotter than Canal's hotplate. This way he had a legitimate reason for being in town and a hundred other guys to take the fall, including us and everybody who ever met Eddie."

"Even so, I hope he gets the same break in court Eddie got." Canal fired up a cigar.

Zagreb got up and opened a window to let out the stench. "Not till he rolls over on Smallwood. Otherwise we can't tie Smallwood to that phony affidavit that kept Eddie in the country. Winston Sweet's dumb enough or scared enough to take that ride alone, and the law can't make him give up his client under oath."

McReary said, "What makes you think Rudnicki will?"

"Just the difference between time off for good behavior and life without parole. *If* he don't make a fight of it tonight. Those capital cops cut their teeth on spies and saboteurs. He makes a fight of it, all we got's another dead cop and a live fixer who makes Frankie Orr's operation look like the Lollipop Guild."

The telephone rang again. Zagreb answered, listened, said "Thanks," hung up. He dug a Chesterfield out of his pack. "He made a fight of it."

After a little while McReary took out the deck of cards.

BIG Band

"You don't have to be Buster Crabbe to choke a dame."

Big Band

Shirley Grabowski had always been one of those women the tabloids called handsome, when a picture accompanied the story and they couldn't smuggle "beauty" past the readers. Her jaw was too square, her nose mannish, and she could never find sunglasses to fit her wide-set eyes. But that was before the war, before she joined the Women's Army Corps. The WAC uniform, with its tailored jacket and skirt and overseas cap set at a rakish angle on her strawberry-blond head, brought everything together. She was, Max Zagreb admitted to himself ruefully, a dish.

He told her as much. She rolled a padded shoulder and pumped the straw in her gin rickey. "It's the government-issue frock: makes men horny, like those Scarlett O'Hara costumes bridesmaids wear. It'd make Olive Oyl look like Lana Turner."

"Now you're just fishing." The Racket Squad lieutenant waited until the Four-F sourpuss in the paper hat turned his back to the counter, then unscrewed his flask and freshened their Cokes. It was past curfew for everyone but cops and their companions. They were the only customers in the Rexall, and the man wanted to close. He'd switched off the radio in the middle of Lowell Thomas to hurry them on their way. "Speaking of bridesmaids, I've heard scuttlebutt."

"You and your stoolies," she said. "Let's hold off on rice rations till the Axis goes belly-up. If Jerry gets me in the family way I won't get to see London."

"Neighborhood's gone downhill since the Luftwaffe moved in, I hear. How is old Jerry? I haven't seen him since the three-legged sack race on Belle Isle."

"Quit your kidding. You never met. You will, if you do me the eensy-weensy favor I dragged you down here to ask."

"What's my end?"

"Old times' sake. You threw me over for a bottle blonde in the Club 666 right in the middle of the 'Five O'Clock Jump.' The way I see it, you owe me a good turn."

"The blonde nicked me for a fin to make change to tip the girl in the powder room and never came back. I figure I paid my debt to society."

"Sap. There aren't any restroom attendants in the 666. There are barely restrooms."

"So I found out when I went looking for her. Okay, I was a drip. How do I square myself?"

"I ship out next week. I want you to keep Jerry out of trouble while I'm away."

"What kind of trouble?"

"The musician kind."

"Sour notes?"

"He never blows 'em. He plays second trumpet with Red Lot's Red Hots, mixed group with a steady gig at the Ruby Lounge on Hastings."

"I know Red. Vice pulled him in on a muggles rap couple of months back."

"Does that sort of thing bother you?"

"It bothers Vice. Those boys sit with their knees together just like their mamas told 'em. Me, I like hooch. I never get in the way of a fellow and his way to hell, so long as it don't involve the rackets."

"Drugs isn't a racket?"

"Only on the supply side. I don't want to know what Satchmo sounds like on Juicy Fruit and grape Nehi."

"I don't mean that kind of trouble. Jerry's a hothead, goes with the job: It takes a few hours to wind down from a good session, and when he gets a few drinks in him, he'd pick a fight with Patton's Third Army."

"I did my bit for Prohibition, Shirl. I've got the lumps to prove it."

"I don't begrudge him a bender now and then. Two sets in the Ruby would turn a teetotaler like Henry Ford into a Class A sot. I just don't want him to catch a fist in the throat some night. He's got his heart set on a slot with the Casa Loma Orchestra, and they aren't hiring men with busted pipes."

"If he likes to fight more than he likes to blow, he should enlist."

"He tried. Glenn Miller said he'd give him an audition for his army band if he showed up, but a crummy doctor at the Light Guard Armory said he had a heart murmur and washed him out."

Zagreb had one of those, too: It kept murmuring *Don't go.* Aloud he said, "I can't babysit him for the duration. The commissioner won't okay the cover charge."

"Well, what *can* you do?"

"Give him an even break if he winds up in the tank."

"Isn't that just going by the book?"

"You know, I never saw a book. I thought they'd hand out copies with the shield, but there was a Depression on and I guess they had to save on the printing bill."

"You know what I think? There isn't a book."

"You'd make a swell detective."

She took the straw out of her glass and slurped liquid off the end. By then it was all gin. "I don't even know if I'll make a good WAC. I just didn't want to pound sheet metal at Chrysler."

"Guess you'll know when you get to London."

"Not London. I can't tell you where they're sending me, but tea and crumpets aren't in it. Can you at least promise me you'll look in on him from time to time? Maybe put the fear of God in him when he steps over the line?"

"What's the skinny, Shirl? Afraid he'll sit under the apple tree with a bottle blonde while you're in the Aleutians?"

She paled. "How did you—? Forget I said that. I fell for a musician. Don't you think I know where to cut my losses? Jerry's a good egg. All he need's a woman who cares enough to trim some of the bark off him. Since it can't be me, I thought I'd draft the Detroit Police Department."

He lit a Chesterfield. The counterman sighed but kept mum. Black marketeers had stuck him up three times for penicillin before he started letting cops order burgers on the cuff. He turned away to flush the soda taps. "You're still aiming high," Zagreb said. "I trained on Tommygunners and axe murderers. Playing Dutch uncle to trumpeters ought to come with combat pay."

She smiled; he remembered she had horse teeth, but now she looked like Katharine Hepburn. Her fingers brushed the back of his hand where it rested on the Formica. "Thanks, Max. I knew I could count on you."

"I didn't—" he said; but she was giving him details.

As they moved toward the door, Paper Hat rang up the sale, sniffed the used glasses, scowled, and plunged them into warm soapy water.

-

The Ruby Lounge had been padlocked once for operating after curfew, but the lieutenant in charge of that detail was a reasonable man with a wife who liked furs and Florida, so it had reopened immediately. It was in full swing when Zagreb dropped in, flashed his shield at the bouncer, and plowed his way to the bar. The atmosphere was so dense he thought it would hold its shape after the walls fell in, a perfect cube of noise and smoke.

Red Lot's Red Hots crowded the bandstand twelve pieces strong. Lot, whose facial congestion matched his thatch of flame-colored hair, leaned heavily on his bass drum, propelling the band through a high-test version of "Let Me Off Uptown." What the girl singer, a light-skinned Negro, lacked in lung power she made up for in body movement. The gyrations of her long slender form in skintight evening dress were incendiary and violated the city ordinance against lewd and lascivious activity. But that one had been passed before a war that had put many things in a different perspective. In any case, that was Vice's headache. Zagreb ordered a double rye and leaned his back against the bar to watch Jerry Dugan blow his horn.

The Racket Squad lieutenant was tone deaf, but he could tell Shirley Grabowski was all wet on the subject of her fella's abilities; he was out of his depth next to the heavyset Negro blasting away at first trumpet. That party climbed the scale to the ear-shattering crescendo with seeming ease, with Dugan stumbling behind in sweaty confusion. Evidently all the best men were in uniform or performing with the USO—or, as in the case of the silver-templed colored player, exempted by age from service until storm troopers invaded Paradise Valley.

Zagreb had no beef with the trombones, reeds, vibes, and piano; but his taste in music began and ended with Bing Crosby.

"Let Me Off Uptown" ended the set, of course. It would have been anticlimactic to follow it with anything but an air raid. The clientele thinned out—entertainment was the draw, not the watered-down black market booze—and Zagreb found space to sidle up next to Jerry Dugan as he called for a Schlitz.

"I always heard you musicians fueled up on ethyl," the lieutenant said by way of opening the conversation.

"I promised my girl I'd ride the wagon a while." The trumpeter was a good-looking kid and knew it. He focused on his reflection behind the bar and smoothed back a sandy lock with an ivory comb. His band jacket was cut to call attention to his narrow waist and square shoulders.

"Tell me which wagon, it lets you blow like that." The department oath came with a license to lie.

"You should hear me when we're jamming. Out in the open I got to hang back or sweep these bush leaguers out the door."

It was going to be impossible to keep this boy out of trouble. "That other trumpeter won't sweep easy."

"Well, Lungs is an institution."

The way he said the name indicated his listener should know it. He made a note to consult McReary. The detective third-grade was the youngest man on the squad and presumably up on current music. "We have a mutual friend. Shirley Grabowski?"

"Shirley's that girl I told you about." Dugan introduced himself and reached across his body to offer his left hand. Fritz Kreisler, the violinist, protected his bow hand that way, they said; but Kreisler needn't fear the return of better musicians when the war was over.

"Max Zagreb."

"How do you know Shirley?"

"We met on a double date. She was out with some loser." No sense naming names.

He felt a hand on his shoulder and looked into the scarlet boozy face of Red Lot. "Hey, there, Lieutenant. How's the boy?"

The bartender had a highball all ready for the bandleader. It wasn't his first or he wouldn't be so chummy. They'd barely spoken while he was being released from the marijuana lockup. Before Zagreb could frame a suitable response, Red was gone with his glass, glad-handing his way from table to table.

Dugan said, "Lieutenant, huh? You on leave?"

"Can't get a pass out of the commissioner."

"Oh. Cop." There was no friendly way to say the phrase.

"Off duty tonight. Only raid polka joints when I'm on."

"Come to think of it, I heard her say she knew a cop. She send you to check up on me?"

"You need checking up on?"

"Shirley thinks so. She don't like to see a man enjoying himself. I'd trade her in for the sport model if she weren't a knockout."

He was liking Dugan better and better—for the draft. "A lot of mugs that like to pop off sometimes could stand having a knockout like her around. I was a hell-raiser myself till my old watch captain took me in hand, and he was ugly as a bag of bricks."

Dugan tipped up his bottle and didn't set it down until it gurgled empty. "Well, you can tell her Jerry-boy's all grown up. She can serve donuts to dogfaces and not give me another thought. Maybe a V-mail now and again to remind me to wear rubbers when it rains. What're you drinking?" The beer was having its effect. Like most mean drunks he was on his way after the second round.

"Rye."

"Make it two, Ace." Dugan slapped the bar.

The bartender, a big Pole who looked as if he'd started out juggling short blocks at Dodge Main, set them up. "Name's Stan. Stanislaus to you, Bugle Boy."

Dugan put back the shot with a jerk, then decided to get mad. Zagreb caught his fist on the cock and twisted his arm behind his back.

"Hey, hey! That's the money arm!" The trumpeter's voice was shrill.

"You should've thought of that before you tried to break it on a bartender named Stanislaus." He fumbled out the folder with his shield and showed it to that individual, who nodded and straightened up from the sawed-off every mixologist in the Arsenal of Democracy kept under the bar. "You going to behave?"

"Yeah, sure. Jesus."

The lieutenant let go, and was ready when Dugan spun around leading with his other fist. He ducked the blow and lifted the boy off his feet in a fireman's carry when the follow-through put him in position. He gripped Dugan's wrists, clamped his other arm around his legs, and opened a path through the crowd of gawkers toward the door. "Fireworks over, folks," he said. "Your tax dollars at work. Be sure and buy war bonds."

-

"Slow news day." Sergeant Canal folded the *Detroit Times*. "You should tell a guy when you moonlight as a bouncer. You won't let me drive a cab."

"Diplomatic decision. The one they have was in the can: Medical deferment. Bad prostates are winning the war for Hitler." Zagreb plunked himself into a chair at a vacant desk, of which the squad was in good supply since before Corregidor. "How'd I come off?"

"Little to the right of Mussolini. Lucky the *Free Press* wasn't there."

"They're pussies. The *Herald* will be screaming for my shield come the next edition." He looked at his watch. "Dugan's made bail by now."

The telephone rang on Canal's desk. The big man answered it and held it out. "Some dame."

"That'll be his bail." He got up to take it. He was right. It was Shirley.

"What happened, Max? Jerry says you sucker-punched him."

"He threw all the punches. It wasn't his fault none of them connected. Well, it was. A guy who can't throw a right jab or a left hook should stick to knitting socks for the marines."

A sigh came down the line. "He's going to be a handful, isn't he?"

"A blowtop like that's wasted outside a torpedo tube. I can't keep the peace and sit on his head too. You need to put more men on the job, but the Hundred-and-First Airborne's busy."

"Is he going to—prison?"

"It'd be one way to keep him in check. Realistically, we could put him on ice for ninety days for assaulting a police officer, but he didn't get that far. Anyway I didn't write it up that way. The judge'll probably fine him for drunk and disorderly, maybe a week shoveling out the stables at Mounted if he's hung over when he hears the case."

"Thank you, Max. If I thought you were all cop I wouldn't have asked the favor."

"Don't bank on that. Jerry's the *Hindenburg* waiting for a spark."

"But you will try to look out for him?"

He blew air. "The Ruby's on my way home. I can use a drink after a hard day snaring saboteurs."

"Maybe if he hangs around you long enough some of the nice guy will rub off on him."

"I heard that last part," Canal said, when he hung up.

"What's it to you?" He was sore at himself, but the sergeant was a bigger target.

"Not a thing, Zag. Maybe you should hire a press agent and get the newshawks off your neck." He sniffed one of his thick black cigars—no one ever said he wasn't a brave man—and put a match to it, clouding the air with the stench of boiling bedpans. "This Grabowski dame must be some tomato."

"I was late finding it out. If I was any kind of detective there wouldn't be any Jerry Dugan in the picture."

"Don't beat yourself up. I dumped a month's salary on forty shares in Hupmobile."

-

Two weeks went by, measured in brawl-bustings, barren stakeouts, and a honey of a double murder over a back-alley tire sale gone bad; not a saboteur to the credit of the fearsome Four Horsemen of the Racket Squad. Zagreb got a picture postcard from Shirley in San Francisco, the jumping-off point before the Aleutians (if the War Department wanted to keep that a secret it shouldn't have stressed their importance in press releases). He dropped in on the Ruby Lounge a half-dozen times, hovering in the background over a glass while Dugan tried to catch up with Chester "Lungs" Nelson, who according to McReary had recorded four sides with Duke Ellington.

"What the hell's he doing playing a dive in Detroit?" Zagreb asked.

"Scuttlebutt is he got the sack for pulling a knife on the Duke. Artistic dispute."

"They sure are sensitive back East. It's how we open negotiations here."

In all that time the lieutenant had no direct contact with Dugan, who'd forked over fifty bucks to the county for the tussle at the bar and seemed to be minding his p's and q's. Anyway he was nursing his beers.

Officer Burke, a big man by any standards that didn't include Canal, braced Zagreb by the five-gallon coffee maker that had crossed the frontier with Fremont, holding a copy of the *News* folded open to the classifieds.

"Pre-war Duesenberg," he said, stabbing a hairy forefinger at the first column. "Four hundred bucks. We can swing that, between us four. I bet we get 'em down to three-fifty."

"Just what's your beef with the Chrysler?" The lieutenant dropped two cubes of something that wasn't sugar into his cup and stirred it with an iron spoon that turned reddish brown when he drew it out.

"It looks like a chamber pot and you can smoke half a pack of Luckies waiting for it to accelerate after you stomp on the pedal. Other than that it's swell."

"You want to drive a kraut car on a public street with U-boats sinking our convoys?"

"We can paint over the insignia and call it a Liberty Car."

Zagreb drank something that wasn't coffee. "Let's just hold off on handing the commish a shovel to bury us with."

McReary entered the squad room as Burke steamed out. The young third-grader looked rakish as usual with his hat tilted on his sadly defoliated head. "Who spit in Burksie's soup? He looks even uglier than always."

"I wasn't listening. Got an aspirin?"

"Nope. Hung over?"

"Too much swing. I don't know how you youngsters stand it."

"I turn down the volume on the Philco. No juke joints for me. I get in my eight hours and punch in fresh as a daisy."

"You'll grow out of it."

The toilet down the hall flushed and Canal came in with the *Racing Form* under his arm. "Burke tell you his brainstorm?" he asked the lieutenant.

"Yeah. Got an aspirin?"

The big man shook his head. "I told him you wouldn't go for it. Next week he'll be asking for a Jap Zero. Hung over?"

"Why's everybody ask that? I heard 'Sing, Sing, Sing' three times this week. Makes me want to puke, puke, puke."

"Mr. First Nighter. You can't go wrong with Guy Lombardo."

Zagreb started going through drawers belonging to unoccupied desks. He found girlie magazines, newspapers folded to sports and crosswords, a half-finished jigsaw puzzle, an unopened package of Trojans, an enema tube attached to a hot-water bottle, and cartridges rolling around loose. At length he came upon an Anacin tin, but it was empty. He ran his finger around the inside and sucked on it. "I'll give either one of you a day off to stand the next watch at the Ruby."

Canal said, "Include me out. One wah-wah and I'm suspended for unnecessary use of deadly force."

McReary said, "What would I do with a day off? I got just enough gas stamps to make it halfway out on the Belle Isle bridge."

"I'll remember you monkeys when they kick me upstairs."

Canal grinned around his cigar. "Okay if I don't start sweating till nineteen sixty?"

The loudspeaker mounted on the wall crackled constantly between radio transmissions that had nothing to do with them. Now the soporific-sounding dispatcher came on to summon cars to an address Zagreb knew on Hastings.

"That's the Ruby," he said.

Canal jerked his chin at McReary. "Burksie does all his sulking by his locker. That's where he parks his flask. Tell him we got a homicide."

"That should cheer him up." McReary left.

-

By day the nightclub looked as empty as the squad room, chairs upended on all the tables; the tobacco-and-liquor reek was a little more pronounced.

A fat, nicotine-stained manager Burke recognized from mug shots conducted them to an upstairs hallway, where they were met by the officers on the scene. One looked too young for military service. His partner was a paunchy grayhead who'd obviously been called up out of retirement. If the draft continued, the department would be excavating them from Mt. Elliott Cemetery.

"Looks open-and-shut, Lieutenant." Grayhead jerked a thumb toward the door behind him. "We got the body and the perp."

Zagreb asked if the detective division was recruiting uniforms that season.

Grayhead looked confused. "No, sir."

"Just curious. If you boys are opening and shutting cases now, this trip wasn't necessary. There's a war on, you know. Gasoline is blood."

"Seems to me I heard that somewhere."

"Next time listen."

"Yes, sir." The response was disgruntled.

The youngster saluted smartly.

"Save it for Eisenhower. Who's the subject?"

The junior officer produced a neat notebook. "Gerald Dugan, no middle. White male, age twenty-six. Says he's a musician."

"You were right not to take his word for it. What else?"

Notebook. "The vic. Griselda Rose Simone, Negro female,

age twenty, according to the manager. Contusions on the throat, tongue extended, body still warm. Parallel longitudinal scars on the abdomen, possibly nail marks. Naked. Sex crime, maybe. That's speculation, sir. I'm not a detective."

"Can't think why anybody'd want to be. You studying to be a doctor?"

He flushed. "Sort of, sir. I hope to enlist with the medical corps."

"Stick around, both of you." Zagreb opened the door.

The Ruby kept a bedroom for the manager to rest when the accounts didn't balance before dawn; that was the official explanation, but liquor and munitions weren't the only business in town. There was an iron-framed bed and a little sitting area to break the ice over a bottle of bonded. Jerry Dugan was sitting there in his undershirt and pegtop slacks with the bottle in one hand. His hair needed his ivory comb and gravity had pulled at his youthful features. Zagreb transferred his attention from him to the unclothed woman on the bed.

The singer wouldn't be gyrating on any more bandstands. She lay lewdly spread-eagled, her evening gown, lacy underthings, and gold-painted heels on the floor and her eyes rolled up toward the low ceiling. Young Dr. Kildare hadn't exaggerated the rest. Strangled bodies didn't look as glamorous in the real world as they did in movies. Her tongue had sought escape from the constriction on her throat and the deep purple lacerations to the left of her navel looked as if they'd been made by a puma.

"Jesus." McReary crossed himself.

"I think He knows already." The lieutenant didn't bother checking for a pulse. He returned to Dugan, snatched the bottle from his hand, held it out for Canal to take, and inspected both sets of fingernails. Then he slapped the trumpeter's face methodically, forehand and backhand. Dugan groaned and tried to stare at the back of his own skull. The slapping stopped and his chin sank back onto his chest.

"Gone as the Kaiser," Zagreb said. "Let's talk to the manager."

McReary fetched him. The man looked annoyed. "I run a decent place. One curfew beef, two solicitation complaints. I canned the girls. I can't be everyplace at once."

"I guess that's why you made bail last time. What happened?"

"Search me. They came early to rehearse a number, they said. They wanted to surprise Red Lot, so they asked to do it up here till it was ready. I trust people, that's my problem. They're up here ten minutes, then I hear screaming. I thought it was a jump tune at first. I got a tin ear. By the time I ran up to check, everything was what you see."

"Dugan drunk when he came in?" Zagreb asked.

"Well, he wasn't bouncing off walls. You can't always tell with musicians. I didn't have any problem with him buying a bottle; to loosen up, he said."

"Okay, beat it."

"No racket stuff here," Canal said when the manager beat it. "Kick it over to Homicide?"

"An ox like Osprey'd just tie it with a cord and hand it to the prosecutor."

Burke said, "What's wrong with that?"

"Ten minutes isn't much time for Dugan to drink himself half into a coma and claw up and strangle a healthy girl."

"Manager could be wrong about the time." McReary kept his gaze away from the corpse. He was looking a little gray. "You said yourself two drinks and Dugan's in Oz."

"Body's still warm. Also his nails are clean. No skin or blood under 'em to match the claw marks on her belly. It's a swell setup, but they worked too fast."

Canal flicked ash off his cigar. "Who's *they*?"

Someone tapped on the door. Zagreb opened it on the kid in uniform. "Band's downstairs, Lieutenant. Send 'em home?"

"No. I'll talk to them downstairs."

-

"Holy smokes." Red Lot, scarlet and sweating in a bright yellow Hawaiian shirt, mopped his face and neck with a silk handkerchief the size of a tablecloth. "Little Grizzy? Holy smokes."

"Yeah." Zagreb had asked the Red Hots to sit, and they'd taken their usual seats on the bandstand, Lot behind his drums. The lieutenant stood before them like a conductor while McReary and Canal straddled chairs they'd taken from tables on the club floor. Burke remained upstairs with Dugan and the corpse. "How did she and Dugan get along?"

"Okay, I guess," Lot said. "I mean, I don't let arguments get out of hand and I got a policy against dating inside the band. That's asking for trouble. But those two never gave me worries either way. They was friendly enough, no more."

"She have a fella?"

"She was up to her hips in stage-door johnnies every night, but she didn't encourage 'em, or any of us either. Just between us, I think she batted left." The bandleader struck a rimshot off his snare. A nervous chuckle rippled through the band.

"Cut that out. This isn't Kay Kyser. We got a dead girl upstairs."

"Sorry." Lot laid aside his sticks.

"The manager of this joint says Dugan and Miss Simone told him they were rehearsing a number they wanted to surprise you with. You know anything about that?"

"Which one said that?"

The lieutenant looked at the fat man leaning on his forearms on the bar. "Dugan," the manager said.

"He was pulling your leg," said Lot. "What do I always say about duets, boys?"

The band raised their voices in chorus. "'If I wanted most of you to sit on your hands, I'd put you in the audience and save a buck.'" The clarinetist added a fillip at the end, lowering his instrument quickly when Zagreb glared at him.

Red Lot nodded, pleased with the harmony. "I guess they cooked up that excuse to play another kind of duet. Maybe I got her wrong, or maybe she made an exception for so-so horn men."

"Why'd you keep him on, he was so bad?"

"Service snapped up all the good ones. Anyway, Lungs likes the kid, and Lungs is what packs 'em in here every night."

Zagreb looked at the colored trumpeter, who took up every inch of his chair with his collar spread and a gold chain around his thick neck from which dangled a tiny gold crucifix. Chester Nelson nodded. "He's okay. I popped off a lot when I was his age. He'll grow out of it; but he'll never be no horn player."

"Did you grow out of it?"

"I guess you mean that mixup with Ellington. There wasn't no knife, I don't know how that got started. Just yellin', boss, that's all. It was his outfit, so it was me that left." He touched the crucifix with one of his big meaty hands as if to swear on it.

"Where've you been the last hour?"

Lungs's eyes widened. "Sportree's. We always drop in there before a gig, to oil up."

"Who's *we*?"

"Us." He swept a hand around the bandstand.

"All of you?" It was a Negro bar. The owner only let the Horsemen in to discourage stickups.

The trumpeter grinned broadly. "They're all honorary coloreds when they're with me."

"Speak for yourself," said one of the men in the trombone section. "I'm temperance."

Zagreb asked him to stand. He was only an inch taller than when sitting, a hollow-cheeked shrimp with arms no bigger around than copper pipe. "Sit down. You couldn't strangle a chipmunk."

"You ain't exactly Tarzan yourself, copper."

"I said sit down. You want us to frisk you for muggles?"

The man sat down. McReary got up and tugged on Zagreb's

coattails, gesturing for him to bend down from the stand. He whispered in his ear. The lieutenant straightened, smiling sourly.

"My colleague reminds me Sportree's is only a five-minute walk from here. There's a fire escape out back, so the manager didn't have to see anything. Any of you guys step out for a leak?"

Lungs said, "Me. I got weak kidneys. I wasn't gone three minutes."

"That sound about right?" The other musicians shrugged. "Anyone go to parochial school?" A few nods. "Okay, you can explain it to the rest. We're checking your nails."

Canal took charge without being asked. He was the least likely member of the squad to encounter resistance. After a few minutes he stepped off the bandstand. "Clean, Zag. Of blood and skin, anyways. Some of these boys could use a lesson in hygiene. Boy on vibes chews his to the elbow." He spoke low.

Zagreb kept his volume down as well. "What about Lungs?"

"Whitest thing about him. He don't leave his barber's without a manicure."

"We can eliminate the slobs. The rest had plenty of time to tidy up." He stared at the sergeant. "You okay?"

"Fine 'n' dandy." His speech was slurred.

Zagreb frowned, then raised his voice to the band. "Leave your names and addresses with Detective McReary, and stick close to home. No show tonight. The place is closed."

"Hey!" The manager stiffened behind the bar.

The lieutenant had already seen his nails. He wouldn't ask the man to make him a sandwich, but it was just dirt. "Tell it to the marines. No, wait—they placed the Ruby off-limits, didn't they?"

Red Lot struck another one off the rim. The fat man flushed and left the room.

The uniforms took Dugan down to 1300, Detroit Police Headquarters, with Zagreb's instructions to book him for suspicion. The trumpeter negotiated the stairs with rubber ankles and an officer holding up each arm. In a little while the medical examiner showed up, humming as he ascended the stairs. The squad repaired to the Chrysler, where the lieutenant touched Burke's arm behind the wheel. "You dating a meter maid?"

"I'm riding the fidelity train just now. Sadie found a cocktail napkin with a phone number in my pocket. Why a meter maid?"

"They aren't making new cars any more. You strip those gears, you'll need to borrow a scooter."

"Be an improvement." But he worked the clutch gently.

"I got a sawbuck says it's Lot," Canal said. "See how red and sweaty he was? Like he just went ten rounds with a fire escape."

Zagreb said, "He always looks like that. My dough's on Lungs. Those hands could throttle a coconut."

"Nuts," said McReary. "Famous people don't do murder."

"Tell it to John Wilkes Booth." Burke flashed his Clark Gable grin at a pair of nurses in a crosswalk. One smiled back. Her companion grabbed her wrist and jerked it like a leash.

"He was just famous on account of he bumped Lincoln."

"He was already boffo box-office in the Raymond Massey picture." Canal blew cigar exhaust out his window.

Not enough. The lieutenant rolled down his, preferring the street odor. It was garbage day. "Anybody can duck out of a dive like Sportree's without being noticed, even a big shot like Lungs. Maybe he objected to Dugan messing with a colored girl."

Burke said, "So why not kill Dugan?"

"He'd be just as sore at them both. Framing Dugan punished him too and took Lungs off the hook for Simone."

"Lucky for him Dugan got a snootful," Burke said.

"It didn't take much. He's an amateur drinker."

"So let's lean on Lungs," Canal said.

"Maybe wait to hear from the M.E." McReary studied law nights. "He'll get the size of the killer's hands from the marks on the neck. You don't have to be Buster Crabbe to choke a dame.

That midget on trombone could've done it if he had time."

"This dame looked plenty healthy on the bandstand," Zagreb said. "Let's drop in on Lungs."

"You're forgetting his fingernails passed inspection. Everybody's did."

The lieutenant looked at the third-grader in the rearview. "You want everything to go together slick as spit, get a job with Ford."

Burke looked at his watch. "He might not be home yet."

"Even better." Zagreb opened the glove compartment and took out a ring of skeleton keys.

-

Chester "Lungs" Nelson kept an apartment on Erskine, above a rib joint they could smell the moment they turned into the block. When they stepped out of the car, Canal stumbled on the curb and caught himself noisily against a cluster of trash cans. Zagreb stared. "You drunk?"

"Just a slug, Zag, honest." The sergeant slid the bottle they'd taken from Dugan out of his coat. Zagreb grabbed it, unscrewed the cap, and sniffed at the contents. "Back in the car," he said.

"What about Lungs?" Burke asked.

"Lungs can wait. We're going to a drugstore."

The nearest drugstore happened to be the one where Zagreb had drunk gin rickeys with Shirley Grabowski. The soda jerk in the paper hat wasn't on duty, but their business was with the pharmacist, a chubby sixty with humorous eyes who heard the request and said, "Don't you boys have your own chemists?"

"Clear up in Lansing," Zagreb said. "Two weeks' minimum. An hour'd be better."

"Well, I don't know. There's so many possibilities, and a different test for each. I'm a little rusty. Mostly I just fill little pill bottles from big ones."

"Start with all the common stuff. We're not looking for Fu Manchu."

The man took the bottle and said he'd do what he could. The Four Horsemen stopped at the counter long enough for Canal to gulp down three cups of coffee, then returned to the squad room and waited for the phone to ring.

Burke shook his head. "How do you do it, Zag? You just yank the handle and the pinball does the rest. Dope in the bottle proves Dugan was set up, just like you said."

"Unless he killed the girl first, then doped himself to make it play that way. But the toilet's on the ground floor, so where'd he clean his nails without the manager seeing him?"

McReary said, "I thought that wasn't important."

"He didn't say that," Burke said. "Manager in on it?"

"Or did it himself," Zagreb said, "but why?"

"Same reason as Lungs. He don't mix his whites with his coloreds. He provided the bottle, didn't he?"

Zagreb said, "It was waiting in the room for the next customer. Anyone who knew what they were up to could've snuck in, spiked the booze, and went back out onto the fire escape to wait for it to work. I'm eliminating Dugan again. No motive."

"It wasn't Lungs."

Everyone looked at Canal, whose voice sounded like a motor trying to start. His broad face was pale and shiny: The cure was worse than the condition. "That's too long to be away from the band at Sportree's and still have time to clean up. Somebody would've noticed he'd been in the can a long time."

"Sure, they'd all cover for him," Burke said. "He's their star attraction."

The phone rang. Zagreb took the call, listened, said thanks, and forked the receiver. "Chloral hydrate. Knockout drops. There was enough in the bottle to stun a moose."

"Lucky it was Canal drunk it," Burke said.

The lieutenant remained seated with the candlestick phone in his lap and his hands resting on it. "Who's good for a search warrant?"

Burke said, "You mean a judge we ain't ticked off lately? Blake just got back from Canada. He was gone a month hunting bears."

"Tail, you mean. We gave him a pass on that underage intern last Christmas. Time to collect." Zagreb started dialing.

Canal rubbed his temples. "What we looking for?"

"I'm not just sure, but it'll be nasty."

-

They tossed the Ruby Lounge from top to bottom, starting with the murder room—minus a corpse now—and finishing in the basement, a dusty monument to Prohibition with what was left of a copper still after the last scrap drive, empty Old Log Cabin crates, and buckets of fusel oil. Canal, recovering now, said he could get up a swell victory party from that alone. But nothing they found was evidence in a homicide investigation.

"Can I open up now?" The fat manager blew his nose. The dust they'd stirred up had set all of them sneezing.

"What'd we miss?" Zagreb asked McReary.

The third-grader shrugged and said something, but a grinding of gears and clanging of metal from outside drowned him out.

"Garbage day!" The lieutenant ran for the stairs.

A prehistoric Mack truck was pulling away from the alley behind the building, its chain drive clattering, when they came out. Burke, moving faster than any of the others had ever seen him, lunged after it and leapt onto the running board, pounding on the door with his shield in his fist. The driver braked, almost throwing him off.

By the time they climbed down from the truck bed, the squad was plastered with coffee grounds, potato skins, and sundry other matter best left mysterious; but Zagreb was grinning, holding a long wooden implement in a hand wrapped in a handkerchief.

"What is it?" asked McReary.

Canal was beaming too. "Before your time, rook. We shut this place down the first time in '37 for gambling. That's one of the rakes the dealers used to scrape in the cash." He pointed to the wooden teeth, stained dark and still glistening. "That what I think it is?"

"Griselda Simone's blood type, or it's back to the beat for me," Zagreb said. "And if we're lucky, somebody's prints on the other end."

The fire door to the Ruby Lounge banged shut. The lock snapped. The manager had been standing in the doorway. Zagreb barked at McReary, who launched himself around the building. He came back three minutes later, panting.

"Out the front and who knows where?" he said. "Tub of lard like him, who'da thought he could run like Seabiscuit?"

"Call box on the corner," Zagreb told Canal, who went that way, fishing for his key. The lieutenant smacked the young detective's shoulder. "No sweat, Mac. What's he going to do, join the navy?"

-

When the man from the lab called Zagreb, he sounded put out. "That set of prints you gave me didn't match the ones on the rake."

"They have to belong to the manager. I got them from his file."

"No dice. Latents on the handle were too small. Ten to one they're a woman's."

"I'll get back to you."

He held up a hand, staying the others from asking questions, and started going through desk drawers—that wartime habit of plopping themselves down in front of any old deserted work station was getting to be a pain. Finally he found the picture postcard and peered at it closely. "Your eyes are younger, Mac. What's it say?" He handed it over, pointing at the postmark.

McReary studied it, passed the card back. "St. Clair Shores."

"Caption says San Francisco."

"She was pulling your leg. She stuck it in a mailbox five miles away. Friend of yours?"

"Cops don't have friends." He picked up the receiver again and asked the long-distance operator for the War Department.

-

Shirley Grabowski had been reported AWOL when she failed to report in California for deployment to Alaska. The fingerprints the War Department sent over matched the prints on the handle of the wooden rake that bore Griselda Simone's blood type on the teeth. The information was given to state police throughout the Great Lakes region and the FBI.

Chester "Lungs" Nelson was brought in, and when Lieutenant Zagreb effectively told him everything that had happened from Lungs's first contact with the WAC, offered no resistance. Disapproving of a "sister" fraternizing with a white man—it had been going on for some time, without Red Lot's notice—he'd brought the affair to Dugan's girlfriend's attention, but swore he'd had nothing to do with the murder. Zagreb was inclined to believe him, especially after Canal had offered to break the trumpeter's jaw in so many places he'd never be able to blow so much as a kazoo. With Shirley still at large, that was where the matter rested until a distant cousin of the fat manager's turned him in to the Toledo Police for failure to pay rent on the use of his couch.

Ohio extradited. The manager, who'd put on more weight while he was shut in, confessed to doping Jerry Dugan's bottle and looking the other way when Shirley Grabowski entered the Ruby and went upstairs. Under what the *News* and the *Times* called "fierce questioning" and the *Free Press* called "the Horsemen's brutal third degree," he insisted that he thought she was planning only to rough up the girl once Dugan was in no condition to prevent her; like Lungs, he hated race-mixing and was interested solely in employing a woman's jealousy toward the solution.

Burke, puffing heavily with his shirtsleeves rolled up to his armpits, said, "What'd you think the rake was for, friendly game of craps?"

"She didn't carry it up. It was in the room. The girl who comes in to clean uses it to hold the door open when she sweeps up. I never even missed it till it showed up in the trash. Why do you think I panicked? The broad went out by the fire escape; she must've ditched it in the can in the alley. I see the body, I'm going to say anything? I already got a record."

-

The story had everything the fact-detective magazines needed to shove Fifth Column spies off the covers. Shirley's picture went up in the post office next to Tokyo Rose's, and Walter Winchell broadcast her description on the radio. When Max Zagreb let himself into his apartment after a night at the Roxy, he'd just seen her face in a newsreel, so when he pulled the chain-switch on the light and saw her sitting in his shabby armchair, he thought at first he was daydreaming.

"Hello, Shirl. How's life on the lam?" He threw his keys on a table.

"Not as glamorous as advertised. A cop ought to have a bobby-pin-proof lock."

"What's a cop got to steal?" He saw she'd traded the trim uniform for a print dress that might have fit her before she lost weight, and her ankles looked thick above shoes with chunky heels. Her shoulder bob needed a good hairdresser and her face was haggard. She'd been right about the military frock; it had given her a kind of beauty she'd never really had.

But then, he was looking at a murderess now. He kept an eye on the handbag she was clutching in her lap.

"Can you see your way clear to fixing me a rickey?" she asked. "I haven't been in a bar in weeks. People get a drink in them and try to collect the bounty. It's up to a thousand now. Be twice as much if I were a man."

"I never saw the sense in that. Women are more dangerous. No Coca-Cola in the icebox, sorry." He took out his flask, seeing her hands flinch on the bag when he went for his pocket.

She hesitated, then pried one loose to accept the flask. As she grasped it, he snatched the bag from her other hand. She made a feeble gesture after it, then relaxed as he undid the clasp and removed a small semiautomatic. "For me?" he said.

"You did a lousy job keeping Jerry out of trouble. But no." She opened the flask, swigged, coughed. "Needs the Coke."

"Be happy with the hospitality. What kind of friend shoots herself in a friend's house? Ever try scrubbing blood and brains out of mohair?"

"I was saving it for later, in case you tried to arrest me. I came to explain. Homely girl thinks she's landed a cute guy—"

"He said you're a knockout."

"I don't believe you, but thanks."

"Nuts to that. He wasn't even happy with you when he said it. Some guys don't like being mothered."

"How about you?"

"I've got a mother. She doesn't like me much. Drink up and let's go downtown." He slid the pistol into his side pocket.

"Whatever happened to old times' sake?"

"You killed a girl, Shirley."

"A woman always blames the other woman, you ought to know that. I'm sorry I did it, though. I didn't plan the—the mutilation, but when I saw that rake—" She shuddered. "Anyway, it wasn't her fault. Who could resist Jerry?" She must have read the answer on his face, because she changed the subject again. "What do you hear from him, by the way?"

"Red Lot gave him the axe. Not for what happened. A better trumpeter got sent home from the Pacific with a hickory leg. Somebody told me Jerry joined the Coast Guard. They're not so particular about heart murmurs. If he's got the brains God gave a cricket he'll throw the horn overboard. As a musician he'll make a swell sailor."

"He isn't Harry James, is he?"

"He isn't even Harry Langdon. And he can't drink. If it weren't for Tojo and Hitler he'd be pumping gas in Garden City."

"What's the song called? 'I'm Looking for a Guy Who Plays Alto and Baritone and Doubles on a Clarinet and Wears a Size 37 Suit'?"

"If Bing didn't sing it, I don't know it."

-

"Manager copped, accessory to assault and battery," Zagreb said, drumming his fingers on the phone in his lap. "They promised him two years, including time tacked on for fleeing and eluding."

"What about Lungs?" McReary asked.

"Nolle prosse. They never had much of a case."

Burke said, "That should make Red Lot happy."

"I doubt it. Lungs put in his notice. USO offered him a tour if he beat the rap. Red already lost his gig at the Ruby. I heard he's taking the band on the road, opening for Jean Goldkette."

A jury rejected Shirley Grabowski's plea of temporary insanity, based on the planning involved: the doped whiskey, the arrangement with the manager, the phony postcard to establish an alibi. Judge James Tolliver Blake sentenced her to life in prison, but her lawyer won a bid for appeal.

"Good thing you ditched her when you did," Canal told the lieutenant. "You dodged a bullet in more ways than one."

"Yeah. Cover for me, will you?"

"Sure, Zag. What's up?"

"Social call."

Zagreb greeted Shirley in the women's facility at the Detroit House of Corrections, where she'd been moved pending a new trial. The matron, whose husband had deserted her for a cigarette girl in the Wolverine Lounge, had pulled strings to get her a jail uniform that fit. In it, she was, Max Zagreb admitted to himself ruefully, a dish.

THE Elevator Man

"God help Omar Bradley when that bunch ships out."

The Elevator Man

John Barrymore had shed blood at the California Hotel.

Then again, maybe not. After destroyers and DeSotos, lurid legends were Detroit's major export.

If the story was true—and an old report at Receiving Hospital of the release of one "Jack Smith" with minor facial lacerations and twenty-three stitches in his right arm was one point in its favor—he was the only guest of his stature ever registered there.

Naming the hotel for the home of Hollywood had failed to attract the glamorous horde the original owner had counted on. When Mary Pickford or Buster Keaton came to town, they had generally stopped at the Pontchartrain, or accepted the hospitality of one of the auto pioneers in Grosse Pointe.

Barrymore may have holed up in the California to elude private detectives hired by his wife. A woman named Ruby LaFlor was booked for soliciting there the same night (rumor had it) the star of *Don Juan* drank too much and walked through the Art Deco glass door of the shower in his suite; but if the events were connected, the publicity value was doubtful.

In any case, that was twenty years in the past. If anyone could shed light on the affair it was Hank, the elevator operator. The hotel staff insisted that the men who'd built the shaft in 1915 had taken his measurements before making the car.

Dan McReary wasn't curious enough to ask Hank, because their average conversation ran four seconds and varied not at all:

"How's it going, old-timer?"

"Good as can be expected, punk."

These exchanges always left the detective third-grade feeling privileged. As far as he knew, the gaunt old man never opened his mouth in the presence of any other member of the Racket Squad. He sat stone-faced on his low stool with his gaze straight ahead and his fist on the lever, wearing what was likely the same brass-buttoned tunic and pillbox hat that had been issued under Woodrow Wilson. From year to year nothing changed, except the length of hair growing out of one of his big pendulous ears and his license in its frame on the elevator wall, renewed on the same day annually.

"What about it, Sarge?" McReary asked once. "Ever get a rise out of old Hank?"

Sergeant Canal worked his cigar, a lonely channel marker bobbing in the sea of his big Slavic face. "I got a grunt out of him when I gave him a portable radio last Christmas. I figured he'd want to keep up on the war, but I never saw it again. Probably sold it on the black market. Now I think about it, it might've been just a burp."

"Maybe he doesn't like to be reminded. Maybe he lost a grandson or somebody overseas."

"His *great*-grandson'd be too old even for the Civil Defense. I think he ran Lincoln up to his box at Ford's Theater."

"You know that doesn't make sense."

Officer Burke, the biggest man on the detail when Canal wasn't around, chuckled from the bed he was stretched out on in shirtsleeves and stocking feet. "Canal never would've made citizen if he didn't take the test next to a smart Mexican."

"I was born here, you Irish S.O.B. Some of us got birth certificates."

"What's it say next to *Father*? 'Player to be named later'?"

Canal shrugged and took out his resentment later on a suspect in a rape.

The California strained a budget already drawn thin by absent department personnel, scattered from Guadalcanal to the Black Forest. The skeleton crew left behind to maintain order patched up the cigarette burns in its uniforms and cannibalized junkyards to keep official cars rolling. Automobile manufacturers were too busy building warplanes and submarines to replace the aging vehicles on the road.

But Sergeant Canal, detectives Burke and McReary, and Max Zagreb, their lieutenant, considered the expense necessary. Cases broke more efficiently without meddling from the brass at 1300 Beaubien, police headquarters. When requisitions were slow, they pooled their paychecks to make rent.

"This time when the bean-counters come through, let's add room service," Burke said. "I'm sick of running out for liquor."

McReary poured a cup of chicory from the pot. "Of all the gall. *I'm* the one does the running. The clerk in the store on the corner thinks I'm a soak, and I never touch the hard stuff."

"Boo. And while I'm at it, hoo. Go cry in your Orange Crush."

"Keep your shirt on, Mac," Zagreb said. "We'll split up the errands, soon as you make a collar on your own."

"How am I supposed to do that, when we're all stuck together at the hip like Siamese quadruplets?"

They were the Four Horsemen in the press. The pro-administration *Detroit News* used the term in the heroic sense, while the reform-conscious *Free Press* thought it appropriate to a quartet of barbarians. Hearst's *Times* straddled the fence. The *Herald*, a radical sheet, pushed for a clean sweep from the mayor on down to the city pound. Commissioner Witherspoon was waiting for a consensus before deciding whether to disband the squad. The fate of the four's draft exemptions rested on the outcome.

"Although God help Omar Bradley when that bunch ships out," Witherspoon confided to his cronies at the Athletic Club.

McReary didn't pursue the Hank subject, and eventually forgot about the discussion. As the youngest Horseman with the least seniority, he had his hands full fetching and carrying for the others when he wasn't contributing to their impressive arrest record. When not much was happening in Europe and the Pacific, they sometimes managed to open for World War II in newsreels.

It was the elevator man himself who stirred his memory.

One day—it was around Thanksgiving, McReary recalled later, because Perry Como was still singing about autumn leaves, but the department stores were already filling up with electric trains and monkey-fur coats—the car came to a sudden stop between floors, with a shudder and a clankity-clank that sounded like a severed cable flapping free: JUNIOR DETECTIVE DIES IN FREAK FALL was the headline that flashed to mind.

But the elevator didn't drop. Hank let go of the lever, which was pushed all the way around to STOP. He looked at his passenger with a glint of life in his matte-finish black eyes.

"Near wet yourself there, young feller. Five floors ain't nothing to old Betsy. Her sister took fifteen in Frisco in ought-six and they put 'er right back on the line with a fresh coat of paint. Not that the six folks that died appreciated it."

"You were in the quake?"

"No, I missed that one. But us lift-jockeys know all the stories. I could curl your hair."

McReary lifted his hat to show his young bald head.

A bony shoulder lifted and fell, but the material of his uniform stayed shrugged. "Think what you save on Brilliantine. I wanted a minute of your time. Betsy's slow, but she ain't that slow. The poor schnook you're working over upstairs won't notice you're late."

"You got the wrong idea, old-timer. That kind of police work went out with bathtub gin."

"Says you. I can fetch you a jug in ten minutes. I seen them jitterbugs go up full of vinegar and come back down two hours later spittin' blood. You can't pull the wool over these eyes, nor get out of me what they seen. A good elevator man is like a priest, only without the dog Latin."

It was more words than he'd heard the old man speak since before Pearl Harbor. "So what's the scoop?" McReary asked. "Selling raffle tickets on a turkey?"

"You mean a pigeon bloated up with water. Government drafted all the turkeys and sent 'em overseas in cans. I'm offering you a cut of a million."

"What would I do with a million turkeys? There ain't enough cranberry sauce in the country."

"Simoleons, you fresh punk. Maybe you can't use it. Maybe you already got a million stashed in the box that twenty-dollar suit came in."

"Eighteen-fifty, from J.L. Hudson's basement. And it came in a paper bag." He pointed at Hank's uniform. "I guess that's gold under the green on those buttons."

"I didn't say I had it. I know where I can get it, but I need help. I don't trust them monkeys you work with. You got an honest face. What you doing Sunday?"

"Taking my mother to church."

"See what I mean? Good boy. Swing by my dump after you eat her fried chicken. Beer's on me." He gave McReary an address on Gratiot and started the elevator back up.

-

"A million, no kidding?" Lieutenant Zagreb lit a Chesterfield and grinned, tilting it toward the squad room ceiling. McReary had gone there when his boss didn't show up at the California.

"I know it's a joke, L.T. I want to hear the punch line, but somebody should know where I am Sunday in case I don't check in. I can handle the old guy, but if he's shilling for somebody with a gripe against the squad"—his smile was uncertain—"anyway, if I told Canal or Burke I'd get the horselaugh. You're the only one don't treat me like Andy Hardy."

"Swell, Mac. Ring me at my place around six. I'll be polishing off a can of string beans. You don't call by quarter after, I'll send in the marines."

"On the level, what's he up to?"

Zagreb scratched the fine sandy hair on his big brainy head. "Probably wants to sell you some swampland in Florida. The Ambassador Bridge is already spoken for."

"As long as it's jake with you we talk."

"Just don't drag the squad into it. All the commish needs is one good excuse to put us all on a troop ship."

-

The apartment was a sawed-off shotgun flat on the third floor of a building Buffalo Bill and the Wild West had paraded past in 1883: one long narrow barely furnished room with a Murphy bed and in the kitchen area an icebox and a hotplate. Hank, nearly unrecognizable in a worn twill shirt, baggy slacks, and suspenders, his white top-thatch exposed, pried the caps off two bottles of Pabst Blue Ribbon and sat down opposite his guest at a folding card table. "Salt?"

McReary looked at the shaker, said no. It wouldn't improve a beverage that tasted to him like propeller wash. The old man shook some salt down the neck of his bottle and swirled it around. "How was church?"

"Long. How do we split up the million?"

"Hold your horses, son. I don't get no company. Let's chew the fat a little."

The detective saw he was in for it, drank beer, sighed. "So tell me about Barrymore."

Hank grinned, swigged, belched. "Hell, that wasn't Barrymore. It was John Gilbert. He was on a cross-country bender after Garbo ditched him at the altar. Ancient history for a sprout like you."

"I'm not as young as everybody thinks. Gilbert washed out when talkies came in, didn't he? Squeaky voice."

"So they say. I ain't been to a picture show since Rin Tin Tin was on the tit. How come you ain't in uniform, strapping boy like you?"

He adjusted to the subject change. "I made detective."

"I mean in the war."

"I'm fighting it right here. Essential service."

"Don't get sore. Me, I'm a pacifist. I done my bit in Cuba, seen the elephant, and spit it out. Voted for Debs twice because I believed him when he said he'd keep us out of the last one. But I knew Roosevelt was a liar. When he said if he was re-elected no American boy would die on foreign soil, I knew we'd be in this one up to our hips inside a year. That's when I stopped paying taxes."

"You haven't paid taxes in two years?"

"They padlocked my house. Why else would I put up in a rat hole like this? That's what I wanted to talk to you about."

McReary sat back cradling his bottle in his lap. "I can't help you, old-timer. That's federal. I can barely fix a parking ticket."

"I know that. I don't care about the house. They can have it, leaky pipes and all. It's what's *in* it I care about."

He hesitated with bottle raised, then thumped it down, rose, and unscrewed the lid from a sugar canister on the counter next to the hotplate. McReary, who was familiar with the Midwestern custom of salting one's beer, wondered if his host was going to sweeten it as well. But the canister was stuffed with paper. Hank rustled among them, found what he wanted, and sat back down, spreading the item between them on the table.

His guest didn't touch the paper. It was about the size of a typewriter sheet, yellow and dog-eared, and tattered at the seams where it had been folded in quarters. It was bordered in filigree, and the bold print near the top was faded but still legible:

THE HENRY FORD MOTOR COMPANY

McReary smiled. "Congratulations. You own a share of Ford stock." The old man had delusions of grandeur.

"We'll come to that. I bought it from Henry himself back in ought-one. It was in the bar of the Russell House, a hotel you never heard of on account of they tore it down before your old man was born. Henry didn't drink, but he had a glass of mineral water to celebrate starting up. How we got to talking I don't remember; one Henry to another, maybe. Times was friendlier then, you struck up acquaintances with strangers. Also I was drunk.

"Celebrating too, you see. My pa had died, miserable man, and I'd sold the fambly farm for a nice piece of change. I wound up buying a thousand shares."

"A thousand—?" McReary set his beer next to the old man's.

Hank, lost in the past, didn't appear to notice. "Don't think I didn't kick myself when I sobered up. I tried to stop payment on the check, but it was already cashed.

"Well, time passed, and I didn't hear anything more about Ford Motors. Not for seven years, till he come up with the Model T. The rest I guess you know. He's the richest man in the world now, and I reckon I'm the richest you're likely to share a beer with."

"I told you I'm not as green as you think. That's no Cadillac you're driving up and down the California."

"You're a smart young feller, I seen that right off; keep your mouth shut while them apes you work with are jabbering. Soak everything in. See, I had a steady job by then, working the elevator at the old Pontchartrain, which was where that auto crowd hung out in their hunnert-dollar suits, puffing two-bit cigars. Smelled like burning money. That wasn't for me. I was married, had a boy. Figured I'd sit on them shares and have something to leave him with to remember his old pa when I was six feet under."

Hank sighed rackingly, pain showing in the faded old eyes. "Life don't always work out the way you planned. Little Hank grew up to be a philanderer. Run out on his wife and baby boy in 1920 for a cooch dancer he met at the Vanity. The wife and the boy went to live with her folks in Indiana. I never laid eyes on either one of them again. The Ponch got tore down, so I moved to the California, and that's the story on me.

"Except," he added, leaning forward with his arthritic hands wrapped around the bottle; and McReary leaned forward also. "I kept sitting on that Ford stock. It'd got to be a habit, you see, like old Scrooge counting his bucks and never spending a cent. I was a widower by then—influenza took my Maggie in nineteen—and there was nobody left to please by throwing in with the idle rich. Fred, that poor little boy whose pa deserted him, was going to get a nice surprise come his twenty-fifth birthday."

McReary picked up his bottle then and drank a slug without thinking. He choked and coughed.

But the old man was still in his world. He sighed again, subsiding in his chair, and the sound was like all the bereaved of wartime America, Europe, and Asia moaning in concert. His face collapsed into a thicket of wrinkles. He looked as old as Canal and Burke thought he was.

"I got the telegram first of this month. I never knew my daughter-in-law cared that much, but I guess under the circumstances she had to keep busy somehow. Fred bought it at Midway. Japanese torpedo caught his destroyer amidship. All hands lost."

"Hank, I'm sorry."

The elevator man rubbed his eyes, looked at his hand, showed it to his guest.

"Pipe that. I'm all dried up like a squoze-out lemon. I never got to know the boy. It's the idea of him I miss. Like saving up for a shiny new bike in a store window and then you find out it's sold. What the hell. I might as well be rich. What else I got?"

"You don't need me to cash in your stock." McReary thought, nodded. "Oh. That's what's locked up in your house."

"Only reason I had this one certificate is I carried it around for luck. But I ain't had none lately." He folded the certificate and put it in his shirt pocket. “The feds are too busy stopping Fifth Column counterfeiters from busting the value of the dollar to follow up on foreclosures. They just stuck a padlock on the door without taking inventory. You and me are the only ones know what's inside.”

“A million seems steep even for a thousand shares in Ford.”

“Not too steep for the man in charge. Years ago he near went broke buying back every share he could find so he wouldn't be beholden to a soul. When he finds out there's a piece of his company he don't own, he'll pay a dollar for a dime's worth to snap it up. They don't call him Crazy Henry just for laughs.”

“What are you going to do, break in?”

“Not me. Too old. You are.”

-

After he left the apartment, McReary used his call-box key and got Zagreb on the line. He heard Jack Benny on a radio playing in the background. The lieutenant asked if he could borrow a couple of hundred thousand till payday. McReary chuckled, but it sounded hollow. “No can do, Zag, sorry.”

“What was the deal?”

“The old guy wanted me to go in with him on the Irish Sweepstakes. He thought it was a sure thing if we bought fifty tickets.”

“Bet he figured he was the first one had that idea.”

“Anyway, the beer was free.”

There was a brief pause, then the radio got quieter. “Why so glum, chum? Don't tell me you thought there was anything to it.”

“No. Some people just have some funny notions about cops.”

“Comes with the badge. See you tomorrow, kid.”

Driving his cranky Model A home, the young detective felt a little bad about the way he'd turned down Hank's proposition. He was still sore he'd been expected to commit burglary, for a cut of a million or a bus token, and risk a federal rap to boot; but the old man's expression, and the pleading way he asked McReary not to tell anyone about their conversation, made him feel sorry for the lonely old soul.

He'd keep silent. It was a bonehead plan anyway, and nothing would come of it.

The next day, and every workday into the new year of 1943, not a word passed between elevator operator and passenger. McReary stopped pitying him. The way Hank seemed to see it, behaving like an honest cop had made him as bad as the rest.

But things changed besides the weather.

At Christmas, McReary's mother burst her appendix and spent six weeks recovering in Detroit Receiving Hospital. The third week of January, his favorite cousin wired him from Toledo for money to bail out her husband, who'd been medically discharged from the army after a jeep accident during basic training and now did all his fighting on a timber leg in gin mills. McReary's savings dwindled. In the mail with the hospital bill came a letter from a government auditor telling him he owed taxes and penalties on undeclared income he'd earned moonlighting as an usher at the Broadway-Capitol Theater.

The Bureau of Internal Revenue, he thought. *How poetic.* He stewed for a week, then went to the California Hotel when the Four Horsemen had no business there and rang for the elevator.

-

"What you do," Hank said, handing him a beer in the apartment on Gratiot, "you use bolt cutters on the padlock. After you come out, you replace it with one from the hardware store. One Yale looks like all the others."

McReary shook his head. "They'd smell a rat the minute their key didn't work, and guess who they'd suspect first? If we're going to do this, it has to be in such a way they never know it happened.

If police work has taught me anything, it's how to slip the latch on a window."

"I didn't know cops and crooks thought so much alike."

"You would if you talked to one once in a while. The guys I work with are the best in the business. If they knew what I was up to, they'd have me busted down to civilian. Maybe not Burke; but he wouldn't snitch an apple off a pushcart."

"What changed your mind? Last time you was here I offered you a fifty-fifty split of a million smackers and you acted like I spit in your face."

"I found out life's a crock. If your grandson joined the army instead of the navy, wrecked a jeep instead of ate a torpedo, you and I never would've got past the elevator." He smiled. "Too deep? Try this: I don't want half. Just enough to put me back in the black."

The old man's mouth fell open. Then his jaw clenched. "That's just dumb. It's my property. I'd rather divvy it up with you than let Uncle Sam blow it on a private train for some fat general."

"That's the deal, Hank. Otherwise no dice."

"Damnedest haggling session I ever heard of. See what I mean about war? It fouls up everything."

They clinked bottles.

-

Dan McReary's first venture into crime was anticlimactic. He'd gotten more thrills during the drive over, swerving around a squirrel.

They went there in broad daylight; it was a working neighborhood on the southwest side, the risk of witnesses at home minimal, and poking around with a flashlight after dark would have invited attention. The house was old enough to have stood outside the original city limits along with a silo and barn—both long gone—and needed everything, from shingles to paint to new windowsills. The government notice tacked to the front door glared white against the discolored wood.

He left Hank in the Model A, to blow the horn if he saw trouble coming, and went around back, where thirty seconds' work with his pocketknife freed a latch from rotted wood. The window stuck, but he put his back into it and raised it far enough to crawl inside.

The place smelled of shut-up house and *eau de* old coot. He found the suitcase where it was supposed to be, shoved back in a bedroom closet hung with stale clothing, heaved it onto a single bed whose springs rocked and creaked, unbuckled the shabby leather straps, and opened it to look at the stacks of stock certificates inside, each bound with a brittle-looking rubber band. Then he fastened it back up and when he was satisfied no one was watching the window he pushed the suitcase through it and followed it out. Resettling the latch and brushing away the yellow wood exposed by his pocketknife took just a little longer than working it loose in the first place.

Hank was standing outside the roadster when he got back and put the suitcase in the rumble seat. The old man looked nervous enough for both of them. "Check it?"

"Sure I checked it. Get in. Patrol's not due for ten minutes on this street, but those beat cops don't always go by their watches." He slid under the wheel, turned the key, and pressed the starter. The loose lifters knocked.

"Any problems?"

McReary sneezed. "Just the dust on my hay fever." He blew his nose and steered away from the curb. "I know less about petty thieves than I did before. I can't see what the shouting's about."

"You call this petty?"

"That's just it. If stealing a million don't give you a charge, why snatch a purse?"

In front of the apartment house he got out to carry the case upstairs, but Hank beat him to it. He hauled it out of the seat and stood on the sidewalk holding it with both hands. "Come on up and I'll give you your cut."

"I'll wait for the cash. *Two* people showing up with shares to sell after all this time would be just begging for attention; the wrong kind."

"Ain't you afraid I'll duck out on you?"

McReary grinned and opened the door on the driver's side. "I'm a detective. Don't you think I could track down the only millionaire elevator operator in the world?"

-

That night he thought he'd dream about being out of debt.

He didn't dream. He didn't even sleep.

At 3:00 A.M. he gave up, brewed a pot of ersatz coffee, and listened to a nasal-voiced radio announcer make guesses about what FDR and Churchill were discussing in Casablanca. There wasn't enough caffeine in a carload of the wartime stuff to keep him awake, but when he tried again later all he did was tangle the sheets. At half-past five he dressed and went to 1300.

Lieutenant Zagreb was already in the squad room, as he knew he would be, chain-smoking Chesterfields and going over the blotter from the night desk. Zag was a professional insomniac who lived on work. McReary hoped to keep his amateur status, which was why he'd decided to talk to his superior.

The leader of the Horsemen pushed his hat back from his bulbous forehead. "You're up with the roosters or still out with the tomcats," he said. "Those steamer trunks under your eyes could go either way."

"I couldn't sleep, L.T. I don't know how you stand it."

"The krauts bombed London fifty-seven days and fifty-seven nights. Anybody can get used to anything. Pour yourself a slug from the pot. It's the McCoy. Bought it off the black market."

"Aren't we supposed to be breaking up the black market?"

"And we never fail. All the more reason to snap up the inventory while it's still available."

He got the coffee and pulled a chair up to the lieutenant's desk. He sipped, but the real thing was wasted on him this morning. Now that he had Zagreb all to himself, he was more reluctant than ever to confide in him. These might be the last friendly moments they ever shared. But the others would be showing up before long, so he started.

-

Zagreb heard him out without interruption. He watched the loudspeaker the whole time and his eyes never blinked. Burke and Canal were fond of saying that that basilisk stare had broken more alibis than all the rubber hoses in the city. When McReary finished, he dealt himself a cigarette and slid the pack toward the detective.

"I don't smoke. You know that."

"Looks like I don't know you at all. Jesus. Yank Uncle Sam's whiskers in the middle of a goddamn war? You *want* to be gang-raped by a better class of con than we got in the state pen?"

"I could be wrong, but I think I'm in the clear with the feds. Not with me, though. Should I turn myself in?"

"That would make the sex consensual."

"You want the collar? It'd draw some of the fire from the squad."

"I'm short-handed enough as it is. You've seen what I got to draw from."

"I stumbled, L.T. I disgraced the shield." He took out his badge folder and put it on the desk.

"I told you I'm low on manpower. You've seen what I got to draw from."

"Any one of 'em would be better than me."

"Pick that up before it scratches the finish." Zagreb extinguished his cigarette in a burn crater. "You think you're the only cop ever stepped off the curb?"

"I'm the first in this outfit."

"Don't be so stuck on yourself. When I was on Vice I ate oysters every night on the Hotel LaSalle. Everybody was doing it. That's why a grand jury got convened. I drew thirty day's suspension without pay, but it was just oysters. The brass with cash were arrested or canned or both. Canal was driving a prowl car, but he got caught up in the same net for delivering policy slips on his beat. He spent six months putting blisters on his feet in Paradise Valley. Burke—oh, hell, what *hasn't* Burke done?"

"You're making this up."

"I had that kind of imagination, I'd be on the radio. The *point* is, we got it out of our systems. I wouldn't play poker with either one of them for big stakes, but when we bust up a brawl in a gin joint I'd rather have them at my back than the Pacific fleet. You, too—if you got this out of your system."

McReary blinked; one of them had to. "Yes, sir! Swear on my mother's life."

"Better not, till she gets the roses back in her cheeks. And call me Zag, or Lieutenant, or L.T., or 'Hey, you, jackass,' but don't call me sir. I work for a living."

"Yes, si-Zag."

"Now pick up that piece of tin before I donate it to a scrap drive."

He scooped up the folder and put it in his pocket. Zagreb smiled for the first time in the meeting.

"I'll say this: You're the only one of us who kicked over the traces for a cut of a million. What's Ford stock look like?"

He described it.

The lieutenant's lids flickered then. "'The Henry Ford Motor Company,' that's what it said? Not 'Ford Motor Company?'"

"I'm sure it was Henry Ford, his whole name."

"When did you say he bought the shares?"

"He said nineteen oh-one. Why?"

Zagreb laughed. The sound of it and the sight of his red face startled McReary. He'd heard his boss chuckle, snicker, let out a 'ha-ha' when someone got off a good one, but this was as close to losing control as the detective had ever witnessed. Canal and Burke came in just as it was winding down.

"Let us in on it, Zag." Canal took the slimy cigar stub out of his mouth. "We ain't heard a Pat-and-Mike story worth repeating in weeks."

The lieutenant wiped his eyes with his handkerchief. "Just a history lesson, boys. Henry Ford finally hit pay dirt in nineteen oh-eight when he built the Model T. Most people don't know he failed the first time. If you own stock issued in nineteen oh-one by The Henry Ford Motor Company, you couldn't buy a stick of gum."

"Lucky I didn't buy any." Canal put back his cigar.

The floor dropped out of McReary's stomach. He'd broken the law, violated his oath, put his job and his freedom on the line, for a suitcase full of junk.

He heard someone else laughing then. It was himself. He couldn't have held it back with both hands.

Burke said, "Stop trying to butter up the boss. It ain't that funny. What's the palaver about, anyway, we're left out? Zag don't care about cars and you ain't interested in history."

McReary caught his breath. "I was hitting up the lieutenant for an advance. I'm busted flat."

Canal grinned. "Yeah, I can see how a fella can get a boot out of that."

-

The next time the Four Horsemen gathered at the California, the detective could tell right away Hank had gotten the news, probably straight from Ford, the company if not the man. His expression was more sour than usual and his grip on the lever would strangle a rhinoceros. When their gazes met, he saw that Hank saw that he knew too.

"How's it going, old-timer?" McReary asked.

"Good as can be expected, punk." The elevator started up.

Sitting

— DUCKS —

"Some guys can sure hold a grudge."

Sitting Ducks

The bomb went off when Officer Burke stepped on the starter button in the Chrysler. He was alone in the car.

The dynamite was old, or had gotten wet, or hadn't been any good to begin with, wartime conditions being what they were, so the only casualties were the hood, the window it broke on the third floor of 1300 Beaubien, Detroit Police Headquarters, and a brief but severe case of tinnitus on Burke's part. His ears were still ringing when he and the rest of the Racket Squad banged the hood back into shape and re-hinged it. Chrysler wouldn't be making any replacement parts for the duration.

"Everybody knows you hate that car," Lieutenant Zagreb told Burke. "Next time you blow it up, remember to get out first."

Detective Third-Grade McReary almost bought it when he parked his Model A and started across Grand Boulevard to the Fisher Theater, where his date was waiting for him in the mezzanine. He was holding his ticket, and when the wind tore it out of his hand and sent it skidding down the street he chased it. The bullet whizzed over his head when he ducked to scoop up the ticket, and smacked Rita Hayworth square between the eyes on the cover of *Life* in the newsstand in front of General Motors.

"Worst part is I missed *Watch on the Rhine*," McReary said.

Sergeant Canal said, "Serves you right for being too cheap to tip the valet."

A Lafayette Coney Island hot dog intended for Lieutenant Zagreb had ketchup on it instead of mustard. He gave it to Canal, who hadn't ordered anything but ate it anyway, got sick, and had a gram of arsenic pumped out of his stomach at Receiving Hospital, along with the hot dog, a gallon of Coca-Cola, a loaf of bread, and most of a ham.

"No wonder it didn't finish you," said Burke. "Two hundred and fifty pounds, and half of it was breakfast."

Zagreb didn't laugh. "Somebody slugged the delivery boy from behind, tied him up in an alley, and hijacked our order. The Four-F dopes downstairs didn't look at the face under the paper hat. Let's go pay our respects to Frankie."

Canal, still a little green after his release, left his cigar unlit. "It ain't Orr's kind of play. Einstein he ain't, but he's smart enough not to try to rub out a cop."

"Let's go anyway. I'm getting flabby. I need to get out and play some handball."

But the genuine English butler in the racketeer's suite in the Book-Cadillac Hotel told them his employer was in Florida, pursuing marlin aboard George Raft's boat.

They frisked the place. Canal flung open the closet doors and nodded. "Yep, his yellow gabardine's missing. That's his fishing outfit."

Burke checked the big sedan for suspicious wires and they got in. "Where to now?" He rested his hairy hands on the wheel.

"I'd say Miami, but the commissioner won't spring for the tickets, especially when there's a chance this punk won't ball it up next time," Zagreb said. "He's been wanting to clear out the squad room for years and put in a pool table. I was Frankie, Florida's where I'd be when it's open season on us."

Canal tossed his masticated cigar out the window and replaced it with a fresh one. "I still don't buy it. Anyway, maybe it ain't just us. Maybe some Four-F sicko got a ticket for parking in a red zone and has it in for all cops."

"He'd start with some flatfoot in Stationary Traffic. So far it's just us. Why don't let's—"

"Hit the dirt!" shouted McReary.

A truck a story and a half high—a Great War veteran, from the clanking of the chain drive—bore down on them, thundering on the wrong side of Michigan.

There was no time to bail. McReary was already on the floor of the back seat. Canal threw himself on top of the third-grader, cracking two ribs, and Burke and Zagreb slumped down below the dash. The collision, a sound effect from a front-line newsreel, crushed the Chrysler's radiator up against the block, sprang the hood yet again, and shoved the sedan back six feet—with Burke's size-fourteen foot pressing the brake pedal to the firewall—into and over a motorcycle parked behind it, turning it into a bucket of spare parts.

-

FOURTH ATTEMPT ON "HORSEMEN"! trumpeted the *News*, with the subhead "Gallant Racket Squad Suffers Injuries in Hit-and-Run Assassination Try."

The *Times* was less certain: QUESTION WHETHER CRASH WAS DELIBERATE OR ACCIDENT.

The anti-administration *Free Press* ran an editorial pointing out that the incident took place in front of gangster Francis Oro's hotel and speculated that the price of graft had grown too steep to pay.

Zagreb, looking like a country preacher in his cervical collar (whiplash), said, "Actually, it was a run-and-hit. Whoever stole that truck took a powder once he got it aimed."

Young McReary, nursing his fractured ribs, said, "*That's* what you picked to squawk about? We're crooks in the *Free Press*."

"We're sitting ducks in the *Times*." Burke had his bandaged foot propped on a swivel chair belonging to a homicide dick currently serving in the Philippines; he'd sprained a ligament. "I don't know which is worse."

Canal was the only member of the famed Four Horsemen who'd emerged without a scratch. McReary had broken his fall, and he maintained a few inches of protective blubber around a frame of thick dense bone and slabbed muscle. "What's 'gallant' mean, anyway? They calling us swishes?"

"Naw, it's one of them words out of books, with pitchers of palookas riding nags dressed up in tin cans." Burke winced. "Jesus, Sarge, pick up that phone, willya? You're the sole survivor of this blitz."

"It ain't ringing, Burksie. That's what you get for not blowing up when you was supposed to."

"Quit riding him," Zagreb said, reaching for the instrument, which was ringing. "We're all chumps here."

The mostly empty squad room reeked of aspirin and Ben-Gay. If the military hadn't left the department short-handed, they'd all be out on medical leave. Canal still couldn't hold down more than half a roast.

The lieutenant hung up. "Car's ready, soon as the paint dries. They don't make 'em like that anymore."

"They don't make 'em anymore, period," Canal reminded him.

Burke said nuts. "I figured totaling that rolling junkyard was the one good thing to come out of this."

Zagreb slid a Chesterfield between his lips, but he couldn't spin the wheel on his Zippo on account of a pinched nerve. He flipped the lighter onto the airman's desk he was using at the moment. "We need to nail this guy. I'm tired of getting sniped at and never getting dead."

"He distracts easy, that we know," said McReary. "Won't try the same thing twice."

Burke said, "Who says he's a *he*? Maybe he's a dame."

Canal asked Burke if he'd talked to his wife lately.

"Uh-uh. We only talk during sex. The phone bill was murder."

"It better not be a dame," Zagreb said. "If she gets lucky and clips one of us and it comes out she's a skirt, we'll lose the *News and* the *Times*."

Canal lit his cigar and blew a cloud of smoke thick enough to bale. "You're starting to sound like the commish. I never heard you give a fig what the rags got to say."

"Right now they're the only thing keeping us in civvies. If they all turn on us, he'll stamp one-A on our foreheads faster than you can say General Patton. Which is what he's been wanting to do right along."

"It ain't a doll," said Canal. "They can't work the clutch on a truck."

"Tell that to Rosie the Riveter." Zagreb stood, tore off the collar, and threw it in a corner. "I'd sooner have the pain in the neck. Let's go down to Records and find out who can drive a rig, shoot a gun, lay hands on poison, and wire a bomb."

"That'd be Wallace Beery, Sergeant York, Lucrezia Borgia, and the Industrial Workers of the World." McReary started to chuckle, then remembered his ribs.

-

The uniform who brought out the stack of mug books was a fat Prohibition beat cop who'd been pulled out of retirement, hearing aid and all, to help fill the hole in personnel. The Four Horsemen sat at the big scarred yellow-oak table and went through the albums of sullen faces like civilians. "I ain't seen so many ugly pans since I washed dishes in Greektown," Canal said. "I think half of these guys is Lon Chaney."

"The wolf man?" McReary asked.

"His father. Just how wet behind the ears *are* you?"

"Young enough to run around an ape like you six times while you're pulling your pants out of your crack."

"Can it, both of you," Zagreb said. "The jerk we're after don't need the help."

"How about Flick Morency?" Burke planted a finger on a flat face in the book he had open. "He fired sharpshooter in France in eighteen. That slug we dug out of the newsstand could've come from a Browning."

"No dice," Canal said. "Flick's doing a dime in Jackson for attempted murder."

"Maybe he crashed out. I seen Bogie do it in a laundry truck in *San Quentin*."

The sergeant shook his big casserole-shaped head. "More like a hearse. Flick was in the infirmary last I heard: terminal cancer."

"How much he serve?"

"Six years."

"Welsher."

Zagreb said, "Here's Ragtime Charlie Potts. Drove a garbage truck, did some hijacking on the side."

"Right up until he ran a hot Diamond Reo into a telephone pole last year on Washington," said Burke. "You remember that, Zag."

"Oh, yeah. Ruptured the gas tank. You could see the flames in Windsor. I need a change of pace. All these lugs are starting to look alike."

Canal said, "We been too hard on our eyeball witnesses. Next time I'll buy 'em a Schlitz."

McReary tapped a dark-skinned party with a shiny shaven head. "What's the scoop on this Mail Train Jefferson, numbers runner on the lam from slipping cyanide into his wife's Orange Julius? Who comes up with these names, Dick Tracy?"

Zagreb said, "Contest editor at the *Times*. Winner gets a toaster. Mail Train's not our man. He couldn't hit the Penobscot Building with a rifle. Also he's colorblind."

"What's being colorblind got to do with the price of eggs?"

"Red and green wires," Canal said. "You mix 'em up building a bomb, the coroner picks you up with a sponge."

"How come you know so much about him, L.T.?"

"I caught him before he could burn his numbers slips when I was with Vice. He did a two-year bit as a habitual offender."

Other candidates were suggested and rejected. After two hours, Burke got up to stretch his legs, circling the room on crutches.

"This is nuts. One guy can make a ten-ton truck stand up and dance a jitterbug, but nobody's ever seen him with a gun, he can't get poison, and he's scared to light a gas stove, never mind monkey with dynamite. Another mug can pick a freckle off a gnat's nose at a hundred yards with anything that loads and fires, but he don't know how to drive and can't spell arsenic, let alone lay hands on it. Mail Train left the Negro football league to run numbers and work as an orderly in the hospital, where a bunch of poison went missing just about the time he gave his wife a permanent mickey and disappeared like Mandrake the Magician, but as to explosives and shooting he's strictly from hunger. This is worse than fifty-one-card poker."

Zagreb rubbed his sore neck. "All these guys did time. We'll pull their prison records, see if they all shared the same cellmate at one point, pooled information."

"I got a better idea."

They all looked at McReary, standing by an open window to duck the atmosphere of Chesterfields, Skoal, and Dutch Masters. He was the junior member of the squad, the kid they sent out for coffee; his idea of an idea was bringing donuts. "Spill," Zagreb said.

"They've got more in common than stir. We're the ones put 'em in. L.T., you busted Mail Train, who poisoned his wife. You're the one who was supposed to eat a loaded hot dog. Burke, you popped Manny 'Boom-Boom' Schultz for possession of explosive devices and booked him a bed in the criminal ward in the loony bin in Ypsi; he's the Mad Bomber of Madison Heights, though you couldn't make that stick. That charge in the Chrysler had your name on it. Jimmy Ray Floyd wasn't in town long enough to pick up a colorful moniker. I nabbed him red-handed drawing a bead on a horse belonging to the Mounted Division when I was in uniform, and good thing, because he was all-state skeet-shooting champ in Kentucky. I spared that nag a bullet, and that runaway ticket spared me another last week. I got a twenty-dollar war bond says they're all back in circulation."

"You forgot me," Canal said. "I didn't know any of them birds. And you left out that truck driver."

"No, I didn't. It was our stakeout, all of us as a squad, put Charlie Potts in a cage up in Marquette for hijacking a load of black market sugar back in forty-two."

Burke sat down, hoisted his foot onto the table. "You weren't listening, kid. Ragtime Charlie barbecued himself when he hit that telephone pole."

"How do we know it was him if he's barbecue?"

"His glass eye didn't burn," Burke said. "One of his fellow brats poked him with a pencil in sixth grade."

"A lot of guys got glass eyes since Pearl Harbor."

Silence settled like a blanket of snow.

Zagreb broke it. "It's too screwy not to make sense. Four men. A squad. Once they're in cuffs we should sue 'em for stealing our act."

-

They were stumped at first for a connection that would hold up in court.

All four were ex-convicts, but they hadn't all been in the same pen at the same time. Worse, neither Emmanuel Schultz—"Boom-Boom" to the press—and neither Charles nor "Ragtime Charlie" Potts ever served in Jackson, and both Marquette and the Ypsilanti State Mental Hospital were unfamiliar territory to Jimmy Ray Floyd and Oscar "Mail Train" Jefferson, who'd fed his wife Mirabelle a lethal dose of cyanide when she taunted him one too many times for getting himself cut from the Motor City Mambas football team.

Then Lieutenant Max Zagreb remembered the Erskine Street Social Club.

It was a blind pig owned and operated by an ex-con named Pop Doheny, catering exclusively to felons on parole, who were prohibited by the terms of their release from patronizing establishments where liquor was served or fraternizing with other convicted criminals. Since the dive was unlicensed anyway, the risks were no worse than even, and the Detroit Police Department left it alone as long as disturbances were kept to a minimum (cue sticks and fists, okay; guns, knives, and broken bottles, not so much); allowing it to remain open provided a convenient place to start looking for fugitives. If the four had ever made contact, that would be a likely spot.

And it was dark enough in the corners for a cop whose face was known to his quarry to set up a stakeout.

Burke's lame foot rendered him useless for tail work, and Canal made too big a black hole to overlook, so Zagreb and McReary took turns nursing beers in the gloom, with the others sitting in the Chrysler outside under a streetlamp that had been burned out since before the war. With air-raid drills taking place every few nights, there wasn't any hurry to replace the bulb.

McReary got lucky at the end of the first week.

He'd committed all the mug shots to memory, and carried copies just in case, but even career criminals rarely resemble photos taken under the bright institutional lights they shunned from habit. Chance timing alone placed him on post the night Jimmy Ray Floyd, the sharpshooter he'd arrested personally, swaggered in, threw a leg over a barstool, and ordered Kentucky rye.

The detective third-grade leaned forward when the bartender, pouring, lowered his head and moved his lips close to Jimmy Ray's ear. Floyd nodded, sat back in a nonchalant pose, then downed his whiskey in one jerk, threw a coin on the bar, and left. McReary abandoned his beer untasted and followed.

He gave the high sign to Canal—spelling the injured Burke behind the wheel—and the sedan crept alongside the curb, headlights extinguished. When Jimmy Ray folded his long lanky form into a 1939 Studebaker Champion, McReary swung open the Chrysler's rear door and got in beside Burke. It was a crisp night, but all the windows were open to dispel the smell of fresh paint.

Canal gave the Studebaker two blocks before switching on the lights.

"Probably meeting some broad," Burke said. "You can only count on luck so far."

"So we brace him and take him back to the California for the full-body treatment," Zagreb said.

"That gin-slinger too," said McReary. "He's the one gave him the message."

Canal grunted. "Bartender? I'd as soon try to crack a coconut with a feather duster."

"Doesn't mean we can't try."

"Stick to being the idea man," said Zagreb. "Leave the heavy lifting to the gorillas."

Burke said, "I resemble that remark."

Jimmy Ray made a left onto East Jefferson Avenue, then swung right onto Riopelle, a street of square block and brick buildings with gridded windows reflecting the moonlight in flat sheets, no illumination inside. Canal followed, dousing the lights.

"Cripes, I love the warehouse district," he said. "Rats big as chimps and every once in a while a body in a burlap sack."

The street ended at the river, where the choppy surface broke the moon into a school of silver minnows. Jimmy Ray left his car by the curb and entered a warehouse, sidling around a rusty barricade made of heavy-gauge steel designed to look like chicken wire. It had been peeled back at one corner as if with a can opener. McReary reached for his door handle.

"Not yet," Zagreb said. "We'll give him a couple minutes to settle in."

"Give us the slip, you mean."

"In peacetime I'd say yeah. Cars are too hard to come by to let one go to the impound."

"What if he boosted it?"

Canal snorted. "Who'd steal a no-nuts machine like that? It's only got six cylinders."

"Sergeant, go on past and swing around at the end, pointing back toward town. I don't like dead ends."

"Yes, sir." The Chrysler edged around the parked car.

"It's a trap!" Burke's voice was hoarse. He was looking through the rear window at a tall tractor cab turning into the street from an alley, towing a flatbed trailer stacked high with wooden crates lashed down with cable. Moonlight struck the white lettering on the door:

CONWAY DEMOLITION

"It's a rolling bomb." The lieutenant's tone was eerily calm. "Pile out, and draw your pieces."

The sedan was still rocking to a stop when all four doors swung wide and they assumed trained positions: McReary and Burke crouching behind the specially installed steel door panels, revolvers aimed through the open windows, wrists braced on the sills; Zagreb and Canal standing, gun arms braced atop the front doors. The truck swung the rest of the way into the street, gears grinding, the engine winding up into the cry of a big cat, headlights blinding, one set of wheels up on the right-hand curb to clear the Studebaker parked on the other side. The driver's-side door popped open.

"Let 'em have it!"

The echo of Zagreb's order was lost in the roar of heavy calibers. One of the truck's headlights went dark, the windshield collapsed in big jagged sheets, puckered holes appeared in the side of the open door. The driver assumed the shape of a bulky shadow against the dim glow of streetlamps on the Jefferson end of the street, one foot on the running board, one hand on the wheel. He leapt free—directly into a grouped ball of four leaden slugs that catapulted him backward and sent him rolling and bouncing down the pavement, just like McReary's theater ticket.

-

But the truck was still coming, weaving from side to side with no one steering and the irregularities in the curb and pavement twisting its wheels this way and that. The Four Horsemen dove for the sidewalks on both sides; Burke delivered an extended and impressive medley of high-pitched curses when his bad foot struck the curb and he fell headlong across crumbling concrete. McReary saw Canal fling himself across Zagreb, thinking, *The son of a bitch is using himself for a shield, just like last time.*

Not that anyone or anything could protect any of them once that truck slammed into something solid and its load went off.

-

Then the left front tire struck a lopsided cube of old cement, a satellite broken off from the curb, and turned, its mate on the right side turning with it. The cab hopped all the way up onto the sidewalk, scraped a fender along the brick building on that side, showering a rooster tail of sparks. Canal and Zagreb scrambled to their feet and out of the truck's path.

For one agonizing instant, the flatbed trailer swung the other direction, snapping like a whip toward the Studebaker, its explosive cargo shuddering in its webwork of cables; McReary squeezed his eyes shut and, comically, stuck his fingers in his ears, his department piece dangling by its trigger guard from the right index.

He heard only the thunder of the truck's motor, the continued screaming of metal against brick.

When he opened his eyes, the trailer had shifted back the other way, obediently following the cab in a straight line along the sidewalk.

McReary, Zagreb, and Canal stood, turning to follow the retreating truck with their eyes. Burke, seated on the curb with his legs splayed in front of him, propped himself up higher to watch. The iron guardrail at the end of the street crumpled like tinfoil. The truck bent in the middle, the cab rolling over the sandbags piled to hold back the Detroit River when it rose; then the cab disappeared, the view blocked by the trailer and its load. Then that, too, vanished.

A second passed, disguised as a week. Then the splash.

It was as loud as everything else connected with the truck, and the wave it made rose stories tall, its top curling white, the hollow of water beneath glittering like a Christmas tree, reflecting every light in the city. It kept curling forward, taking a bow, then struck the street with a nasty splat that soaked the Four Horsemen from hat to heels.

-

They reasoned later the four thugs had drawn straws. Jimmy Ray Floyd was the bait, Ragtime Charlie Potts the hammer. Whether the others were even present remained a mystery. The survivors weren't talking.

"We weren't the only ones figured the Erskine was the place to stake out," Zagreb said. "As crooks went, they weren't any smarter than the usual run, but four half-wits make two decent noggins."

The border guards on the Canadian side of the Ambassador Bridge, alerted by radio by the U.S. guards, stopped Jimmy Ray driving a stolen Hudson coupe, the day after the bomb squad rescued fifty cases of water-logged dynamite from the river, each stick capped by an expert.

Ragtime Charlie Potts, resurrected from the dead thanks to a case of mistaken identity, stayed there this time, with a hole in his chest the size of a softball and a crushed skull when he landed on the street.

Canal said, "Seems he just walked right into the lot at Conway Demolition, found a load ready to go, and drove out the front gate. Stopped just long enough to sign the bill of lading with a name belonging to a driver who was out with the sniffles. We'll sweat those out of him in the California Hotel."

Zagreb said, "What would we hold him on? Taking a fin to call in sick?"

The Department of the Army did Detroit the favor of turning over Manny Schultz, the putative Mad Bomber of Madison Heights, after he tried enlisting in Springfield, Ohio, under a fictitious name and his fingerprints were checked in Washington.

"I hear he asked for a mine detail," McReary said.

Mail Train Jefferson, long sought by the FBI for interstate flight to avoid prosecution, didn't make it out of Michigan this time. Responding to complaints of an offensive odor by guests in a residential hotel in Dearborn, the desk clerk found him in his bed, dead about a week. The coroner discovered enough arsenic in his system to ground the Luftwaffe.

"That's that." Zagreb hung up the telephone. "Some guys can sure hold a grudge. You'd think they'd find something better to do with a war on."

Canal said, "Maybe they knitted socks for the troops when they wasn't trying to put us on ice."

"Who cares? My neck's feeling better. How about you, Mac?"

"Tape came off yesterday. Took my first deep breath in two weeks." He looked at Canal, striking a match off the seat of his pants. "I saw what you did, you know."

The big sergeant hoisted his bushy brows, lighting a cigar. "What's that, little-bit?"

"Down by the river. Just like the last time, only then it was me safe under a tub of lard."

"Bushwah. I can't help it if guys keep getting in the way when I'm saving my skin."

"My foot's killing me," Burke said. "Sprained it all over again when I tripped on the city of Detroit. Thanks for asking."

Zagreb played with a Chesterfield. "Forget it, Officer. Mac's the man of the hour. That was straight thinking there in Records, figuring out it was four instead of one. You ought to think about becoming a detective."

"Go boil your head," said McReary. "Sir."

TIN Cop

"If they don't want guys threatening to jump off buildings, why do they put ledges on 'em in the first place?"

Tin Cop

"Well, hello, there, Officer O'Shea. Long time no see."

McReary looked around, but whoever Burke had addressed was nowhere in sight. "Mac" was slimy with sweat, his shirtsleeves rolled, and his hands black as a stove. As the junior member of the Detroit Racket Squad, he'd been tagged with cleaning the basement storage room at 1300, Detroit Police Headquarters, along with the big detective, who was being punished for failure to feed the coffee kitty: "We're supposed to *pay* for that ersatz swill?" had been his defense. "I thought somebody followed the Mounted Division around with a shovel."

"You'll wish you had one soon enough," Lieutenant Zagreb had said. "The last annual spring cleaning was in nineteen thirty-nine." It was 1944.

The handsome Italianate architecture ended at ground level. Beneath was a concrete enclosure as big as an underground parking garage, with a steel post every few yards, sweaty concrete walls, and piles of broken and discarded police equipment in the storage room. Not so long ago it had been a dungeon, where Burke said reluctant suspects were "given the Ameche."

"What's that?"

"Well, you know Don Ameche played Alexander Graham Bell. What you do, you get an old-fashioned crank telephone, clip the wires to their nipples, and every time you don't like the answer to a question, you give the crank a turn. It's like putting their nips in a light bulb socket: like the sixty-four-dollar question, only the prize is you don't scream and wet your drawers. But somebody beefed, so now it's just a root cellar without the roots."

There were mountains of broken chairs, shards of blackboard slate, parts of moldy uniforms, piles of bulletproof vests—the old-fashioned kind with steel plates sewed inside quilts made of wire mesh—cartons of ancient arrest reports chewed up by mice and deposited here and there in confetti balled into nests, leaky coffee-pots, a couple of crank telephones (McReary hadn't really bought that story until he came upon these), bales of *Police Gazettes*, assorted girlie magazines, sawed-off shotgun barrels, silhouette targets with holes punched in them, a forty-six-star American flag, and crates of tear-gas canisters, among other detritus made unidentifiable by age and decay.

"Mind them rusty canisters," Burke said. "Drop one, we both get off this detail double-quick, except we won't enjoy the personal time."

Carefully, McReary started stacking the crates. "What about rats?"

"You got something against unrationed meat?"

"This is uniform work. Why don't they get someone in a blue bag?"

"Most of 'em are too busy cleaning out machine-gun nests on the Siegfried Line. What's left is out pounding the beat. Gripe less, work more. I don't want to spend Christmas down here any more than you."

A few minutes later was when Burke greeted the invisible Officer O'Shea.

"I'll bite," McReary said finally. "Who is he, and how long's he been holding his breath under all this crap?"

Burke stooped, grunted, and tipped something up from the slab floor. McReary looked at the cutout image of a cartoon policeman with a bulbous nose and a crooked Killarney grin, wearing an old-fashioned harness uniform topped by a peaked cap. It was two inches thick, as wide as a pair of cops standing shoulder to shoulder, and judging by the sound of the big man's exertions as heavy as lead. There were two rectangular holes where the eyes belonged.

"Looks like a lot of scrap iron for a Halloween decoration. What is it?"

"It's from before I came on the job. The old-timers were still talking about it then. The department had it run up by the drop-forge team at the Ford plant. It was supposed to give cover when the riot squad charged Bolsheviks and anarchists forted up somewhere back around twenty, but it was only used once, when Baboon Magoon knocked over the Motor City Savings and Loan solo and somebody tripped the alarm. He got off three before they cut him down." Reaching around the edge, Burke pointed out three deep circular dents where a flesh-and-blood cop's heart would be. "Boiler plate."

McReary stepped over a case of empty Old Log Cabin bottles and behind the big metal slab, which Burke was holding upright by an iron handle riveted to the back, which was blank. He saw then it was mounted on casters.

"It should've been donated," McReary said. "It'd be a lot more useful as part of a Sherman tank."

"Oh, you never know. Imagine going to a Nazi Bund rally in Grand Circus Park and laying eyes on this thing trundling your way pushed by two cops with Tommy guns." The big detective rolled it forward, then back, the hard rubber wheels squeaking. "A little oil and Officer O'Shea's ready to report for duty."

"Why O'Shea?"

"First name's Rick."

"Oh. Ha-ha. Wheel it over to that pile we set aside for the scrap drive."

"Damn shame. He should be decorated, a wound like that."

"What's the matter, too tuckered?"

"Take my place, you fresh kid. Feel how it was to be the city's finest before we wound up rousting Four-F troublemakers out of the beer gardens downtown."

McReary took hold of the handle, which was big enough for two hands. When Burke let go, it almost fell on top of the smaller detective. He was lining his eyes up with the holes in the iron head when a gun barked, an explosion in the enclosed quarters, followed by a *spang* and a blow he felt in his hands on the handle. He craned his neck to see around the effigy. Burke had a sheepish look on his face and his .38 revolver in his hand.

"What the *hell*!"

"Accident. I was shooting at one of them rats you're so concerned about."

"You calling me a rat?"

"He came running along the bottom of the wall. I missed." Turning, Burke pointed at a chip in the concrete near the floor. McReary looked from it to the fresh dent in Officer O'Shea's painted tunic.

McReary let go. The slab of iron hit the floor with a crash and the younger detective tackled Burke, knocking the gun out of his grasp and carrying him down onto a pile of trash. They gouged and bit and rolled.

A shrill whistle ended the wrestling match. They separated and looked at Lieutenant Max Zagreb standing on the stairs. He took his fingers from his mouth and scowled.

"If you girls are through dancing, we got us a situation downtown."

-

"He's been up there since noon, his boss says." Zagreb handed Burke his binoculars.

The detective focused on the forty-sixth floor of the Penobscot Building, the highest but one in a skyscraper towering over the rest of the city with the blinking light of a radio tower on top. The man standing on the ledge was in his shirtsleeves, his necktie snapping like a pennant in the wind. He looked to be in his thirties. A square semiautomatic pistol dangled from his right hand. At street level, barricades manned by officers in uniform kept a crowd clear of the block.

Burke passed the binoculars to McReary. "Who'd he shoot?"

"Nobody, yet. Name's Kenneth Spills, cooks the books for an outfit that makes paper for General Eisenhower to doodle on while he's chasing Hitler. His wife left him this morning."

"Who, Eisenhower's?" McReary offered the binoculars to Sergeant Canal, the fourth member of the Racket Squad and the biggest, Burke included. He shook his enormous head; he'd seen everything already.

"Spills's, dummy," Canal said. "When his boss tried to stop him from climbing out the window, he pulled a rod on him. Says he'll shoot anybody who tries to keep him from jumping."

Burke said, "I don't get it. If they don't want guys threatening to jump off buildings, why do they put ledges on 'em in the first place?"

"What's our end?" McReary asked. "This should be the uniform division's baby."

"Commissioner says us. All us Home Fronters have to pull together." Zagreb took back his binoculars. "Any ideas?"

Canal shifted his cigar from one side of his mouth to the other. "We got a deer rifle in the trunk. I can pick him off from here."

"Any ideas that don't stick us with a murder rap?"

"Don't the fire department usually show up with a net for this kind of deal?" Burke asked.

"They're using it in Redford," the lieutenant said. "Some punk got turned down for enlistment and set fire to an apartment house to register his disappointment. We could rush him, but that might startle him into a swan dive. I don't care about that so much, but he might plug one of us before he does. Be nice to talk him inside, though. Make the department look good and get the commish off our backs for a while."

Canal said, "Hell, if we was any good at that we'd be with the diplomatic corps. Where's the shrink? Get him to say why he hates his mother and wipe his nose when he steps back in."

"The one we had's doing that for the navy. He got Admiral Halsey to admit he wet the bed and that's how we won at Midway." Zagreb touched his lighter to a Chesterfield. The wind blew out the flame and he threw the cigarette into the gutter. "We need to come up with something before—"

"—Kenneth spills," Canal finished.

McReary said, "I just had a thought."

Burke grinned. "How'd that feel?"

"You want to finish what we started?"

"Say when, rook."

"One war at a time, boys," Zagreb said. "What you got, Mac?"

McReary told him.

"We still got that? I thought we gave it to the government."

"If we did, I wouldn't be standing here." The detective third-grade glared at Burke.

"It's only half an idea. What's to keep him from taking a brodie?"

"I said it was a thought, not a brainstorm."

"Oh, looky," Canal said.

A black Packard squished to a stop at the end of the block. Police Commissioner Witherspoon, a sphincter with eyeglasses, got out on the passenger's side, stepped around the barricades, glanced up at the man on the ledge, and jerked his chin at the lieutenant.

"What's the situation?" he demanded when Zagreb joined him.

"Same as when we found it, sir. That's not a gargoyle up there."

"Don't be insubordinate! What's your plan?"

"I was just discussing it with Detective McReary."

"Care to let me in on it?"

"Mac?"

McReary joined them. Witherspoon heard him out. His sour look curdled further. "A splendid solution, if it were your job to save your own skins. Meanwhile we're stuck with a bookkeeper waiting for the DPW to scrape him off Griswold Street."

A fourth party appeared, wearing a press card in his hatband. He had a broad, humorous face and gin blossoms on his ample nose. "Van Croker, Commissioner: the *News*."

"I know damn well who you are, Croker. Those barricades are as much for the press as the citizenry."

"I'm a citizen too."

"Excuse me, sir," Zagreb said. "I'll handle it."

"By all means. I'll send a man up to ask Mr. Spills to stay put while you *handle* things."

Zagreb and Croker stepped out of earshot. "How'd you get past Sergeant Dix?"

"I had a little help from Alexander Hamilton."

"He's raised his prices. His wife must be expecting another kid."

"What's the scuttlebutt, Lieutenant? Stock market crash again?" Croker jerked a thumb at the top of the skyscraper.

"Trouble at home. He's got a roscoe."

"Use it on the old lady, did he?"

"Be easier on all of us if he did." Zagreb started to say something else, then fell silent. "Huh."

"Can I quote you?" The reporter waited.

"Van, we still jake with your editorial board?"

"Touch-and-go. Right now they're inclined to let the current administration stay in office for another month or two. Why?"

"You still got that airplane gizmo?"

"Autogyro. We put it in mothballs after FDR declared war

on the world. Gasoline's blood, according to the OPA. So's shoe leather, but it's all we have now to scoop the *Times* and *Free Press*."

"Can it be broke out?"

"I'm the one supposed to ask the questions."

"What if I said I might wangle the *News* a *T* sticker?"

"That's for truckers; unlimited fuel. You dating Eleanor Roosevelt?"

"I can't promise it. Rockbottom, whatever pops, the Racket Squad calls the *News* first."

"Starting now?"

"Starting now. How much does that whirligig hold?"

"One pound past four hundred and it won't leave the ground."

"That lets out Canal and Burke, counting the pilot." Zagreb caught McReary's eye. He came over.

"Thanks, L.T. Witherspoon's worse company than usual."

"He was born three drinks behind. What do you weigh stripped, about one-sixty?"

The detective hesitated. "Why do I think I won't like where this conversation's headed?"

-

They loaded Officer O'Shea into a paddy wagon, and Burke and Canal rolled him into the Penobscot through the delivery entrance. The elevator operator, one legged and draft exempt, gave the iron effigy a curious glance on the way up.

"He's fresh from the academy," Canal explained. "We're short-handed."

-

"Of all the harebrained notions," Witherspoon said. "Zagreb, I wash my hands. When it blows up in your face it won't be me carrying a duffel up the gangplank of a Liberty ship. Who invited this man?" He glared at Van Croker.

"Some mick," Zagreb said. "Bill O'Rights."

"Here comes Buck Rogers." Croker nudged his photographer, who loaded a plate into his Speed Graphic.

The aircraft swept in low over the skyline, a weird sail-winged craft built of balsa and canvas with rotor blades whirling atop the fuselage, sounding like the love child of an air corps glider and a Waring blender. The crowd outside the barricades made the appropriate noises of spectators at a fireworks exhibition; no one there had seen the contraption since the days of Prohibition and Depression, when Croker and his colleagues had outmaneuvered every other paper in town covering gang shootings, labor strikes, and breadlines around the block. Every head turned when it climbed and made a wide graceful loop into the wind flapping Kenneth Spills's hair and necktie. The would-be suicide lifted his chin, his weapon, too, following the autogyro with the muzzle.

"Lieutenant, if he shoots down a member of the press—"

Zagreb interrupted the commissioner. "Not to mention one of the Four Horsemen."

"That name is not sanctioned by this department! A Racket Squad with a fancy *nom de guerre* is still a bevy of thugs with shields."

Croker asked if he could quote him.

Witherspoon's face took on a deeper shade of apoplexy. "It's off the record! I warn you, First Amendment or not—"

"Tom, get a shot of the commissioner. I'm going to ask the chief to run it in color. I think it's what Sylvia's got in mind to paint the kitchen."

The photographer lifted his bulky camera and exploded the flash in Witherspoon's face.

That official blinked, tore off his spectacles, rubbed his eyes. "If you run that, I'll yank your credentials!"

"Put it on the wire, Tom. There's a credit line in it for you in *Time*."

Grinning, the man stashed the exposed plate in one of his voluminous pockets, replaced it, and plugged in a fresh bulb. “Not the Pulitzer, though. That’s coming.” He aimed the lens at the aircraft, which was circling perilously close to the radio tower.

“Keep your shirt on,” Zagreb said. “You ain’t seen nothing yet.”

The sound of a shot reached them, warped by wind and distance. The man on the ledge had fired at the autogyro.

“Not to worry,” said Croker. “Jack Dance emptied a clip at it back in thirty-one, escorting a load of hooch across the bridge from Windsor. That fabric’s dosed with creosote; bullets just skid around it.”

“I’m calling an end to this immediately! Get Spills’s wife here. We’ll put her on a bullhorn and talk him down.”

“Too late,” Zagreb told the commissioner. “Unless you’re politician enough to explain to these good people what *that’s* about.” He pointed.

A fresh whoop from the crowd accompanied the sight of the man emerging from the open door of the flying machine. McReary, the junior member of the Racket Squad, wearing a one-piece flight suit and a leather helmet, perched on the floor of the craft the better part of a minute while it hovered, then stepped out into empty air. The rope attached to his chest harness uncoiled, jerked him up several feet when it came to an end, and dropped him the same distance while he hung on to the harness with both hands.

Zagreb cupped his hands around his mouth and shouted at the top of his lungs. “Hang on, Mac! I’m bumping you up to first-grade!”

“. . . *you*, L.T.!” Half the response was torn away by the wind.

“I didn’t catch that,” Witherspoon said.

Zagreb grinned. “I’ll fill in the blank back at Thirteen Hundred.”

Tom, the photographer, steadied his camera, took a deep breath, and pressed the shutter button. Next day, the picture made every front page in the country, bumping Monte Cassino below the fold.

-

"Police! Freeze!"

Canal and Burke had gone rock-paper-scissors for who'd get to say it; Burke won.

They'd used a passkey, and opened the door slowly to avoid distracting the man standing outside the window with a sudden movement. At Burke's shout, Kenneth Spills wheeled, nearly lost his footing on the ledge, steadied himself, and fired. The slug struck Officer Rick O'Shea square between the eyes, which was too close for Canal's comfort, having drawn the duty of peering through the rectangular holes beneath the tin cop's comical brows. But both men showed remarkable restraint, aiming their weapons around its edges without pulling the triggers.

Spills opened his hand, letting his .45 drop forty-six stories, appeared to brace himself, and fell away from the building.

Square into the arms of Detective Third-Grade McReary, dangling like a baited hook from an aircraft that hadn't had a shakedown flight since before Pearl Harbor.

"Kenneth," he said, "If you had anything heavier than a poached egg for breakfast, I'm going to extradite you from hell in the next life."

Spills struggled, but McReary's grip, increased by fear, was as strong as Patton's Third Army. He succumbed. "No problem, mister," he said. "I haven't seen an egg since Guadalcanal."

-

Kenneth Spills accepted commitment to the Ypsilanti State Mental Hospital, which allowed him to plead guilty to a reduced charge of creating a public disturbance. His impassioned testimony convinced the judge that he never intended to shoot anyone.

"Not counting the crate I was riding," McReary said, when the decision was announced. "What was to stop him from taking a potshot at me when I was hanging there like the tail on a kite?"

Zagreb said, "I put a sniper on top of the Dime Building, if Spills drew a bead. He invalided home after picking off thirty-six of Tojo's monkeys on Guam."

"Been nice if I'd known that when I was up there."

"Quit your bellyaching. You know how hard it is to swing a stateside promotion in wartime? You're getting an extra twenty bucks a month. You can afford to move your dear old ma out of that rat-trap apartment and into one of them houses Henry Ford built for Joe Lunchpail."

"I offered. She turned me down. She named all the rats. They're her pets now."

Burke said, "In that case, I'm glad I missed that one in the basement."

They were sitting in the squad room, occupying chairs belonging to men subsisting on K-rations in Europe and the Pacific. Canal blew the exhaust from one of his worn-out tractor tires out an open window. "What's the commish up to?"

"Tanning his hide in the spotlight," Zagreb said. "He held off a half hour before calling a press conference. I was impressed."

Burke said, "What about Officer O'Shea? He took five slugs in the line of duty. I make that five Purple Hearts, a Distinguished Service Cross, and a by-god Congressional Medal of Honor."

"Close," said Zagreb. "He went to the smelters. This time next week, he'll be on his way to Italy in the prow of a destroyer."

"God help Mussolini." Burke lifted his flask.

KILL Fee

"Just don't throw any pineapples in Detroit, that's all we ask."

Kill Fee

Zagreb snatched up the receiver on the first ring. The Four Horsemen were expecting a search warrant from Judge Springer.

"For you." He held it out to Burke. "Grady from downstairs."

"What's up, Mel? I was catching up on my knuckle-cracking." As the big detective listened, his face grew dark. "Who says he's a friend? Well, let 'im rot. Jesus." He banged down the receiver.

Sergeant Canal, who was bigger yet, skinned the cellophane off a cigar. "Been reading Dale Carnegie?"

"They tanked Asa Organdy for d-and-d. He wants me to bail him out."

"Makes sense." Dan McReary licked and sealed a V-mail envelope. He had a cousin in boot camp at Fort Dix. "Zag and Canal sold him a U-boat sighting in Lake St. Clair, and he never remembers my name. You're the only one hasn't done him a bad turn lately that he knows."

"Drunk-and-disorderly's baby stuff," Lieutenant Zagreb said. "Let's chip in. We can use a friend on the *Herald*."

"That's fifty bucks wasted. His editor hates the mayor worse than Yamamoto. Organdy's been trying to pin something on us since Dunkirk."

"See what he wants. It'll give us something to do while we're waiting for Judge 'Spring 'em' to make up his mind. Pony up, boys. Yesterday was payday and we pulled a double shift, so I know you're still flush. Who can you bank on these days if not the press?"

-

Organdy had written a regular column for the *Detroit Herald* until too many bum steers from Zagreb's Racket Squad busted him down to obituaries. He'd spent eighteen months building himself up to man-on-the-street reporter; although truth be told he conducted most of his interviews in bars and brothels. His drinking history had left lesions on a face that was mostly nose under a hat that was beyond brushing and blocking. He scribbled his name on a receipt for his personal effects, distributed them among his various pockets, and Burke accompanied him from the jail to nearby Greektown, where the journalist ordered a bourbon and branch from the big Macedonian behind the Pegasus bar.

"What about you, Officer?" asked the bartender.

"Draw me a beer. I'm on duty. Put it on my friend's tab."

Organdy scowled, then shrugged. The bartender served their drinks. "You know, we settle up first of every month. That's tomorrow."

"I ever stiff you, Connie?"

"Depends on what you call stiff. Every time a new month comes around, I don't see you till it's half gone."

"Well, the first don't always come on payday." The reporter searched all his pockets, came up with a couple of crumpled bills, a handful of change, half a roll of Tums, and a streetcar token. "Take out what looks like currency and leave the rest."

The Macedonian rang up the sale and sat on a stool on the other end of the bar, snapping open a Greek newspaper.

"Why put the arm on me?" Burke asked Organdy. "No friends on your rag?"

"I got fired yesterday, that's why I went off on a bat. Before that I was four weeks off the sauce."

"That don't answer the question how come me."

"Best way to make a friend is to put yourself in his debt. I'll make good on it, don't you worry."

"I'm not as dumb as that bartender. You didn't show him that fiver you picked up with the rest of your stuff."

"Don't you want to know why I got the sack?"

"I don't guess that Nazi sub in the lake helped."

"Go on, ride me. That's why I went on the wagon. I'd been sober at the time, Zagreb and Canal wouldn't've put it over. I'm giving you boys a pass on that, seeing as how it was me screwed up. I got a warning: One more slip and I might as well enlist and write for *Stars and Stripes*."

"What'd you do, spot Josef Goebbels cutting a rug with Ginger Rogers in the Oriole Terrace?"

"My piece never saw print. My editor shitcanned it and me with it. It was a hundred percent accurate and he threw me out on my ass. No kill fee, no nothing. Just the air."

Burke drank off half his beer, wiped the foam from his stubble. "You spilling military secrets now? I don't mind bending an ordinance or two, but when it comes to treason you can step off that scaffold all on your lonesome."

"Where would I get military secrets? It was human-interest, that's all: a thousand words on a big-time industrialist in Cleveland. Word is he bankrolled the Norden bombsight out of his own pocket."

"What's his moniker, Daddy Warbucks?"

"Abner Elias Smallwood."

"Drink up," Burke said after a moment. "We're going to Thirteen Hundred."

"Whoa! I didn't ask you to get me out of the clink just to wind up at police headquarters."

A pair of handcuffs struck the bar with a bang. "You got three choices: Put 'em on, I put 'em on for you, you come along without 'em. Personally I'd choose number one over number two. When I put 'em on, it takes half a day to feel your fingers after you're sprung."

Organdy tossed back his bourbon. "Number three."

Burke gathered up the cuffs and dropped them in his side pocket. "They always pick three. I should be a pitchman for Lux Flakes."

-

"He's in holding," Burke told Zagreb. "I thought you'd want to talk about how we go at him first."

"I want this bird Smallwood. I wanted him ever since he helped set up that hit on Eddie the Carp last year."

Canal said, "Screw Karpalov. One less cop killer."

"We almost got tagged with that one. To begin with I don't like guys getting set up on our watch and to end with I don't like almost getting stuck with the rap and I don't like guys setting up kills for cash and then walking away like it didn't happen to begin with."

Burke shook his head. "I should've skipped that beer. You got me dizzy enough."

McReary got up from his chair and paced the almost-empty squad room. "Frankie Orr says this Smallwood's a go-between, running errands for jillionaires with procurement big shots in Washington. If he didn't step outside his specialty to peddle Eddie's head for a U.S. marshal, we'd never have heard of him. He's way outside our league."

Zagreb said, "I can't prove it, but I got a pain in my knee says Smallwood arranged for the marshal to go down fighting arrest so he couldn't testify against him. Bunny Belsen knocked a chip off that knee with a .32 when I was on foot patrol. It hurts when it rains or somebody pulls a fast one. I say it's time for some interleague play."

Burke resumed cracking his knuckles. "Let's go down and put Organdy in the batting cage."

They took the elevator down to third-floor Holding, where Burke goggled at the man in the cell, a middle-ager about Organdy's build, but with a flushed face that didn't match his.

The detective buttonholed a man who was too old for active duty and too skinny for his uniform. "Where's the guy I put in here? I left orders not to book him."

"He went home. His wife posted bail."

"His wife ran off three years ago with a sword-swallower with Ringling Brothers." Burke looked again at the man in the cell. "Where'd you get those clothes, buddy?"

-

Zagreb put a five-dollar bill on the commissioner's desk. "Burke saw it in Organdy's hand, torn corner and all. The arresting officers emptied the pockets of the d-and-d in holding, and he was wearing a brown leather jacket and dungarees when they put him in with the newshawk. When Organdy found out the guy's wife was on the way with bail, he greased his palm, switched clothes with him, and walked out with Sherlock here."

"How did they manage it in a room filled with policemen?" Commissioner Witherspoon was looking at the skinny officer.

"It's dark in that cell. Bulb burned out."

"He's right, sir," Zagreb said. "Been that way a year. Replacements are tough to come by on account of the war."

"Good cops, too. You're dismissed, Officer." Witherspoon turned to the Horsemen. "Where is the prisoner now?"

Canal said, "He left with his old lady."

The commissioner's face reddened. It looked like a peach pit wearing glasses. "You let him go after he helped a man break jail?"

"Technically it wasn't a break," Burke said. "Organdy wasn't under arrest. I just parked him there so I could fill the lieutenant in before we questioned him on this Smallwood business."

"I take it he changed his mind."

"He wasn't crazy about the idea to begin with. I didn't exactly give him a choice."

"So on top of embarrassing this department by losing a witness in custody, you've opened it up to a suit for unlawful incarceration."

Zagreb said, "That's a lot to hope for. If he sobered up enough to take a powder, hopping the first freight to anyplace that isn't Detroit or Cleveland would be his next bright thought. Guys like Smallwood don't get rich throwing their money around. He'd sooner invest in a shooter than a press agent."

"APB, sir?" It was McReary's first contribution to the conversation.

"Absolutely not. The less noise we make over this mess, the better. Forget Smallwood, all of you." His scowl got worse. "Lieutenant, I've told you before not to smoke in this office."

"Sorry." Zagreb put his Chesterfield back in the pack. "I wanted to cover the stink. It's the first time I was ordered off a case of murder in our own jurisdiction."

"The Karpalov case is closed. The man responsible was shot to death by the police in Washington, D.C., when he resisted arrest."

"He made a deal with Smallwood to set Karpalov up. He had a personal score to settle and he cashed in his war bonds to meet his fee."

"All you have to base that on is the word of a slimy Ohio attorney and a dead deputy U.S. marshal, a disgrace to his shield. Organdy's editor is right. We've got nothing on the man that will stick, and he's in a position to make things hot for us if we start making accusations without evidence."

-

A young uniform who was expecting his call-up any day intercepted the Four Horsemen on the stairs. He was holding a long envelope. "Messenger brought it from the county building, Lieutenant."

Zagreb opened it, glanced at the contents, and put them and the envelope in an inside pocket. "The warrant from Springer. That one can wait."

"What for?" McReary asked. "A little while ago we were bitching about how long it was taking."

"A little while ago all we cared about was a shipment of black market sardines."

"We're ignoring a direct order from the police commissioner?"

Canal lit Zagreb's cigarette, then his own cigar. "Cheer up, rook. All he can do is sack us. We got to get all the insubordination out of our system before the draft. They shoot you for it over there."

-

The *Detroit Herald* operated out of two floors in the Guardian Building, a brick pile designed in the modern Dutch style on Griswold. The paper's circulation was commonly assigned to Bolsheviks, anarchists, and Republicans, who since war was declared had dropped their subscriptions to avoid showing up on subversive lists, but skulked about the sidewalk newsstands when they thought no one was looking.

The Racket Squad was a favorite target. The publisher and managing editor, Hillary Squant, retired from the National Guard with the rank of major, had a brother-in-law who'd been passed over for commissioner, and a nephew currently serving a three-year sentence in the state penitentiary in Jackson for selling contraband out of the trunk of his car in defense plant parking lots: The headlines covering his arrest in the *News* and *Free Press* had been among the first to feature the Horsemen.

But Squant was a paper tiger who hid behind his fire-breathing columns. In person, he was a meek gnome with a wrinkled bald head and a silver beard and moustache waxed into tridentlike points. He greeted the squad in his glass office, decorated with framed portraits of Horace Greeley, Joseph Pulitzer, and—for reasons known only to him—Walt Disney. He had on a double-breasted vest over a candy-striped shirt with a cutthroat Edwardian collar. "What can I do for you boys?" He raised his voice above the din of typewriters and file drawers in the city room.

The four visitors exchanged glances.

"How about giving us a hinge at that think piece that got Asa Organdy canned?" Zagreb asked.

"I'm surprised he told you about that. It's a tragedy to see a brilliant journalistic career brought low by drink. I destroyed the article. Put it in the incinerator myself."

"That hot to touch, was it?"

"For the future of this journal, yes. If one word of that piece ever got into print, the lawsuit would bankrupt this institution."

Canal said, "I guess all the reliable triggermen are in uniform."

Squant's face darkened. "That's just the kind of reckless statement that obliged me to let Organdy go. I don't know what gin mill he was in when he heard all that guff, or if he just picked the man's name out of the Social Register and decided to whip up a pulp story, but he'd have been better off making up a name and offering it to *Dime Detective*."

"If you read it, you must remember what he wrote," Zagreb said. "That's what we're here for, to horse-trade."

"Why take up my time? If Organdy told you what happened, he can tell you what he wrote."

"We were going to do just that when he took it on the ankles. His landlord hasn't seen him and we called all his favorite bars, which I mean to tell you is a lot of nickels. You wouldn't be hiding him, would you, a material witness in a homicide investigation?"

"Are you implying you believe his cock-and-bull story?"

"The judge did." Zagreb slid the long envelope from his pocket and thumbed out a corner of the warrant signed by the Honorable Vernon Springer.

-

"That's all?" Zagreb asked, when Squant finished talking. "Smallwood bankrolls gambling interests in Detroit?"

"That's what Organdy wrote."

"Horseshit," Burke said. "Smallwood's big-time. What he rakes off wouldn't pay his office expenses."

"One more reason to disregard everything in the article," said the publisher. "I've held up my end of the bargain, Lieutenant. Now put away that warrant."

"Relax, Major. Who cares if you got a drum or two of unrationed gas hid amongst the rolls of newsprint? Nobody—*if* you can name the source of the gambling story."

"I resent the implication." But the publisher chewed on the corners of his moustache. "It must never get back to him who told you. He doesn't come downtown often, but according to the copy filed by my police reporters, he's dangerously unstable."

"You ought to take a crack at a Doc Savage yarn yourself," Burke said. "They fried Pittsburgh Phil last year."

"We don't give up our snitches," said Zagreb.

"A loathsome word." Squant drummed his fingers on the desk, then leaned forward, gesturing to the lieutenant, who leaned forward also. He whispered in his ear.

-

The joint was on Hastings, one of those blank-faced one-story buildings with a flat roof people drove past every day on their way to work and never noticed. That description didn't apply to the man who opened the door. He was bigger than Sergeant Canal, deep brown, with hundreds of stitches crisscrossing his shaven scalp. His head looked like a medicine ball.

The rest of the man was all slabbed muscle under a striped jersey and a pair of overalls. A meat tenderizer dangled from his left hand at his side, a steel hammer with ridges on the striking surface.

"Who wants him?" The voice rumbled like a sunken tramp steamer sliding off a submerged shoal.

"Us." Zagreb flashed his gold shield.

"You can wait." The door thumped into its frame. It was a fire door, brown-painted steel.

Canal reached up, rapped a nearby window, and got a dull ring. "Steel shutters. They ought to donate the place to a scrap drive."

"Not just yet." Zagreb pointed out a ragged line of chips in the building's concrete façade. "Frankie Orr tried to take over the policy business back in thirty-nine; he lost half his guys and decided to lay off. That don't mean he won't try again when the boys are back from the fighting. Every bike messenger and scrubwoman in the Black Bottom plays numbers."

"Lothar there ain't holding 'em off with his toy hammer," Burke said.

"He just softens up the gristle. His boss makes the best chitlins in town, but I wouldn't risk eating 'em after he's just had a run-in with the competition."

Canal said, "If he's such a hot ticket, how come this here's our first visit?"

"Up till now, the only guts he's cooked belonged to hogs and hoods."

"How do we know that ain't still true?"

"We don't, which is why we're here. Also I got a yen for collard greens."

The door opened again and the big man stepped aside, the hammer still hanging from his fist.

Inside, a haze of smoke obscured the details of the room, which took up most of the building. The corners were stacked with stout cartons and what appeared to be party streamers hung from steel trusses overhead. Canal smacked into one of the streamers. It turned out to be a plucked chicken hanging head down, its feet tied with twine. He impugned someone's parentage and wiped his face with a handkerchief.

A voice came from the haze. "Ain't no way to greet a man in his place of bidness."

Zagreb said, "Jesus, Little Bob. You think you might open a window?" His eyes stung and his nose was running from the fried-pepper fumes lacing the smell of hot grease.

"Reuben."

Metal clanked, a hinge squeaked. Gradually the fog of smoke dissipated, drawn into the draft from the open shutters. Little by little, the room identified itself as a vast kitchen, containing a twelve-burner stove, a heavy oaken door with a thick pane of frosted glass, and a white enamel sink big enough to conduct an autopsy. The dead fowl strung up from the beams stirred in the current of air.

"Little Bob. Sergeant Canal and Detectives Burke and McReary. Boys, say hello to Robert Robideux, the Chef Boy-Ar-Dee of the Black Bottom."

"Nuts to that. What I cook would eat right through the can."

The black man stood behind a butcher block bigger than the commissioner's desk, but he still had to bend almost double to flay open the carcass atop it from belly to gullet with one swift motion; the curved blade was as big as a bowie's but looked like a penknife in his grasp. He was nearly as broad as he was tall, all hard fat in a bloodstained apron that could double as a sheet and a straw boater tipped to one side. His face was round, ringed with extra chins, and seemed about to break into a barn-door grin, but never did while the Racket Squad was in his presence.

Canal whistled. "If you're Little Bob, I'm Prince Kong."

"They called me that ever since my daddy was alive. He was Big Nabob to folks that knew him."

Burke said, "I thought I saw the resemblance. I was there when they put Big Nabob into the ground in a piano crate."

"Thass a damn lie. The boys chipped in and had it made special in a furniture factory in Grand Rapids. Solid African hardwood with a pink satin lining, cost thirty grand."

"Not to mention what it set you back to plug all those holes

Frankie Orr put in him," Zagreb said. "Of course, numbers is just Little Bob's hobby now. He supplies every colored restaurant in the state."

"Not just yet. Coupla places in the Thumb ain't got the message yet."

"Just don't throw any pineapples in Detroit, that's all we ask." The lieutenant pointed his chin at the big pile of entrails in the sink. "Anybody we know?"

"Ain't nobody here but us chickens, boss. I'm catering Linus Washington's wedding Saturday. I done all his nuptials since the first. Damn!" The chicken he was gutting stirred suddenly. He strangled it one-handed without laying down the knife. "Thass a shame. She'd of made good breeding stock for cockfights."

McReary excused himself and went out. He came back in a few moments later, just in time to see Reuben pounding the freshly killed hen with his steel hammer. He excused himself again.

"Department's recruiting vegetarians now, I reckon," Little Bob said when he returned, pale as a pillowcase. The big man mopped his bloody hands on his apron. "What can I do for you gents today?"

Zagreb drew the envelope out of his pocket. "Vice is even shorter-handed than we are. This is a warrant to search the joint for gambling paraphernalia."

"Aw, hell. I'm all paid up till the end of the month."

"Next time make sure the cop you give the dough to isn't due to ship out. Where are the slips, Bob? I'd hate to bust up all this fine black market equipment looking for 'em."

"I got a side of pork ready to barbecue. What say I treat you fellas to a feast?"

"Any of you boys hungry?"

Canal said, "I'm on a diet. Doc says I got to shed fifty pounds."

Burke said, "I gave up meat for Lent."

"Mac?"

McReary was still a watery shade of green. "C'mon, L.T."

"I just ate," Zagreb said. "Tell you what: Clue us in on what you told Asa Organdy about a bird named Smallwood, and this warrant got lost in the mail."

"Reuben."

When Medicine Ball turned his way, Little Bob threw him a carcass from the pile. He caught it against his chest.

"Run over to Poletown and deliver that to Mike Kubelski in the Warsaw Market. I accidentally shortchanged him yesterday."

The man pulled a section of butcher wrap off a roller mounted on the drainboard, wrapped the chicken quickly, pulled on a leather bomber jacket, and went out the back door with the package under one arm.

Little Bob slit another carcass. "I don't know if you fellas noticed, but that man Organdy ain't exactly Ernie Pyle when it comes to laying down facts. I never set eyes on Smallwood."

Zagreb said, "You know him, though. We're just looking for a place to start, Bob. Where we got it don't have to leave this kitchen."

"I ain't saying I got anything to hide. My sister's boy Duane's in the navy, and don't he look fine in his whites. I don't mess in no racket that'd deny him what he needs over there."

"Policy slips, then. I pulled your file. You're on parole for that bookmaking operation you ran a couple years back. You don't want to have to finish out your time just when you got this thriving enterprise going. Somehow I don't see Reuben managing it while you're gone."

"Don't let them stitches fool you. He went through a Corsair windshield in forty-one."

"He was a pilot?" McReary said.

"Thass open to debate. It was his first solo landing in training at Tuskegee. He was wasted there. That boy can stun a steer with just his elbow." With a sudden movement, he switched grips on the knife, underhand to overhand, and thrust it point first into the butcher block, sinking it almost to its hilt. His eyes met Zagreb's. "Boss, I tell you what I know about Smallwood, you tear up that warrant and don't come round here six months. Thass the deal."

The lieutenant slid a Chesterfield along his lower lip. "The war could be over in six months, Bob. That's enough time to push over every colored restaurant and numbers parlor in the Midwest."

"I'm too fat for that kind of ambition. All's I axe is time to build my honest bidness without a gang of shirkers in uniform coming round busting it up just for sumpin to do."

"Six weeks."

"Three months."

"Two." Zagreb slid out the envelope and held it between his hands.

Little Bob Robideux tipped his boater. The lieutenant tore the envelope in half.

-

Back on the sidewalk, McReary asked, "What are you going to tell Judge Springer when he asks what became of his warrant?"

"Oh, we'll serve it." Zagreb took it out and held it up, intact. "There wasn't anything in the envelope. I learned how to work a shell game when I was with Vice. I'll miss this piece of paper, though. No telling how much more mileage we might've gotten out of it."

Burke kicked a tire on the Chrysler parked at the curb. "I hope these skins'll hold up to Cleveland and back."

"Who says we're going to Cleveland?" Zagreb asked.

"Big Little Bob just told us he swapped Smallwood half the Detroit numbers territory for half of Cleveland's. Ain't that ammo enough to pump Smallwood?"

"Not coming from a known criminal. Guys like Smallwood don't go to the pictures without consulting a gang of lawyers. You want to spend the rest of the war in court?"

"Brother, I don't want to spend it in Cleveland. Where, then?"

"The California Hotel."

Burke said, "Why? We only go there when we got a suspect to bounce off the walls."

"So let's bounce Asa Organdy."

The World War I–era hotel was just around the corner. Walking there, McReary said, "How do you know he's in the California? We had him on the rails headed out of town."

"Too many people knew he was writing about Smallwood. He's a dumb cluck, but not so dumb he'd let himself be seen at a train station with a target stamped on his forehead. He can't go home, and the law says the hotels have to keep their registrations up to date."

Canal grinned. "The California's last registration book is on display at the Henry Ford Museum, with General Pershing's name on it."

"Organdy knows that. No thug in town would go near the place, and no cop would think to look for him in our own joint."

"No cop except you," McReary said.

"Yeah. I guess when my time comes they'll have to screw me into the ground."

-

The desk clerk wore a rusty morning coat over a gray vest closed with a safety pin and a collar he'd inherited from Calvin Coolidge. He combed his hair away from a widening center part with a spatula.

"You boys never stop at the desk," he said by way of greeting. "Don't tell me you lost your key."

The lieutenant put his hands in his pockets. "Can't a guy say hello to an old friend? How's it going, Quinn? Sniff any girls' bicycle seats lately?"

"Aw, I'm clean six years now. The shrinks cured me up in Jackson."

"How'd you like to go back and visit?"

Quinn's natural pallor increased. He almost faded into the wallpaper. "C'mon, you start with that? When'd I ever steer you boys wrong?"

"You're right. Been a rough day. Where'd you stash Organdy?"

"Who's that?"

Canal reached across the desk and lifted him by his greasy lapels. Zagreb touched his arm.

"My mistake, Sergeant. The *Herald* stopped running his picture when it took away his column, and he wouldn't be using his name. Put him down." When Canal obeyed: "Rat-faced mook, his nose shows up five minutes before the rest of him. Last seen wearing a brown leather jacket and dungarees."

Quinn adjusted his clothes, snatched a key off the pegboard behind him, and smacked it on the desk. "You cops. I didn't have a bad ear I'd be in a submarine instead of here."

"What'd he pay you with?" Zagreb asked.

"He showed me a press card, said he was doing a what-you-call exposé on infractions in the hotel industry, and did I want to be the cover boy?"

The key belonged to room 1002, directly below the one the squad used for interrogation. They took positions on either side of the door, .38s in hand. Zagreb reached over and knocked. "Open up, Asa."

"Go away!" The voice was muffled behind the door. "I got a gun!"

"Put it back in your BVDs and open up. Wash your hands first. You weren't heeled at Thirteen Hundred, you haven't been home, and you gave your last fin to the guy you switched clothes with. Pawnbrokers don't take IOUs, and they don't shake up as easy as hotel clerks."

"Zagreb?"

"Who else? I don't want to shoot the lock off. You'll lose your deposit."

"Who's with you?"

Canal squared off in front of the door and kicked. The door flew open, taking with it part of the frame. "Guess."

Organdy stood in the middle of the room, hands raised to his shoulders, palms forward. "Make yourself at home, fellas. You didn't happen to bring along a bottle, by any chance?"

-

McReary returned carrying a pint of Old Grand-Dad in a paper sack. The others dealt themselves Dixie cups from the bathroom dispenser and drank to the boys overseas.

Zagreb paged through his notepad. "Who gave you all these names?"

"You know I talked to Little Bob." Organdy, sitting up in the bed with ankles crossed in his socks, drained his cup and reached again for the bottle. "I can't give up my sources. I have to work in this town. If you can get 'em all to sign statements, you can tie an anchor around Smallwood's neck and sink him in Lake Erie, and the sooner the better. Once they're public property, I can show my face."

"And get your column back," said the lieutenant. "Even Squant can't argue with these names. All we have to do to round 'em up is stop by the next charity event. Smallwood's still respectable. If we play it right, we'll get one or two of 'em to spill their connections before they find out he's a notorious character. Some of the rest'll cooperate when it comes to racing each other to a plea deal."

Burke said, "It'll take a heap of time. We got to show he's investing his numbers capital in the black market, and getting these square citizens to pony up clearance from Washington so he can lay hold of the merchandise. The grand jury won't adjourn before nineteen fifty."

"Jake with me." Zagreb put away his notebook and patted his pocket. "That's six years we won't be digging foxholes."

Organdy frowned over his Dixie cup. "You fellas realize I got to keep ragging you. We kiss and make up in public, somebody's going to tumble to the fact we're hitched before you're ready to make arrests, and I'll be on my way to the bottom of the river dressed to kill in concrete. What I write won't mean nothing, though. We'll know we're tight."

"Jesus." Canal refilled his own cup. "Asa Organdy and the Horsemen. That's got to be the weirdest partnership since FDR and Stalin."

Recommended Sources

I've been writing about Detroit for more than thirty years, and have amassed several shelves of indispensable books on the city and its history, as well as of history in general. (You'll note I make no reference to the Internet, which is more than sporadically unreliable; and therefore useless for my purposes.) Here are a few that have contributed to the Four Horsemen stories, along with other less stationary venues:

Annis, Sheldon. *Detroit: A Young Guide to the City*. Detroit: Speedball, 1970.

It's terribly outdated now, and its smart-ass approach is just annoying, but I return to it nearly as often as *All Our Yesterdays* (which see), for its rundown of long-established places to visit (many of them gone now) and such rebellious features as "Historical Spots Without Markers," showcasing some local history the Chamber of Commerce would rather forget. In Studs Terkel fashion, "Four Personal Histories of Modern Detroit" allows eyewitnesses to local history to recount what they saw, heard, and felt at pivotal points, in their own words. Ordinary folks don't know what's important and what isn't, so they lay it all out, and thank God for them.

Auto Editors of Consumer Guide. *Cars of the Fascinating '40s: A Decade of Challenges and Changes*. Publications International, 2002.

Not as gee-whiz as the title implies, this handsome coffee-table book delivers sharp full-color and monochrome photos of hundreds of makes and models, vintage advertisements, and a lively, informative text, with an eleven-page photographic spread on the industry's weapons of war. You'll find the Four Horsemen's much-maligned (by Burke) Chrysler Royal on page 8.

Barfknecht, Gary W. *Murder, Michigan*. Davison, Mich.: Friede Publications, 1983.

The "true crime" genre has contributed salacious voyeurism and solid investigative reporting in equal parts. This is one of its high points. The passage of any geographical place from wilderness days to our high-tech age offers its share of sanguinary episodes; the history of Detroit, for all its virtues, is a history of violence. What separates serious scholarship from exploitation is a balanced view of the eras in which atrocities took place.

Beasley, Norman, and Stark, George W. *Made in Detroit*. New York: Putnam's, 1957.

Beasley wrote for the old *Detroit Journal* from 1907–1919, Stark for the *Detroit News* for more than fifty years. They're gone now, of course, but from this enthralling book we get an on-the-scene report of a great population center's coming-of-age, told with objectivity and attention to detail by two no-nonsense professional reporters. (By comparison, today's "electronic journalists" appear to be in the employ of the city council.) The index is compact but utilitarian.

Bingay, Malcolm W. *Detroit Is My Own Home Town.* Indianapolis: Bobbs-Merrill, 1946.

Bingay, a beloved local journalist, was one of those eyewitnesses mentioned earlier, and the publication date of his folksy memoirs promises—and delivers—material on the 1940s local scene still fresh in mind. There's no index, damn it, and chapter titles like "He Fell Into the River" are scarcely helpful in locating specific incidents necessary to my endeavor; but it's the next best thing to listening to an old-timer gas on captivatingly about the past.

Bjorn, Lars, with Jim Gallert. *Before Motown: A History of Jazz in Detroit, 1920–1960.* Ann Arbor: University of Michigan, 2001.

Although I take issue with their title, which suggests that the city's brief love affair with 1960s soul was more significant than its six decades on the jazz scene, Bjorn and Gallert provide invaluable information on the artists, clubs, and theaters that made the Motor City jump throughout its heyday. It's always fun to plop Zagreb, Canal, Burke, and McReary inside one of these smoky, splashy, blaring places and see what develops.

Board of County Auditors. *Manual County of Wayne 1930.* Detroit: (publisher unknown), 1930.

One of my best finds, a sturdy leather-bound volume "compiled with the intent of providing a reliable and authoritative source of information relative to the activities of the county government" (from a letter written by the secretary of the Wayne County Board of Auditors to Chris Wagner, an executive with the legendary Kern's department store; tipped into my copy along with an envelope bearing a two-cent stamp). Depression-era pictures, names of officials, and a breakdown of all branches of the government of the county where Detroit resides, appear nowhere else in this quantity and in this much detail. I return most often to the section on the Coroner's Court Building (better known as the Wayne County Morgue), which is still operating after more than ninety years. The Four Horsemen would have known the place well.

The Book of Knowledge: The Children's Encyclopedia. New York: Grolier, 1963.

I can't speak too highly of this source. My parents bought it for their sons on the installment plan, one volume at a time until we had all twenty. It's aimed toward elementary-school pupils; but anyone who knows children's literature knows the importance of clarity and accuracy. I turn to it as often as Random House's *American College Dictionary*, also a gift from my parents, and found detailed information lacking in every other encyclopedia I've consulted. Detroit alone figures in four volumes, with a concise one-paragraph description of the city in the index.

Box, Rob de la Rive. *The Complete Encyclopedia of Antique Cars*. Edison, NJ: Chartwell, 1998.

I've devoted many years to filling my shelves with automotive books for research, and this is the first that's suited all my requirements. Alphabetical by the names of the manufacturers, then broken down year by model year from the beginning to nearly the close of the twentieth century. Too much of this literature is devoted to foreign makes—pretty pieces of work, but technically inferior to the USA's.

Catton, Bruce. *Michigan: A Bicentennial History*. New York: W.W. Norton, 1976.

Catton, a native Upper Peninsulan whose multiple-volume history of the Civil War is the last word on its subject (sorry, Shelby Foote), accepted a commission to write this breezy, meticulously researched chronicle as part of the States and the Nation Series, and I've found none to equal it. There were no scales on Catton's eyes: He wrote early in the scandalous career of Mayor Coleman A. Young, and had a prescient idea of where Detroit and its state were headed under that kind of leadership.

Collier, Peter, and Horowitz, David. *The Fords: An American Epic*. New York: Simon & Schuster, 1987.

To do this seminal family complete justice would require an encyclopedic study; but this compelling book is as thorough a one-volume history of the American automobile industry as the researcher can hope for. "The Elevator Man" in particular owes much to it, as well as my entire Detroit Series of historical fiction.

Detroit Institute of Arts, 5200 Woodward Avenue, Detroit.

Art and historical treasures from around the globe, classic films, rare documentaries, and an accommodating staff make this world-class museum one of the city's best-kept secrets.

Detroit Public Library Main Branch, 5201 Woodward Avenue, Detroit.

A no-brainer, it would seem; libraries are the human circulatory system of the research world; but I'd place this institution in competition with the best in the world. Its location directly across the street from the Detroit Institute of Arts guarantees a day lost from whatever else you're doing with your life. I've worn a path on the marble floor from the entrance to the microfilm section. The staff is enthusiastic and wonderfully helpful.

Ferry, W. Hawkins. *The Legacy of Albert Kahn*. Detroit: Wayne State University Press, 1970.

Kahn spent fifty years stamping his personal trademark on the city. His soaring, sprawling neoclassical and Art Deco buildings, including the Fisher, the structures that formerly housed the *News* and *Free Press*, the police department, all of the auto factories, and the Ford Willow Run aircraft plant (among scores of others), pay tribute to an era of overweening confidence in America's future. Even in Detroit's present extremity, a stroll downtown among his towering skyscrapers reminds one on a visceral level that it was once great. (Reference books without indexes, like this one, are a pet peeve; but the table of contents is specific and helps make up for that omission.)

Gentry, Curt. *J. Edgar Hoover: The Man and the Secrets*. New York: W.W. Norton, 1991.

Grun, Bernard. *The Timetables of History: A Horizontal Linkage of People and Events*. New York: Simon & Schuster, 1979.

The ultimate quick-flip source, stretching back to ancient times. I only wish the monthly dates were included with the years.

Henrickson, Wilma Wood, editor. *Detroit Perspectives: Crossroads and Turning Points*. Detroit: Wayne State University Press, 1991.

A book completely free of editorial bias, Wood's effort contains contemporary accounts of the city's development from Cadillac's reports upon its founding through its continuing struggle to survive in the last decade of the twentieth century.

Holli, Melvin G., editor. *Detroit*. New York: New Viewpoints, 1976.

Another valuable tour of the city's history, through contemporary essays, retrospectives, maps, and statistics.

Jackson, H.C.L. *It Happened in Detroit*. Detroit: Conjure House, 1947.

As with Bingay, the date says it all on the subject of fresh memory. Also as with Bingay, the nonexistent index and avuncular and unenlightening chapter headings lead to a lot of time lost paging back and forth in pursuit of a particular reference. It's worth the time, intermittently; Jackson, a longtime columnist with the *Detroit News*, certainly knows what he's writing about, but he spends an inordinate amount of ink on mildly amusing nonentities.

Kavieff, Paul R. *The Purple Gang: Organized Crime in Detroit 1910–1945*. New York: Barricade Books, 2000.

What it says it is. Michigan went dry a year before the rest of the nation, by which time the Purples had the bootlegging situation nailed down so tight they could afford to outsource hired killers to Al Capone and points east and west. Ostensibly shattered by grand jury proceedings and a newspaper-fed crackdown, they had clout enough still to run the wartime black market and gambling and narcotics traffic into our own time. Kavieff's local origins gave him unique insight into this homegrown den of thieves and killers.

Kavieff, Paul R. *The Violent Years: Prohibition and the Detroit Mobs*. Fort Lee, NJ: Barricade, 2001.

More sharp reporting from Kavieff. From the Purples through my own Frankie Orr to twenty-first-century drug gangs, organized crime in Detroit owes everything to these Tommy-toting pioneers. To understand them is to combat them.

Langworth, Richard M., and Norbye, Jan P. *The Complete History of General Motors 1908–1986*. Skokie, Ill.: Publications International, 1986.

In additional to providing a year-by-year history of its automobile output, this massive volume includes four densely printed pages on GM's involvement in the industrial defense effort.

Lutz, William W. *The News of Detroit: How a Newspaper and a City Grew Together*. Boston: Little, Brown, 1973.

You can't beat this history presented from the perspective of one of the twentieth century's great newspapers. Here, through a lively text and two substantial pictorial inserts, we get to follow Detroit's passage from the world's leading wagon- and stove-maker to grim Murder City. It reads like a novel—a thriller—and offers luscious anecdotes involving Ty Cobb, Henry Ford, the Purple Gang—and the *News*'s marvelous autogyro, the envy of all its competitors and a star of "Tin Cop."

Maltin, Leonard. *Leonard Maltin's Classic Movie Guide*. London: Penguin, 2005.

When the proliferating Hollywood product created a space problem in his annual *Movie Guide* staple, the remarkable Maltin addressed it by sequestering most of the great classics in a separate volume. I don't always agree with his opinions (I still think *The Philadelphia Story* is vastly overrated; it isn't even funny), but I respect them. He and his staff have blessed us with unimpeachably accurate dates and credits of some 9,000 films produced from the silent period through 1959. With this entertaining and absorbing book at hand, I can state with confidence what might be playing in one of Detroit's motion-picture palaces while the Horsemen are on the prowl.

Mason, Philip P. *Rum Running and the Roaring Twenties: Prohibition on the Michigan-Ontario Waterway*. Detroit: Wayne State University Press, 1995.

This handsome coffee-table book is one of the first to chronicle the importance of Detroit's proximity to Canada circa 1919–1933. If not for historians of Mason's stamp, the world might have gone on thinking that the beer wars were contained to Chicago—a piker, when you consider that Capone got his merchandise by way of the Ambassador Bridge, the Detroit-Windsor Tunnel, and the naval battleground of Lake St. Clair, and imported his hit men from Detroit. The World War II black market benefited beyond measure from the lessons of its Prohibition forefathers.

Meyer, Katharine Mattingly, editor. *Detroit Architecture*. Detroit: Wayne State University Press, 1971.

W. Hawkins Ferry, author of *The Legacy of Albert Kahn*, furnished much of the text as well as an introduction. Thanks to this meticulously laid-out guide (divided into handy geographical sections listed building by building in the index), I'm reminded by photographs exactly what the Book-Cadillac Hotel looks like without a time-consuming visit to the scene, and the addresses, architects' names, and descriptions of the structures are dealt with in pithy captions. The project was sponsored by the American Institute of Architects. I return to it regularly.

McCutcheon, Marc. *The Writer's Guide to Everyday Life from Prohibition through World War II.* Cincinnati: Writer's Digest Books, 1995.

The title says it all. This series is somewhat facile, but when I need to know which ration-stamp designation provided unlimited gasoline, or what a "baby vamp" is, it saves hours of pulling books from my ludicrously huge library on the various eras and slogging through thousands of pages.

Peterson, Joyce Shaw. *American Automobile Workers: 1900–1933.* Albany: State University of New York Press, 1987.

Although it cuts off before the events dramatized in this collection, this concise study of the American labor movement in microcosm has paid back its modest cover price in years of dividends. After all, the Horsemen weren't born full grown at the time of the attack on Pearl Harbor.

Pflieger, Elmer F., Schoen, Frederick Elbert, and John W. Pritchard, editors. *Detroit: A Manual for Citizens.* Detroit: Board of Education, 1968.

This school textbook lays out all the city's departments of government, including the police, as they existed at time of publication, and had since before the 1940s. Much has changed in the interval, but it still speaks to those interested in the decades at issue.

Powers, Tom. *Michigan in Quotes.* Davison, Michigan: Friede Publications, 1994.

An entertaining book to flip through in idle moments, and a bonanza of verbal snapshots of Detroit from its pioneer days into the twentieth century. (I'm embarrassed to say I'm represented throughout; but it's impossible to write about a place for three decades and not attract local notice.)

Rubenstein, Bruce A., and Ziewacz, Lawrence E. *Three Bullets Sealed His Lips.* Michigan State University Press, 1987.

This gimlet-eyed scrutiny of the 1943 murder of corrupt Michigan State Senator Warren Hooper on the eve of his testimony before a grand jury probing organized crime is a marvel of investigative journalism; a lost art in today's world of advocacy reporting. Reporters post-Woodward-and-Bernstein are sycophantic stenographers compared to Rubenstein and Ziewacz.

Theoharis, Athan G., with Tony G. Poveda, Susan Rosenfeld, and Richard Gid Powers. *The FBI: A Comprehensive Reference Guide.* Phoenix: Oryx, 1999. An excellent quick-flip reference to the Bureau's history, methods, and technology.

Time-Life editors. *This Fabulous Century: 1940–1950*. New York: Time-Life Books, 1969.

Like many such projects assembled by committee, Time-Life has endured criticism regarding some of its sources and facts; but pictures don't lie (or at least they didn't when these volumes were produced, before Photoshop), and the 1940s had a look all their own, preserved here. I'd back its version against anything on the Internet (the same source that insisted whales and dolphins migrated regularly through the Great Lakes; it's a circus without a ringleader).

Various. *The Detroit News*. Detroit: 1941–1945.

Various. *The Detroit Free Press*. Detroit: 1941–1945.

Various. *The Detroit Times*. Detroit: 1941–1945.

Newspapers were no more accurate then than they are now: "Literature in a hurry" routinely throws truth under the bus of expedience, but at least those old-time reporters didn't cloak themselves in the mystique of a noble profession; back then, hypocrisy went only so far. When it comes to immersing oneself in an era, there's nothing like spending a few hours with old editions. Advertisements (What's playing at the movies? Where do we eat? Who's in town?), photos, and contemporary editorial policies (William Randolph Hearst's *Times* is a period gem, for the best comic strips and a guaranteed puff piece on Marion Davies' latest film) mark a time and place more vividly than any chronicle written from the distance of years. The microfilm readers in the Detroit Public Library are time machines. You can go backward and forward in history at the turn of a crank.

Various. *New York Herald Tribune Front Page History of the Second World War*. New York: Tribune, 1946.

Actually, any of these retrospectives is valuable; most of the major dailies have issued at least one. The *Tribune*'s stands out for its chronology at the back. While my Racket Squad was fighting its own war on the streets, the Allies were hammering the Axis in both hemispheres, and almost everyone in the world was desperate to keep abreast of the situation. Television was still in the future, radio reports were colored by the commentators, and theatrical newsreels were outdated upon release—although they have value now, moving pictures of Alexander, Napoleon, and the Crimean War being unavailable. These headlines, dates, and breathlessly hammered-out accounts have helped me tie wartime Detroit to events abroad.

Widick, B.J. *Detroit: City of Race and Class Violence, Revised Edition*. Detroit: Wayne State University Press, 1989.

You can't do better than Wayne State when it comes to understanding this city. Its emphasis on race is an excellent peg upon which to hang any serious study of Detroit's modern history. That said, Widick's grim view is tainted by his premise, that everything bad that has happened in America's racial history is linked inextricably to Detroit.

Woodford, Frank B., and Woodford, Arthur M. *All Our Yesterdays: A Brief History of Detroit.* Detroit: Wayne State University Press, 1969.

I snagged this prize when I began the Amos Walker series in 1979, and have worn the covers off it. From its earliest period (when Daniel Boone escaped from an Iroquois camp) through the 1968 World Series, the Woodfords, father and son, race through all the highlights in the city's progress (and regression), with an enormously useful chronology and an exhaustive index at the end. Considering all that's befallen Detroit since 1969, this one begs for an update; but it's been my most dependable workhorse from the beginning.

Wrynn, V. Dennis. *Detroit Goes to War: The American Automobile Industry in World War II.* Osceola, WI: Motorbooks International, 1993.

Hardly comprehensive, but a good sketch of an industry in sweeping transition, Wrynn's coffee-table book is striking for its slick four-color and black-and-white reproductions of propaganda-style advertisements that were actually intended to assure the public that the auto business hadn't gone away forever. There are useful statistics and quick-search dates, but its greatest contribution is to instill the reader with a feel for the era.

-

Although I wouldn't embarrass their memories with a formal listing, I'm grateful to my parents, Leauvett and Louise Estleman, who lived through two world wars, Prohibition, and the Great Depression, and shared colorful stories of their experiences and observations, repeating them often so my brother and I would be sure to remember them. I'm still reaping the benefits.

Valedictory Note

Elmore "Dutch" Leonard's crime novels set in Detroit have educated more readers on the city's character than scores of exhaustive histories. *Newsweek* christened him, in a rare cover article featuring a novelist, as "The Dickens of Detroit." *Swag, Stick, 52 Pickup, City Primeval: High Noon in Detroit, Rum Punch, Out of Sight, Get Shorty*—to explore them all even briefly would hoist the production values of *Detroit Is Our Beat* well beyond the budget. (*Up in Honey's Room* is a sly tribute to the era of interest to this book.) His westerns alone, including the seminal *Hombre*, would mark his place in the Yankee canon; then he raised the ante when he redirected his gimlet eye to our own time. American literature—and Detroit—lost a powerful voice when Leonard left us at the age of 87 in 2013. Thanks for the boogie ride, Dutch.